BARONESS MOLLY: BI-SEXUAL DOMINATRIX AND OTHER EROTIC STORIES

VOLUME 2

Elizabeth Rebecca Shaw

This book is a work of fiction. All the characters and events portrayed in this book are either products of the author's imagination or are used fictitiously.

CONTENTS

TONI'S FIRST LESBIAN EXPERIENCE

Antonia Brown was sitting on a stool at the bar, hunched over and looking at her furtive appearance in the polished mirror behind the bar; she had a concoction that they called a pink cosmopolitan with a straw stuck through a piece of pineapple and a cherry sitting in front of her. She wasn't sure that she liked the taste of it but she was quite young, just nineteen, and didn't have much experience in drinking. She also had zero experience in what she was here to learn about and was having serious second thoughts about what she was doing. She was about to chicken out and leave when she felt a light touch on her right shoulder. She looked over and there was a short woman in her early thirties standing there beside her.

"Hi there" the woman said pleasantly, giving the startled Toni a bright smile. "You're new here. If you don't mind me saying, you look a little lost." She indicated the stool beside Toni and asked "Do you mind if I sit down here beside you and talk with you?" Toni just mutely shook her head negatively as she formed her impression of the other woman. She was dark-haired with a pretty face, had a wide red lipsticked mouth, a long slightly pointed nose and pale blue eyes. She was about five three or four with a curvy figure that was carrying a couple of extra pounds that looked quite good on her. She had a short skirt that came down to about a hand span from her crotch and a blue silk top that showed her red lacy bra off. Toni reflected on how she herself looked with her short black dress with spaghetti straps that showed off her legs and cleavage. She knew that she didn't have nearly as much to be proud of as this older woman but with her five foot seven inch height and dirty blonde hair, felt she could compete with her somewhat. Then Toni mentally shook her head to clear them of competitive thoughts; that was not what she was in this bar for. The woman watched with amusement as Toni looked her over. She'd been watching the girl from her table of friends for about ten minutes before she decided to approach her.

She climbed up onto the tall stool, ensuring that she flashed the white lacy tops of her stockings as she did and wiggled her plump ass around to get more comfortable. She was aware of Toni looking her over but trying to be very circumspect about it. She leaned in a little closer to the girl, breathing in her fresh scent and cheap perfume and giving the girl a chance to smell her own very expensive scent and asked quietly "Do you understand what type of bar you are in?"

Toni nodded and tried to answer, she failed. She cleared her throat and tried again, replying "This is a lesbian bar."

The brunette nodded encouragingly and said "Good. At least you're not as lost as I thought you might be. Do I take it that you are here tonight to meet with a lesbian?"

Toni thought about her answer for about thirty seconds as she contemplated if she should admit that or just get up, walk out and forget about this experience. She knew that she would probably regret leaving for the rest of her life so she admitted "Yes, I did hope to meet a lesbian."

"Well, pleased to meet you" the woman said joyously, smiling widely and stuck out her hand for Toni to shake. Toni eyed her hand briefly and then reached out and shook the slim hand tentatively; this pretty, outgoing woman was not what she expected at all when she thought about lesbians. Then she noticed that the other woman was wearing an engagement ring with a big diamond and a wedding band on her left hand. The woman grinned at her as she saw where Toni's eyes were focused.

"You caught me" she said playfully with a smirk as she raised her left hand and wiggled her fingers in front of Toni. "I'm married. But my husband is fully aware of where I am and what I am doing. He's busy taking care of our two children so I can be out here having fun." Then she looked at Toni with a touch of concern on her face and asked "Does that make a difference for you?"

Toni paused and thought about it for a moment; what difference did it truly make to her if the woman was married, she considered, realizing that it really didn't matter. Then another thought struck her and she blurted it out without thinking "But then you're really not a lesbian."

The woman shrugged her shoulders, causing her breasts to bounce enticingly and stated "I guess that I'm not. I'm bi-sexual." She peered a little closer at Toni and asked "Did you want me to introduce you to a strict lesbian then?"

"No, that's fine" Toni admitted as she recognized that the other woman's bi-sexuality was on par with her being married; neither meant anything to Toni. "I was just a little surprised" she said, feeling a little more confident.

The woman could see they younger blonde beginning to loosen up and feel more at ease with herself and was pleased about the fact. She decided that she should just straight out ask the girl what she was looking for so she asked "Are you here for anything in particular? Looking to repeat an experience you had when you were younger or anything? I'm a regular here and I know who may give you your best experience if you're looking for something specific." She stopped and looked Toni in the eyes.

Toni blushed a fetching reddish colour, ducked her head a bit away from the other woman's eyes and admitted "I've never had a lesbian experience and don't know what I am looking for. I was just hoping that maybe someone could teach me about being with another woman. I've been attracted to women since puberty but haven't acted on it. My few experiences with men have been disastrous and unsatisfying." She looked up to give Abigail a winsome smile and quietly said "I'm hoping that I'll enjoy being with a woman more. I'm feeling fairly horny and masturbating is just exasperating the situation."

"Well" Abigail said with a slight chortle. "I guess that I can guide you a little if you are interested in listening to me. First things first. Do you like that drink that you have in front of you? I know it is the house specialty but I've always found it to be disgusting, myself."

Toni looked at her with surprise and admitted "Not really. Could you recommend something then?"

Abigail gave her a huge smile and called over one of the pretty bartenders. "Two White Russians and take this crap away" she ordered as she pointed at Toni's drink. She laid a twenty dollar bill on the bar to pay for the drinks. Toni began to protest but she waved the younger woman away. "My husband makes very good money and I can easily afford this better than you." The bartender left to fill the order, taking the drink with her and Abigail turned to Toni and asked "What would you like to be called? Some women in here go by nicknames or names other than their own so if you want to be a little more anonymous, feel free."

"My name is Antonia Brown but I like to be called Toni" Toni said smiling.

"My name is Abigail and I don't like to be called Abby or Gail" Abigail told her returning the smile. "If you don't mind, I'd like to keep my last name a secret for now. I'll tell it to you if we get to know each other better. So, Toni, what would you like to get out of tonight? Do you want to meet a woman who'll fuck you hard with a dildo? Do you want to have your pussy eaten? Or maybe get a chance to eat a pussy?"

Toni thought about matters for a moment as the bartender brought back the drinks. When the drink was in front of her, Toni took a thoughtful sip and was surprised at the smooth, pleasant taste of it. "It's good" she said brightly to Abigail who just smiled in return. "I guess I'd have to ask what, if anything, you might be interested in doing with me" she offered to Abigail.

"Well" said Abigail, very pleased with the offer. "I'm more of a femme than butch and you don't look to be very butch either. Besides, when I want to ride a dildo, I prefer to have an experienced partner. So, if you're willing, we'll borrow one of the smaller upstairs rooms where I'll let you taste my pussy to see if you like doing that. I want a promise out of you that you'll try it for at least five minutes before making up your mind about doing it. I don't expect that you'll be able to make me orgasm, so don't worry about that. After that, I'll eat your pussy and since I have much more experience doing that, I expect that I'll make you cum." She smiled confidently at the younger blonde and continued "In fact, I'm willing to bet that I can make you howl like a banshee." Toni smiled brightly and held out her hand; Abigail got off her stool and led Toni over to the door where the stairs up were, grabbing one of the keys from the hooks by there.

When Abigail led her into the small bedroom, Toni looked around in interest; there was a small bed covered in a fitted sheet and a shelf holding more sheets in there. Abigail grabbed the top sheet and flicked it out over the bed before patting it down more firmly. Toni attempted to help with making up the bed but Abigail just laughed and said "We only put down the sheet loosely so that we can lie on it without dirtying the rest of the bed. Once we are finished we'll take off this sheet and put it in the hamper. They'll wash it and put it back up here to use again. Now, I want to undress you first so I can admire your pretty body and I'll play with you a bit before you undress me. Okay?" Toni nodded her head eagerly in agreement and Abigail came over and grabbed the hem of her short black dress. She lifted it up to Toni's waist and then guided the blonde to bend over so that she could more easily remove it over her head.

She was disappointed to see that Toni was wearing panties and a bra; a pretty girl like her shouldn't be wearing underwear when she went out to a place like this she thought. She instructed Toni over that fact and the blonde quickly promised that she wouldn't in the future. Abigail rapidly divested her of the underwear and felt the younger woman's firm young tits; she liked how the blonde's pink nipples popped up when caressed, even lightly. She ran her hand down the other woman's belly and lightly ran her finger along her slit. She could begin to smell Toni's arousal and was quite pleased with her. Toni pursed her full lips and let out a moan to let Abigail know that she was enjoying the touching. Toni was beginning to think that this experience was the most wonderful thing that she had ever enjoyed. Abigail didn't want the other girl to be too aroused so she stopped playing with her and said "Your turn to undress me. I would prefer if you didn't take too much time because I really want to feel your pretty tongue in me. We can play with each other when we're done the pussy eating." So Toni quickly helped Abigail off with her skirt, top and bra, just holding the full weight of the brunette's right tit for a moment to enjoy its feel before releasing it.

"How come you wear a bra when you tell me not to" she asked a bit teasingly.

"Because if I didn't wear a bra to support these babies" Abigail said, indicating her heavy tits, "my tits would end up in my skirt." Toni recognized that Abigail was exaggerating somewhat but that she did require the support of a bra, whereas Toni did not. Then Abigail arranged herself on the bed and encouraged Toni to join her. Toni did so and the brunette arranged her positioning so that Toni could lick her pussy. Toni moved her head up between the older woman's legs hesitantly and took a sniff. She could scent the older woman's natural odour underneath her expensive perfume. She took a moment to analyze the smell and decided that it was actually very pleasant and arousing. She pushed her head closer and ran her tongue along Abigail's slit before backing off to once again analyze matters. The taste was both sweet and slightly tangy, she thought and realized that she could enjoy it. She quickly went back down for another taste and Abigail lightly grabbed her shoulders, steadying her a bit. She ran her tongue up and down the other woman's pussy and decided that she liked what she was doing. So she increased her pace and Abigail held her head closer to her crotch, encouraging the younger girl to do more. "Stick that pretty, wet tongue deep into me" Abigail encouraged her and let out a soft moan of approval. Toni pushed her face right into the brunette's pussy hair and sent her tongue up into the wet cunt as far as she could. She wiggled it energetically causing Abigail to moan approvingly. About ten minutes went by without Toni even noticing it because she was so absorbed in what she was doing. Finally, Abigail pushed her lightly away from her because she wanted to spend some time eating the younger blonde's cunt. "That was very nice, honeypie" she said sweetly. "You're not going to make me cum because you have to learn to improve your technique in order to achieve that but I really appreciate the effort. It's pretty obvious that you don't have any problems with eating pussy but we'll have to teach you how to do it better. I want to spend some time with my tongue in your pussy now so that you know what that feels like. So lie back here so I can do that."

Toni immediately followed the instructions and Abigail soon had her tongue up against the blonde's pussy. Toni recognized the other woman's experience compared to her own earlier attempts; Abigail quickly excited Toni's cunt and had her dripping in no time. She ran her tongue all around Toni's crotch area, searching for more sensitive areas to exploit. Toni soon began to feel that she was about to orgasm and said breathily "I'm about to cum."

"I know you are, honeypie" the brunette replied, lifting her head briefly and reaching up with her right hand to give Toni's tit a firm squeeze. "Just go ahead and do that. That is what I want you to do." So Toni bit her lip slightly, gave a small squeal and orgasmed. Abigail quickly cleaned off the small amount of liquid from Toni's crotch. "We're also going to have to teach you to orgasm more freely" she told the panting blonde. "But that was quite nice for a first time together. Did you enjoy yourself?" Toni nodded and gave a sigh of contentment. She'd enjoyed her experience tremendously. Abigail gave her a light slap on the inner thigh and said "Once you're a bit more experienced with this and comfortable with yourself, I'll see if I can find a man to teach you how to get fucked by a man." Toni looked at her in utter surprise. Abigail smiled and said "We really should see if you are bi-sexual or not. I think that maybe you've had to put up with inexperienced selfish men and the right man could make you enjoy yourself. If you'll allow me to mentor you in your sex life, I think that you would really learn a lot and enjoy the benefits. It is something that you can think about. I have to go home to my husband and kids now but I will be back here at the bar in two nights if you are interested." She then gathered up her clothes and put them on quickly; as soon as she was done, she gave Toni a final smile and left. Toni lay there, feeling too tired to leave at the moment but it was a wonderful type of tired that she'd never experienced before. She looked forward to further sex lessons.

JANE AND HER TWO ROOMMATES

Jane fumbled with her keys as she opened the door to the three bedroom apartment she shared with two other girls. She paid most of the rent so she got the master bedroom while the other two made do with the smaller bedrooms. She also bought most of the groceries and treated the other two to some better meals than they would have been able to afford on their own; she didn't mind the arrangement most days since she was the one making money, although not really a tremendous amount, while they were still taking classes at the university. Jane had endured an extremely bad day at work and was pissed off mightily. When she entered the apartment, she was struck by something that she couldn't quite identify but seemed out of place to her. She did notice that neither of her roommates were in the living room but that wasn't terribly unusual. She paused to gaze around and listen intently to try to determine what had spooked her; there it was, she realized that she was hearing a faint noise and she attempted to track it down and classify what it was. She walked forward a few silent steps in her heels and determined that it was coming from her right; it was emanating from Amber's bedroom. She listened to it for a moment and decided that it sounded like a soft sighing moan. She wondered briefly whether or not Amber was having sex with a man in there but decided that it was probably unlikely because Amber didn't have a current boyfriend and she wasn't the type to put out on the first date. Jane figured that she'd risk the embarrassment of interrupting a good fuck by calling out to Amber to ascertain that she was all right and not being held captive in there or anything.

"Amber, are you all right?" she called through the closed door. She heard a small cry of dismay from in the room and then some soft whispering too low for her to make out what was being said. "Amber, please let me know if you need any help" she called with some worry. She tried to doorknob and found out that it was locked; she pondered trying to force the door. Suddenly, it opened and Amber stood there, holding the door close to her so that Jane couldn't see inside. Jane looked her over very carefully, noticing that she was extremely sweaty and flushed. Her tshirt and sweatpants looked as though they'd been pulled on hastily, she wasn't wearing a bra because Jane could see her nipples poking the fabric and her blonde hair was a tangled mess. Jane frowned grumpily at her; they had a policy of texting each other when they were bringing a man home so that the other two girls could hole up in their rooms while the deed was done and avoid confrontations like this one. Amber hadn't bothered to text her. She decided to say something about it. "Why didn't you text me if you were going to be fucking someone?" she asked quietly but commandingly. "Where's Cici? Did you text her and not me?" She discerned a flash of something cross the pretty blonde's face; guilt, she thought when she analyzed it. Why would she be feeling so guilty when I asked about Cici, she wondered silently, it can't be because she warned her and not me. Then it struck her like a thunderbolt as she examined the blushing girl in front of her.

She reached over the shorter blonde's left shoulder and pushed the door open; Amber just let her meekly do that. "Cici" she called into the room. "I know you're in there, honey. Why don't you come out here and the three of us can sit in the living room and discuss matters." She paused to see what would happen, scrutinizing Amber as the blonde cringed and looked down at the floor. Brunette Cici slid quietly out of the room, brushing by the immobile Amber; she too did not want to meet Jane's eyes. Jane regarded the pair of them silently and then pointed towards the living room; both of them caught the flicker of movement and registered the gesture. The three women walked silently into the large living room.

Jane plopped herself down on the comfortable leather sofa and pulled one of the large red silk cushions to lean her tired back against. Amber and Cici remained standing, unsure of where they should sit. Jane crossed one sheer nylon encased leg over the other and noted that Cici gazed at her slim legs as she was doing that; so, Jane thought with some satisfaction, Cici was the more gay one of the pair. The two women still stood there and then Jane sighed in exasperation and patted the sofa near her. "Cici, you come sit over here beside me. Amber, I could use a glass of red wine before you sit down. Be a dear and fetch one for me, will you?" she commanded. Amber gave her a quick look of defiance, they'd never treated each other like Jane was doing and she wasn't happy about it, but Jane overrode it with a stern stare. Amber quickly crumbled and went to get the wine, feeling frightfully guilty about being caught with Cici. While she was gone, Jane examined the meek brunette with intensity; she knew that Amber had the stronger of the personalities of the two and undoubtedly was the one being eaten. She also thought that she could see a trace of liquid still marking up Cici's puckered mouth. She reached out and raised the other woman's chin before brushing one of her fingers against the mark to check it out. Cici blushed furiously as she recognized that Jane could see the evidence of what she'd been up to in the room. Jane simply held her damp finger in front of the pretty mouth. Cici appeared to be unsure of what the other woman wanted her to do and hesitated, looking at the finger in a confused manner.

Suddenly she realized what Jane wanted and began to lick the finger clean. Once she had her tongue against it, Jane rotated her hand so that she could put the finger right into the warm, wet mouth. Amber returned with the bottle of red wine and three glasses and stood still in the doorway, watching the performance before her. She felt a surge of jealousy that Jane would automatically assume dominance over the pretty brunette; it had been her pussy that the other woman had been licking just moments before, she thought, furious.

Jane looked Amber over quite carefully, she'd seen the flash of jealousy cross the blonde's features and she gave quiet contemplation to whether or not she wanted the blonde to remain in that state. She could probably assume dominance over both women while giving Amber a measure of mastery over Cici. That would likely keep Amber compliant. Or she could make the blonde fight her over control of the pretty brunette. It might be a whole load of fun to constantly be showing the blonde who her mistress was by spanking and whipping her to get her to submit. She decided that she could make that decision at a later date, today was just to get the two women comfortable with the knowledge that she knew about their relationship and that she intended to participate in it. She took her finger out of Cici's mouth and beckoned Amber over with that hand. When the blonde approached she motioned for her to sit on the floor by her feet, on the other side from Cici. Amber looked at her in confusion and then defiance once she realized what Jane intended. The two women faced off against each other for a couple of moments.

Jane made her decision; Amber had to learn her place, she decided. After a quick glance at Cici, Jane looked Amber right in the eyes and then backhanded Cici across her plump mouth. Both Amber and Cici stared at Jane in disbelief; Jane had hit Cici hard enough to draw a trickle of blood but not hard enough to do any real damage. After a few seconds of surprise though, Cici began sobbing loudly, cradling her face in her hands; she couldn't believe that Jane would be so mean to her. Jane kept her eyes locked on Ambers, smiling with superiority and daring the blonde to do something about what she'd done to Cici. Amber realized that she couldn't do anything; Jane had proven that she was the meaner, more ruthless person. As Amber slumped her shoulders in defeat, Jane recognized it and snapped her fingers while pointing to the spot on the floor. Amber wasted no time in scrambling into position; she didn't want to see Cici hurt again. Jane motioned for Amber to pour them all a glass of wine and turned to comfort the pretty brunette she'd struck. It sent a small shiver of satisfaction when Cici flinched away initially from her attention. She grasped the brunette by the chin, lifted her head and inspected the injury; it looked like a tooth had caught her lip to create the bleeding and her plump lips were likely a little bruised but no more damage than that.

Jane pulled the other woman forward and smashed her mouth against the bruised lips causing Cici to moan in pain but the brunette quickly responded and was soon sliding her plump lips all over Jane's mouth. Jane was a bit surprised by how forward the other woman was; she was attempting to force her tongue into Jane's mouth but decided that she quite liked it. After a moment, Jane could hear Amber moaning in frustration and jealousy about being left out. She separated from the pleasant situation in order to look at the blonde. Amber was still where she'd placed her but was watching the two of them kissing quite intently and had an extreme look of displeasure on her face. Jane thought about just letting the other woman stew but decided that it would probably be better if she became more pliable and controllable. She thought that she understood the feelings that Amber was having and determined that showing her some sympathy might get the other two women to accept what she wanted of them easier. She reached out and tousled the blonde's disarrayed hair before putting her hand on the back of Amber's head and guiding her up to join them. Amber eagerly raised herself up and leaned forward to join them in the kissing. Jane shared a number of wet kisses with each of them and also let them kiss one another.

After about five minutes, Jane leaned back and directed the pair of them to continue kissing as she pondered the situation and what she intended to do about it. She knew that she was going to make the two women serve her sexually but had yet to determine the specifics of the situation. She'd thought that the best path would have been to make Cici a total slave bitch and let Amber have some fun with her while Jane retained dominance over both of them but after the kissing, she suspected that Cici would actually show some backbone. She was now of the opinion that the two women would react fairly similar to each other and neither would be happy being the bitch all the time. As she watched them kiss, she could see that Cici was pushing Amber slightly to get her to accept being the more submissive. Jane decided that she'd have to try them both out in roles a little more before making a final determination. That was going to be fun, she thought; wondering how far they'd let her push them.

Jane could sense that Amber was tiring of trying to hold her position and needed to change it; besides, Jane was growing weary of watching them. She reached out and moved Amber back before turning to Cici. "Stand up, bitch" she commanded roughly. When Cici stood up, Jane gave them both a very obvious inspection; she tutted to herself as she catalogued their faults and was ecstatic that they blushed with embarrassment. It was so much fun in making other pretty women believe that you were better than them, she thought happily and quickly pushed the intruding thoughts about her own deficiencies out of her mind. "Strip" she demanded. Cici enthusiastically started removing her clothes while Amber hesitated just slightly before doing the same. Jane ensured that she looked Amber right in her eyes so that she could enforce her dominance over her while the blonde disrobed. Jane was totally amused by the fact that Cici, for all her strength shown during the kissing, was quickly nude and exhibiting all signs of being completely aroused about being naked in front of the other two women. Her long nipples stood firmly at attention on top of her surprisingly plump breasts and Jane could see new evidence that her pussy was wet as there was a sheen of liquid coating her inner thighs. She also had a huge grin on her face and her eyes sparkled delightfully. Amber on the other hand, was a little more reluctant to show herself off and was actually trying to cover her pussy with clasped hands in front of her. "Amber, get your hands by your sides and spread your legs some more. Cici, stop bouncing around and stand still. I'll get seasick watching your tits bouncing up and down" Jane groused. The two women quickly complied and Jane was able to regard their assets in all their splendor. She looked Amber over first since it was quite evident that Cici wanted the attention. The blonde was short and possibly could be considered to be a bit chunky with her large breasts, thick waist and broad hips but Jane thought that her curves were very nice. She had a fairly thick blonde pussy that looked a little matted, undoubtedly from Cici's recent attention to it. The blonde's aureoles and nipples were pale pink and fairly large; Jane thought that she'd enjoy fastening clamps to that sensitive flesh. Jane now turned her attention to Cici, whom she noticed smiled invitingly at her. Cici was taller than Amber by a couple of inches and was a deal slimmer than her. She had a nice rack, a toned waist and slim hips; her black bush was trimmed and shaved down to a patch smaller than her tiny hands and Jane could see her gaping slit easily. Jane could feel a stirring deep in her loins as she imagined what she would be doing with these two.

But she didn't want them to get swell heads about the whole thing, so she sighed with fake disappointment after she'd examined their naked bodies. She could see Amber flush and twitch to try to cover her hairy bush once again before she regained control; even Cici frowned at her with a look of confusion. "I guess if that's the best that you look, it'll have to do" she said softly. "Well, there's nothing to be done about it right now and I've had a hard day and deserve a little pampering. I want both of you kneeling here in front of me. Take off my shoes and massage my feet for me. The girl that I determine does the best job gets a treat while the other one gets punished." She fixed them with a hard glare as she asked "Do you understand me?" Both women nodded and leapt to follow her bidding.

At first, both women were just using their hands to rub her nylon clad feet and then Cici broke out in an insolent grin and began rubbing Jan's foot against her fleshy tit. Jane swore that she could feel the stiff nipple stroking against her skin but dismissed that as wishful thinking. It did feel quite nice though and was an interesting touch. Amber noticed that Jane approved of this and was determined to outdo the brunette; she wrapped both of her large breasts around Jane's foot and stroked it up and down in a fleshy cocoon. Jane had to supress a chortle of glee so that they wouldn't see exactly how much she was enjoying their actions; she needed for them to be constantly seeking her approval. Cici upped the ante by pulling Jane's foot between her thighs and rubbing it against her damp crotch. Jane gave her a half nod of approval even though she was very pleased by the action. Amber gave Cici a look of anger and then placed Jane's foot between her plump thighs; Jane was shocked when Amber chose to guide her big toe up into her cunt. Both Jane and Cici watched for a moment or two as Amber rocked her hips while she engulfed the tip of Jane's foot in her pussy. Jane was aroused by the warm, damp cavern that covered her foot and wiggled her big toe around a bit causing Amber to look up at her with a look of enjoyment on her screwed up face. Cici gave a small hmmph of unhappiness, knowing that Jane was going to award the treat to Jane; she couldn't think of too much else to do. Then it came to her, she took Jane's foot out from between Amber's thighs and started sucking on the wet toes. She looked up to meet Jane's gaze as she worked her mouth around the entire end of her foot.

Jane gave a laugh of approval but said "That's not enough to win you the treat this time, Cici. Amber was much more inventive so she wins the treat." She smiled in a somewhat cruel manner and said flatly "You get the punishment." Jane was quite pleased about how it had turned out; she'd expected Cici to be the more forward one and to be rewarded but she was intrigued that it was Amber who had taken advantage. She patted her lap to indicate to Cici that she should position her nude body across it. She intended on spanking the brunette and was wondering how many times she should choose to do it on this initial attempt. She didn't want it to be too many but she needed for it to remind the girl of her status for a couple of days. She had no idea if Cici had ever done this before and wasn't about to break the mood by asking. She came to the conclusion that fifteen would be a good number to start with. Cici arrayed herself over Jane's lap and the way that she wriggled her ass to get into position Jane came to the conclusion that Cici had done this before and liked it. She had to resist the strong urge to stroke the brunette's nice round ass; she was supposed to be punishing her, not worshiping her.

"I'm gonna spank your ass fifteen times" she told Cici.

"Fifteen" the girl whined piteously. She was so convincing that Jane had second thoughts about the number and was considering reducing the amount. She was thinking about this when Cici began rubbing her damp pussy all over Jane's lap; Jane could tell that the girl wasn't really afraid but was tremendously excited about the spanking. She determined that she'd let the number stand. She would learn from this experience how to handle the brunette in the future.

"I may have to add more for insolence" she threatened. "I want to hear you count out the strokes nice and loud" she commanded firmly. She raised her right hand and smacked down hard on Cici's nicely padded ass.

"One" counted Cici with a small whimper. "Two" she stated with a moan as Jane quickly spanked her again. Jane rained down blows rapidly as Cici counted them up to the completion of nine before she chose to pause. Cici lay across her lap crying loudly as Jane surveyed her handiwork. The woman's ass was a pattern of red splotches from where Jane's hand had contacted her. Once again, Jane was concerned about the number being too much. She gave Cici's ass a quick little rub to hearten the girl and was quite surprised that Cici immediately wiggled it for her. Hmmm, she thought, this little bitch is faking her distress; apparently she likes this quite a bit. She smacked the brunette hard three more times in rapid succession. Cici squealed but remembered to count them out. Jane hesitated again because her hand was getting a bit sore; Cici's butt looked well-padded but she had some definite muscle under there, Jane thought. After waiting a moment, both to get some feeling back into her hand and to make the girl anticipate things a little longer, Jane quickly finished the spanking with Cici calling out the blows. It looked to Jane as though she'd delivered some bruising to Cici's ass and that she'd have some discomfort with sitting down for the next couple of days. She was quite satisfied that she'd conveyed her message very well.

"You may get up now, Cici" she said as she ran her hand over the other woman's smooth ass. "You may go over and let Amber rub your ass for you for five minutes. When that time is up, you're going to eat her pussy while I watch. You have ten minutes to make her orgasm. If there is no climax by that time, you'll have to stick your tongue up her asshole for two minutes and then up mine for a further two minutes." She paused as she gave some thought about making it more difficult for Cici by instructing Amber that she'd receive some punishment if she let Cici orgasm her. But she eventually decided that it complicated things too much for the very first time they were having sex together. She also pondered what she'd get one or both of them to do for her. She decided that she had time to think about it while watching them in action. She said nothing further to them but just shooed Cici off of her lap and got into a comfortable position to watch the other two women perform.

Cici went over and knelt in front of Amber so that the blonde could stroke her ass for her. Amber obediently used both of her hands to caress the beaten ass while Jane watched, feeling her pleasure growing. She could sense that she was starting to get her panties quite wet and was seriously considering stripping off her clothes. She decided that she would at least open her blouse and pull up her bra so that she could massage her own breasts while watching the erotic scene in front of her. As she was doing so, she saw Cici whispering something very softly to Amber; she was too far away to hear what was said and was about to demand that they tell her when Amber began wetly kissing areas of the abused buttocks. Jane decided that she was amused and somewhat aroused by their actions so she didn't bother to make an issue of it. Realizing that she was the only one who should be keeping aware of the clock, she looked over and noticed that at least six minutes had gone by. "Time's up" she commanded. Cici looked over her shoulder that was away from Amber and gave her a dissatisfied scowl; she made Jane very aware that she would've liked for Amber to go on some more with her commiseration. Jane just imperiously looked back at her and made a motion for her to get on with matters. This performance was for her pleasure, not Cici's, Jane thought. Cici flushed slightly and then began to get prepared to eat Amber's pussy for the second time that day. As she looked around, she noticed the ottoman and decided that it would work wonderfully to support Amber while she sucked on her pussy. She quickly crawled over and retrieved it. She got Amber well positioned on the low piece of furniture and made sure that Jane had a good line of sight. She bent her head to the task eagerly; Amber had been near her orgasm but hadn't quite achieved it when Jane interrupted them by coming home early. Cici rapidly found the spot that she knew Amber was particularly sensitive to because of her experience with her earlier in the day. She darted a stiffened tongue swiftly and repeatedly against the blonde's aroused clitoris. Amber moaned her approval and Cici could feel and see the liquids that she was producing from her pussy. Cici raked her sharp little front teeth over the sensitive organ, eliciting an extremely excited squeal of delight from Amber who began begging the brunette to use her harder. Cici did a quick check over her shoulder to gauge how Jane was liking this action; she sensed that the outwardly composed woman was feeling very aroused. She noticed that Jane had exposed her breasts to fondle them and was very interested in examining them but was aware that she was on a time limit and would undoubtedly need all of that time to achieve the task set before her. Not that she imagined that Amber would be extremely hard to orgasm but she knew from past experience with other women that it took a little time; they were not like men, who usually could get off in two minutes. So she got back down to the task; she didn't want to have to stick her tongue up anyone's ass today, she didn't greatly object to the task, it was her pride that made her want to please the other two women on this first get-together. She pursed her plump lips and sucked along Amber's nice little slit, slurping up the juices loudly. Amber wiggled her hips and whimpered happily; it was obvious to Cici that her mind was feeding her erotic thoughts to go along with the sensations her body was relaying to her. Cici worked Amber over fairly hard but she sensed that she was still going to lose the race with time; she pondered what action she could take to improve her odds and then realized what would probably send the blonde over the edge. She sucked Amber's pert, aroused clit into her warm, wet mouth and closed her teeth over it. She didn't bite down hard but did it just firmly enough to frighten Amber into thinking that she would. Amber shouted her alarm and tried to sit up to free herself from the assault; as she did, she lost control over her body and it proceeded to orgasm. Although Amber tried to push Cici's head away from her pussy, Cici grabbed a tight hold on the other woman's hips and held herself in place. She gently sucked up all of the juices and Amber eventually settled back down to enjoy what was being done to her. Jane had been almost as startled as

Amber had been but she marveled at what Cici had done; it really turned her on and she decided to disrobe completely while the brunette was finishing up her undertaking. When Cici was completed, she reached out and helped the tired Amber into a sitting position and both of them faced Jane to see what else she had in mind.

Jane sat on the sofa in front of them, nude and lightly stroking her pussy with her right hand while her left squeezed her left breast and wondered about what she wanted to do with them next. She knew, that to be fair, she should probably let Cici watch while Amber ate her out; the big problem with that was that she desperately wanted to feel Cici's tongue on her hot cunt. She pondered if she had enough energy to let them both lick her pussy and decided that the hard day had taken too much out of her. With that in mind, she made her decision.

"Cici, you come over here and eat my pussy" she commanded as she lay back to get comfortable and give the brunette plenty of access. "Amber, you use your fingers on Cici's pussy and make sure you give her plenty of action. I want to hear and feel her squeal into my dripping pussy." The two women moved keenly over to do as she demanded although Cici insisted on kissing Jane on the lips before going down on her. Jane could taste the remnants of Amber's cum on those plump lips but she wasn't upset about it but was actually intrigued. Jane had found that she didn't like reciprocating too much by eating another woman's pussy; she liked to have her own eaten and fucked and would generally just fuck the other woman with a strap-on. But she was very surprised to find that she liked the taste of Amber that lingered on Cici's mouth; she'd have to see if she wanted to do a real taste test on the actual pussy. Cici moved down and began slowly sliding her tongue along the outer lips of Jane's mostly shaven pussy and was pleased by the response. Jane murmured her approval and her outer lips started swelling; Cici hummed in happiness. Once Cici had arranged herself in position, Amber slid her fingers into her eager pussy; she started with a single finger to work the other woman open enough to accept more. She liked how easily her finger slid in and out of Cici; she'd only ever fingered her own pussy before and found it to be an awkward reach. It was very pleasant to watch how effortlessly another woman's pussy accepted her finger, she was intrigued by the squishiness of Cici's folds. She kept an eye on the action going on at Jane's cunt and when Cici ramped up her efforts of licking Jane's pussy, Amber slid another finger into Cici's cunt. Cici was in heaven and she moaned loudly to let all know; Amber varied her fingering technique, sometimes going deeper and sometimes changing the angle; she became quite fascinated as to Cici's responses to what she did to her. Cici was having some trouble remembering what her responsibilities were because her brain was insisting that it needed to monitor what was happening in her own cunt but she overrode it so that she could enjoy her eating of Jane's sweet hole. This action went on for over five minutes with the only sounds being the squishy response to Amber's fingers, the slurping of Cici's mouth and the moans of enjoyment from the two women. Amber managed to work three of her fingers into Cic's tight cunt and was trying to get her to take the fourth; she was having some trouble getting that job done and then suddenly, Cici exploded in orgasm. Cici tried to twist her hips as she was lost in the throes of her climax and Amber rapidly rescued her trapped hand to prevent any injury to it. Cici writhed around for a moment or two as she enjoyed the sensations emanating from her pussy. Jane had been close to orgasming herself but watched with interest as the brunette tossed herself around; she found herself quite amused by the process and gave Amber a smile when she caught her eyes. The two women watched silently as Cici expended her orgasm; both of them were quite aroused by the sight and each of them stroked their own pussies in reaction.

Right after most of the results of her climax finished with her body, Cici climbed back up to her position between Jane's legs and resumed her licking. She could feel the pleasant aftershocks still rocketing through her but was determined that Jane would soon be in the same position. Jane welcomed her enthusiastically, somewhat amazed that she had the presence of mind to do that, and tousled her sweaty hair. As aroused as Jane was by all that had happened that afternoon, it only took Cici a couple of moments to make Jane climax. Jane wasn't as expressive in her orgasm as Cici had been but there was no mistaking when she'd been pushed over the edge. She caught her breath and let loose a low keening sound as she screwed up her face in effort. Cici watched, feeling the satisfaction of achievement, and gave in to her own feelings; she moaned and panted in delayed reaction to her own orgasm, feeling well satisfied. Amber moved in and massaged gently each of the other women's shoulders as they displayed their bliss about their conditions. She was surprised that rather than feeling like a third wheel, she was truly happy for both of them and incredibly aroused by the sight and smell of them. Cici decided that she'd recovered enough of her strength to crawl back up and clean up Jane's messy pussy. She was doing a good job on it when Amber startled her by pushing her warm mouth against Cici's cunt; Amber hadn't licked too many pussies before but she decided that now was the right time to see if she liked it because she was still incredibly aroused by the other two women. She was surprised that she found Cici's pussy to be sweet and pleasant rather than icky. She recognized that she had no technique but was convinced that the other two women would be more than happy to teach her and let her practice on them.

After a couple of minutes, Amber decided that she'd had enough for her first time and removed her mouth; she stroked Cici's lower back and ass as the brunette continued in her cleanup job. When Cici finished a few minutes later, she sat up and grinned at Jane before turning and kissing Amber on the mouth for being such a good sport about things. Jane watched the two of them kiss for a moment, somewhat amused, and then realized that she was missing out on a good thing. She joined the pair of them and they spent a few moments in a three-way liplock. When they broke from that, they looked at each other to decide what they wanted to do next. By mutual agreement, they determined that all of them had performed enough for that first time and assured each other that there would be many more. The three women left the sofa and headed into the kitchen to begin preparing their evening meal. None of them bothered to put any of their clothing back on.

THE BARONESS MEETS
A BRIDE TO BE

Baroness Molly was waiting for her limousine to be driven around to pick up her and four of their female employees; they were going shopping for some new lingerie and since it was a nice morning, she waited on the sidewalk. A pretty, young blonde woman called to her from a few feet away on the sidewalk.

"Baroness, please may I talk with you" the young woman asked eagerly. The Baroness looked the woman over; she was quite tall, had a slim but nice figure, great legs, a striking face and brilliant blue-grey eyes. Baroness Molly estimated that she was about an inch taller than the other woman who was dressed in a nice short blue dress that really showed off her long, toned legs. She beckoned the young woman forward and looked her in the eyes. "Thank you for listening to me. My name is Tamilin. I want to get married but my boyfriend and I have no hope of paying for the wedding that I want. I've heard a bit about you and your husband from some friends of mine and I'd like a chance to negotiate with you into paying for my wedding" the woman babbled out.

"Why on earth would we be interested in paying for your wedding. We are not a charity. Be away with you" Baroness Molly snapped, waving her hand imperiously at the young blonde.

"Because I'd be willing to exchange anything in order to achieve it" the young woman said softly but firmly. "I know what you and your husband like to do to pretty, young women and I'd be very willing to subject myself to it in order to achieve my goals." She sidled closer and whispered "I'll literally kiss your ass, eat your pussy and let you beat the crap out of me if you'll help me out. I know that's some of what you like." The Baroness took a closer look at the young woman, seeing that she was very serious about her offer and decided that she liked what she saw. She determined that she could easily ascertain the young woman's willingness to do what she claimed that she would by inviting her to join them in the limousine and be their plaything for the afternoon; that should show whether or not the young bitch was serious about her proposal or not.

"Then I guess you should join us on our shopping trip" the Baroness told the young beauty. "But I want to see you in just your heels after you get in" she commanded. The blonde nodded eagerly, excited at the chance she was getting. The limousine drove up about thirty seconds later and the women waited to let Tamilin enter it first so that she could begin stripping off her clothes. By the time that the Baroness entered the vehicle, Tamilin was lying across one leather seat, wiggling her ass around as she worked her panties down her hips. The Baroness and the other women looked her over with acute interest. When she'd gotten her panties off, she put her heels back on and sat there, back straight to show off her plump tits and legs spread wide to show off her neatly trimmed blonde pussy; she was very proud of how she looked and knew that other people found her to be very attractive. Desdemona was seated nearest her and she reached out with her right hand to cup Tamilin's large right breast; the Baroness was happy to see that Tamilin didn't shy from the groping hand but rather pressed herself further towards the other woman. Hmmm, she thought, this was promising to be an even more interesting day than she had thought it would be when she proposed it that morning.

The three women seated across the front seat encouraged Tamilin to lay her nude body across their laps so that they could all stroke and play with her and the blonde quickly did just that. The Baroness was quite impressed that the girl was intelligent enough to realize that the Baroness would want to see her in action with the other women before she bothered to partake of her favours herself. The Baroness settled back in her seat, taking the glass of champagne Jill poured for her and watched as the three women ran their hands over Tamilin's soft skin. Tamilin moaned and writhed as their hands ran over her more sensitive areas; it was obvious to Molly that the young woman was enjoying the attention paid to her. Desdemona had worked three of her fingers into the naked young blonde and was occupied with stroking them in and out of her slick cunt. She offered those fingers to Tamilin and the girl eagerly sucked her own juices off the digits with immense satisfaction. Paula leaned forward and sampled the girl's juices from Desdemona's fingers as well; when she did, Tamilin stole a quick kiss from the brunette and she responded. The rest of the women watched in amusement as the two women locked up with each other and spent about five minutes swapping kisses. The Baroness noted that they had arrived at the lingerie store and were slowing down in front of it. She realized that she couldn't expect Tamilin to march into the store naked even though she was amused at the thought of that but she really didn't want the blonde to put her clothes back on. Jill had anticipated the problem and was shrugging out of her smart trench coat so that Tamilin could wear it and still remain naked underneath it. The Baroness smiled at the other woman, impressed that she'd quietly come up with the perfect solution and the newer brunette grinned back at her.

They almost had to drag Tamilin and Paula apart in order to get the blonde into the trench coat so that they could get her into the store. None of them were very upset about the fact and, in fact, they found the situation extremely amusing. It took nearly five minutes for them to disembark and get into the store. Tamilin and the four women were giggling wildly as they stormed through the doors into the shop and the Baroness trailed them more sedately, fighting the urge to break out into laughter like the others; she had to maintain a modicum of dignity, she thought seriously, considering her position as Baroness. She didn't begrudge the women their giddiness and found it fairly enjoyable; she looked forward to their antics during the rest of their visit.

When the four women stormed in, the middle-aged owner of the store started storming over, intent on dressing the group down before she realized that they were with the Baroness. Since the Baroness was such a good customer and bought a great deal of items during the year, never quibbling about the prices, she was prepared to put up with a lot from anyone associated with the Baroness. She quickly changed her expression from one of anger to one of welcome and greeted the Baroness; the group was late for their appointment, something she would have remarked on to a lesser customer, but she ignored the fact, saying "Welcome, Baroness. I've arranged for your group to be accommodated in the back room so that you won't be disturbed by the rest of the customers." She noticed Tamilin and said "Oh, I didn't realize that you'd added another girl to your little group." Then she frowned and recalled what items she'd selected for them to try on before saying "I don't recall that you told me her measurements so I could arrange some items for her to try on." She smiled and said hastily "I'm sure that we just missed the change and I apologize for that. We'll need her measurements so that we can quickly select some goods for her."

"No need to apologize, Mrs. Appletree. I didn't tell you about her because she was a last minute addition to our group. I wouldn't mind seeing her in a few items but there's no rush in getting them for her since we surprised you with her. I know that you have a business to run and we put a bit of a strain on your capabilities when we visit." She smiled genuinely at the older woman before continuing "I know that you take real good care of us and appreciate my business but I don't want you to have to put yourself out too much for us."

"Maybe we could just get her rough measurements quickly out here so that we can begin selecting" Mrs. Appletree suggested.

"Uhh, we'll have to wait until we get into the back room, I think, Mrs. Appletree" she replied, chortling slightly as the other five women giggled loudly. "She's not wearing any clothing under that coat and we don't want to scandalize your other customers any more than we already are now, do we?" She smiled when the other woman stiffened slightly at the words but quickly changed her attitude back to one of acceptance; she knew that the Baroness was a person who loved to live her life in a really different manner from most people. You had to be prepared for anything around the beautiful redhead, she thought with a slight bit of approval. She smiled her acceptance of the matter and nodded in understanding before calling forward her prettiest assistant, whom she'd detailed the service for the Baroness to earlier. The very pretty blonde assistant led them back to where she'd set up the items for them.

The assistant quickly went over to pour another glass of champagne for Tamilin and then distributed the flutes to all of the women; the Baroness made for the comfortable chair that they set up for her so that she could watch all the women trying on the lingerie. The assistant approached Tamilin with a tape measure and asked her to remove the trench coat so that she could take the blonde's measurements. She quickly and efficiently took and recorded the measurements onto a client card that they used for all women who visited their shop. She took this information over to another assistant who would be responsible for going out to select the items for the new blonde to try on. The pretty assistant's task was to make sure that the Baroness and her party had everything that they desired. The assistant watched with interest as the rest of the Baroness's beautiful entourage began disrobing; she knew that the women were used to showing off their pretty bodies and weren't embarrassed by her looking them over. She didn't do that with regular customers, in fear of making them uneasy, but these women had made it plain very early on in their visits that she was quite welcome to look. Of course, before they finished, she would be naked as well so that they could return the favour to her; she accepted that as part of her duties and the Baroness made it very worth her while to do that. The assistant was a discreet lesbian in a very serious seven year relationship; she liked looking at these women and showing herself off to them but had no sexual contact with them. The Baroness understood her position and had absolutely no problems with it. The assistant perused Tamilin, giving her an encouraging smile and the blonde grinned back at her.

The four women with the Baroness were now completely naked and were standing easily sipping at their flutes of champagne as they waited for the Baroness to direct them to try on the outfits that were waiting for them. The Baroness was in no rush to have them try on the various items as she sat there leisurely looking them over; she wanted Tamilin to understand that she was not the only one who would spend the majority of her time in front of the Baroness, naked. The women were unconcerned about their nudity because the Baroness frequently required it of them. The women often served tea and cakes to their mistress and her friends in nothing more than stockings and heels. Molly decided that they had waited long enough and that she'd made her point to Tamilin, so she commanded "Paula, you may have the honour of modeling the first outfit." Then she settled back to watch the woman put it on.

The assistant was called over to the entrance of the room and passed the initial selection of outfits for Tamilin; there was a quiet exchange between her and the second employee. The assistant walked over to beside the Baroness and asked, respectfully "Baroness, I'm sorry for disturbing you but we need to know how many outfits you'd like to see the new blonde try on." She waved her hand to indicate Tamilin. "Also, is there a price range that you'd prefer for her?"

The Baroness smiled at the young assistant, she understood that the woman didn't want to interfere with her enjoyment of the situation but that she needed information to do her job in the proper manner. The Baroness had no quibbles with anyone who was seeking to make her life flow in a more organized fashion. "I think we'll limit it to seven or eight outfits. They should be in the lower-medium price range for now. If I require the girl to have more expensive items later, we will come back for another fitting. I know that I'm making an imposition on you by springing her on you without sufficient warning but trust that you'll be able to accommodate me on this. I, of course, will express my gratitude in the usual fashion." Paula had stopped while the Baroness was having the conversation with the assistant and stood there with the bra half on; she knew that the Baroness would want to watch her fitting the lacy item to herself. Once the matter was attended to and the Baroness had returned her attention to her, Paula pushed her breasts into the cups of the bra and fastened it behind her back. She then displayed to the Baroness how well it fit her and how wonderful she looked in it by arching her back and bending forward a few times. Molly watched her contort her upper body with some interest; she never tired of looking at a pretty woman, no matter how many times she'd seen or touched her before. The other women watched with varying degrees of interest as they waited for their turn; of course, Tamilin was quite interested, being new to the process but Desdemona was a little bored because she had spent quite a bit of that morning sucking and playing with Paula's tits.

The other women soon got their turn to show off what the assistant had picked out for them to try on and the Baroness liked most of the items; the few that she didn't, she made her choice obvious pretty much immediately and told the woman wearing it to put it in the reject pile. The accepted pile of lingerie was about six or seven times greater than the rejected pile; the store was very good about picking out items that they thought the Baroness would like to see on her women and the Baroness had a great range that she liked. Shortly after the women had all tried on their second outfits, they began to demand that the assistant disrobe so that she would be naked like they were. The assistant knew the game and initially rejected their suggestion but did so with a show of reluctance when they kept insisting. Tamilin watched the process unfold with a look of confusion until Paula whispered to her that this went on every visit. She then smiled and got in on the action. The Baroness watched her join in the fun with her other girls with a fair bit of amusement; she was quite pleased that the young woman was willing to go as far as them without too much prodding. She'd also liked how the young blonde looked in the outfits that had been chosen for her and wondered briefly if it would be advantageous to see if the woman would delay her proposed marriage to become one of her bitches. Then the Baroness decided that she was being unfair in thinking that way; she should be encouraging the young bride to be to go ahead with her wedding. She knew that she didn't mind playing with another married woman and if the husband was amiable, he might be fun to play with as well. She gave some quick thought to having a threesome with Tamilin and her prospective husband and enjoyed the thought immensely. The visit went by quite quickly and soon it was time for them to leave. They waited while all of their purchases were rung up and packaged for them.

The limousine was waiting at the curb for them and the shop girls filled the huge trunk with all of their purchases as the party got into the spacious passenger compartment. Tamilin had left the store the same way that she had entered it; namely nude under Jill's trench coat. Paula quickly helped her to take it off once they were in the car and resumed playing with the pretty, younger woman. Tamilin enjoyed the attention and was soon being fondled by all of the Baroness's women. She'd decided that she was no longer participating just to get her wedding paid for but because she truly did love what was being done to her. She worried for a bit about what that might mean for her marriage but determined that she would examine those feelings in more detail at a later date and would enjoy herself in the meanwhile. Soon they arrived back at the apartment building where the Baron and Baroness occupied the top two floors.

The Baroness told Tamilin to put Jill's trench coat on once more so that she could enter the building without alarming the other occupants. She told Tamilin that they would be the first ones to go to the penthouse and that the other women would bring up the purchases and join them later. She remembered to instruct Jill to gather up Tamilin's clothing from where it remained strewn around the limousine; she would need her clothing later in the day.

So the Baroness had the pleasure of leading Tamilin into the penthouse; once they were inside the door, she immediately told Tamilin to take off the coat and led her nude down to the living room. The Baroness pulled forward one of the armless chairs that had a plush seat on it and sat down upon it; she knew that this chair would allow her a wide range of movement and had used it before. She looked Tamilin over slowly and then commanded "Sit here at my feet. You may begin kissing up my legs from the knee onwards." She cocked her eyebrow at the young blonde and asked, a little archly "You're not going to balk, are you? I want to feel how well you eat pussy. If I enjoy your attempt, I want to watch you eat out all of my girls." Tamilin nodded eagerly and began placing soft kisses on the Baroness's knees. She slowly worked her way up, using her hands to gently push the Baroness's legs open so she could kiss her upper inside thighs. The Baroness cooperated, watching the blonde's performance with interest. It was obviously not the girl's first time eating pussy and she seemed to be enjoying what she was doing. When Tamilin was within a hand span of the Baroness's flame red pussy, the other women arrived, having finished their tasks. They quickly stripped down to their stockings and heels, which was their normal outfits for the penthouse and arranged themselves around the two women so that they could watch the proceedings. Tamilin was initially distracted by their arrival and looked around at them but the Baroness took her face in her two hands and guided her back to her task. Tamilin settled back into what she was doing quickly.

Soon Tamilin was at the Baroness's cunt, she had pushed the other woman's short dress up to get access to her pussy; she didn't hesitate but started running the tip of her tongue along the Baroness's cunt. After nearly a moment she paused to relish the taste and aroma of the redhead; she found both to be quite intoxicating. She'd had a fair amount of practice eating pussy but she found this to be one of her best ever experiences. She was very excited, her own pussy tingled and twitched as her arousal built; she was thinking how nice it would be for someone to stick a cock in her and ride her while she was doing this. She was a bit surprised that she thought this way because she'd never experienced a three way like that; her two experiences had been with two men. She tried to push that aside so that she could concentrate on giving the Baroness the best experience she could; she recognized now that she wanted something more out of this than just having a wedding paid for. She wondered how best to approach the Baroness about joining her household in some way and then wondered how her fiancé would feel about matters; he knew that she'd enjoyed some lesbian experiences before but would be shocked to find out how much she now wanted to pursue that side of things.

She gently pushed the tip of her tongue into the Baroness and wiggled it as much as she could; the Baroness murmured appreciation and urged her to continue. She ran her tongue up and down the slightly drooling slit, wetting down the curly pussy hairs; the Baroness was exuding a nice musky smell as she increased her flow of juices. Tamilin isolated the Baroness's clit hood and began rubbing her sharp little teeth over it, causing the redhead to flinch slightly and gasp in surprise. Tamilin was a little shocked as well when the Baroness grabbed the back of her blonde head and pushed it hard against her red haired pussy, wanting more from the blonde. Tamilin responded by increasing her slurping. Molly was enjoying the other woman's actions and could feel that she was building towards an orgasm; it was a bit unusual for her to climax with a totally new girl, usually she had to teach the other woman how to get the most out of her. The Baroness could feel her nipples aching for attention and she didn't want Tamilin to stop what she was doing to her pussy so she called Paula over to suck on them for her. Paula came over rapidly to do her mistress's bidding and while she was sucking on the redhead's tits, she took the opportunity to stroke the pretty rear end of Tamilin. Tamilin noticed Paula's attention to her but she didn't object and just continued licking the Baroness's pussy, trying hard to make her climax.

Baroness Molly was whining and twisting her hips somewhat as the blonde continued to lick her and push her closer to climax; the feeling of Tamilin's tongue probing her aroused and drooling cunt and of Paula sucking on her nipples were driving her to a frenzy. This feels utterly fantastic, she thought. A few more minutes of attention and the Baroness gave a small, sharp shriek as she orgasmed all over Tamilin's face. Paula moved up to the Baroness's face and started kissing her mouth as the redhead panted for air; the Baroness loved being distracted by what Paula was doing to her as her body reacted to her orgasm. She could feel a second one just in the offing and murmured softly to Paula "I think I'll come again if you go down and lick me hard. I think Tamilin might be a little too worn out at the moment to achieve it." So Paula eased aside Tamilin, telling her to go up and kiss the Baroness's face, and took her spot between the redhead's legs. She could immediately tell that it wasn't going to take her too much effort to drive her mistress into a second orgasm. The Baroness was fully primed. After five minutes of licking, the Baroness came a second time with an ear-splitting cry of triumph. She so loved it when her girls could make her orgasm multiple times.

The other women had been watching them intently, aroused and stroking themselves as they enjoyed the spectacle. Baroness Molly decided that she and Tamilin needed some time to recover and deserved a little entertainment so she commanded her girls to daisy chain and lick each other to orgasm while she and the blonde bride to be watched them. The girls were very eager to do as commanded and soon the air was filled with their moans as they attempted to make another girl orgasm before they themselves were forced to cum. After nearly eight minutes, all the girls were panting as they attempted to hold back their orgasms and then it was like dominos. One of the girls gave a shriek and orgasmed, quickly followed by two others as they lost control and then the final girl surrendered about thirty seconds later. The four girls lay in a collapsed, intertwined pile as each of them savoured how good they felt. Tamilin looked keenly at the Baroness, she wanted to go in to taste all of the girls; the Baroness immediately understood her intent, smiled at her and nodded her head to give her permission. Tamilin winnowed her way into the pile and started slurping up the juices of all the girls.

Baroness Molly watched the proceedings raptly, thinking how well this pretty young blonde fit in. She decided that she would help the girl to get married in the venue she wanted if that was her desire. She knew that she would work hard at convincing Tamilin that she should join her entourage and would attempt to get her husband to be to join as well. What a pleasant day this turned out to be, she thought happily.

ALL HALLOWS EVE

Kelly was feeling a bit drunk, here at this bar on Halloween as it neared midnight; she'd been guzzling back the beers in order to forget the fact that her boyfriend was supposed to be with her tonight but she had just caught him screwing another girl, just two days ago. She'd considered not bothering to come to the bar, even though she's bought her ticket more than two weeks ago and had spent a good portion of that time creating her costume. She'd always liked Halloween and the fun of dressing up; the last six or so years, she'd come up with some very sexy costumes, even though she was not quite twenty yet. She'd blossomed fairly early and liked making the most of it when she could hide her actual face and identity. She found that enticing men had been extremely stimulating, especially when she could flirt outrageously with them and then say no to their advances. She loved the look of disappointment on their faces when she made it plain that she had absolutely no intention of fulfilling their fantasies. It made her feel superior. But this night she hadn't been able to focus on that mission, she felt too sorry for herself. She took another swig of the somewhat warm beer and sighed deeply, looking down into her glass.

She was enormously surprised when a slim, elegant hand reached in, grabbed her chin and tilted her head up. She found herself looking into the cool grey eyes of another woman. The other woman looked at her quite curiously and then she extended her fingers and brushed the two rather large fake warts from Kelly's nose and right cheek. "There, that's much better" the woman murmured softly, almost to herself. Kelly found that the woman was tilting her head from side to side as she examined her face; she tried to speak in order to protest her treatment but the woman shook her head and she found that she couldn't. Kelly had the stray thought that she should bat the other woman's hand away from her chin but found that she didn't seem to want to do that either. She just stood there mutely. When the other woman reached up with her thumb to trace along Kelly's plump, lipsticked lips, Kelly darted the tip of her tongue at that thumb, shocking the hell out of herself. The woman grunted slightly with pleasure at the response that Kelly was making and Kelly felt a flush of embarrassment start to rush to her pretty face and, to her total astonishment, a deep warmth starting to form deep in her hips. Kelly couldn't understand what was happening to her, she'd always liked men and had never been attracted in any way to another woman before. She wondered if this was just some sort of temporary reaction to her boyfriend's betrayal; at least she kind of hoped that that was what it was.

As she herself was being examined, she looked over the other woman intently. The woman in front of her had long dark hair that flowed to her waist and a narrow, oval face with a wide slash of a mouth and a small, pointed nose. Her cheekbones flared her face out a bit under her rather deepset eyes that peeped out from under a tall, smooth forehead. Kelly noticed that the woman had a tiny bit of a unibrow going as she hadn't bothered to pluck the sparse hairs growing between her gorgeous eyes. Kelly was pretty sure that, unlike the fairly ratty black wig that she was wearing, the woman's hair was her own and it was a beautiful fall of shiny black. Kelly found that she wanted to tilt her chin so that she could get a better look at the other woman's body but her own body refused to obey her commands and she was forced to just look into her face instead. Her cornflower blue eyes finally met the woman's grey ones and Kelly gasped loudly, feeling as though an electric shock had just run up her spine. She frowned from the confusion over what was happening to her and the woman laughed in a slightly tinkling way. "You show confusion, little one" she said to Kelly in a husky, sexy voice. "You dress in that manner on All Hallows Eve and don't expect to get called on it by a practitioner of the dark arts? Surely even you can't be so naïve to think that you could get away with it. I claim you as my own and you will do everything that I bid until I release you from your obligation." She waved her fingers in front of Kelly's staring eyes in a very intricate manner and Kelly's eyes followed them hypnotically. The woman then snapped her fingers and Kelly began smiling very suggestively.

The woman released Kelly's chin and stepped back to look at her body better, therefore giving Kelly a chance to look her over as well. Kelly gave herself a shock as she mmm'd with approval as she took in the dark haired woman in front of her; the woman smiled approvingly at her and thrust out her chest a touch more. Kelly estimated that she had the bigger, rounder chest of the two of them but there was definitely nothing wrong with what the other woman had. Kelly was nearly six foot tall, broad shouldered, big busted with a somewhat thick waist, wide deep hips and long toned legs. She estimated the brunette to be just a half inch shorter than her and of a slimmer build on all aspects but nowhere near skinny. Kelly was astonished to note that she was brazenly looking over the brunette and enjoying it immensely. She ran her long, pink tongue out over her lips to coat their suddenly dry surface. She then noticed that even though the other woman was no longer holding her chin in place, she still didn't seem to be able to move from her spot; she could only seem to cast her eyes about. As she thought about it, she recognized briefly that she should be worried about that fact but her mind kept telling her not to worry about such trivial matters.

Kelly became aware that the other woman was examining her carefully. Kelly had designed her outfit to attract men so it was extremely tight on her, was high up on her long, luscious legs and exposed a huge amount of cleavage. Kelly wasn't wearing a bra or any other support and had been threatening to spill out of her low top all night. She hadn't been more aware of it than the moment the brunette locked her eyes on Kelly's remarkable chest and Kelly was totally conscious that she wanted it to happen. She was wearing a fringed dress that was cut so high that she exposed her bare crotch when she tried to sit on a stool and she'd managed to give quite a number of handsome men a quick little look at her blonde fringe down there. She was also wearing black, silk stockings with the white lace tops fully exposed; in fact she was exposing about an inch of bare thigh above the tops of the stockings most of the time. She was also wearing black leather boots that came up about four inches above her knees and had seven inch heels on them; they made here sway precipitously from side to side when she wasn't drunk and tonight she could barely stand up in them. She'd seen lots of men stop to watch her go by as the evening progressed and her ass bounced around even more. The only real good thing had been that she'd caked on quite a bit of makeup and was sure that only her boyfriend and one or two other men she knew would have been able to identify her. She noticed the brunette take all of this in with a smile of approval and what appeared to be lust. Kelly noticed that the other woman was also dressed as a witch but the outfit wasn't as blatant as Kelly's was. Kelly was surprised that the other woman seemed at home in the outfit, like it wasn't a costume for Halloween at all. She also noted that the brunette had on only a little makeup and no fake blemishes at all.

The woman lifted up Kelly's long pointed black hat and pulled off the ratty wig from underneath, dropping it to the floor, before replacing the hat on Kelly's blonde hair. The wig had covered her shoulder length hair so well that Kelly hadn't bothered to tie her hair up. The brunette once again showed her teeth and said evenly "That looks a little better. I can tell that you're actually quite a beauty under all that gunk on your face and can't wait to get you someplace where we can remove it. But until then, I'll just have to focus on the loveliness under the crap. My name is Witch Hazel and you will refer to me as that or as Mistress. Do you understand?" Kelly was astonished to find herself nodding vigorously but she couldn't seem to stop. "Fine" the brunette purred. "You will be coming home with me tonight. We will lick each other's cunts, play with each other's tits and I'll ream your pussy for you with an oversize dildo. Then I'm going to light some candles and pour hot wax all over your large tits so that you writhe in pain before picking it off with a sharp needle. Doesn't that sound like fun?" Kelly was now almost nodding her head off in agreement; she felt like she should be objecting to something but she couldn't quite seem to pin down what it was. "But I think that maybe I'd enjoy dancing with you for a bit before that. Follow me."

Witch Hazel grabbed Kelly's hand and led her up onto the dance floor; the bar was crowded and they had to push through a number of people to get to the tiled area. Kelly was surprised that no one seemed to brush against the brunette as they made their way because all of the men and more than half the women in their path seemed to push their bodies up against her. She'd felt more than a dozen hands explore her plump ass as Witch Hazel pulled her along; she was very tempted to spike the offender's feet hard with her boots but was hauled by them too fast to do so. Witch Hazel found a clear spot for them to prepare to dance and she pulled Kelly's head down so that it rested on top of her left shoulder; she ground her tits against Kelly's, enjoying the soft plumpness of them and began nibbling on Kelly's earlobe. Kelly muttered her pleasure over her treatment and attempted to mold her big body into the slightly smaller woman. Witch Hazel took a quick peek around to see how closely anyone was watching them and then slid her right hand down the opening in Kelly's top; she slid the fabric down enough that Kelly's large tit popped out. She squeezed the malleable flesh hard with her strong hand and was rewarded with Kelly's nipple growing erect; she rolled and twisted the sensitive nub as Kelly gasped and groaned over her pleasure at what Witch Hazel was doing to her. She didn't seem to mind that it was all happening right in front of everyone. Witch Hazel liked the responsiveness of the big pink nipple and dipped her head down to suck it into her mouth; she raked her sharp teeth across it, eliciting moans of joy from the larger blonde. She kept this up for a few minutes while bumping their two bodies together before she decided to put the breast back into place. Kelly was amazed that no one else in the place had paid any attention to them while that was going on. They sure seemed to be looking at them now, she thought.

"Okay, enough with this. I've had enough foreplay for now. I want to take you someplace where I can get your clothes off so that I can enjoy the rest of your body. You're ready for that, aren't you?" Once again, Kelly felt like one of those toy dogs in the back windows off some cars, nodding their heads aimlessly. She felt a tremendous dampness sliding down her thighs as she gave thought to how rough this woman was going to treat her. Witch Hazel smiled quite cruelly at her and then tugged her towards the exit. They came out onto the cold street and Kelly could feel herself shiver; her outer clothing was still in the bar and she was about to protest the fact when the brunette led her over to a sleek black Jaguar sitting just down the street. Witch Hazel opened the passenger door and guided the tall blonde into it before going around and jumping into the driver's seat. She started the car and Kelly was astounded that warm air started blowing around them right away. Her shivers ceased and her goosebumps retreated.

Witch Hazel drove expertly to a tall, well-light glass building; she led Kelly in through the front entrance and past the well-mannered doormen, who simply nodded at them. They took the elevator up to the penthouse and Kelly gaped at the size of the room that it emptied into; it was huge, more than half of the entire building size. She could see that the far walls were complete glass and it looked like the view would be fabulous in the daytime; at night, it was a huge array of lights and colours from all over the city. When she could tear her eyes away from the outside, she looked at all the small groupings of furniture that dotted the room; the place looked like it had been set up for a gathering of many smaller more intimate groups that just happened to want to be in the same room. She noticed a lot of expensive leather furniture and a number of items that looked like they must be very valuable antiques. Witch Hazel simply stood and watched Kelly's expressive face as she took all of the information in; she felt a small surge of pride that the blonde was so impressed by her lair. She took Kelly by the right arm and guided her over to a stout leather couch that looked like it had come from a psychiatrist's office; it was black, intricately stitched and butter soft. She sat the other woman down on it and began rapidly removing her clothes; Kelly didn't protest and moved around to assist in the removal. Witch Hazel then found a makeup removal cloth and proceeded to wipe away all of the makeup coating Kelly's face; she smiled as Kelly's very pretty features began to emerge. She noted that the blonde was still a bit unfocused in her awareness and knew that she would appear more normal as time passed and she got used to what Witch Hazel had done to her.

She lay Kelly back so that her upper torso was still supported and got in between her long, beautiful legs. She put her face close to the wonderful fringe of blonde hair there at the junction of those gorgeous legs and sniffed daintily, enjoying the musky aroma like a wine connoisseur. She felt her mouth begin to water and a heat form deep inside her hips. This young woman in front of her was ripe and ready for the picking, she thought gleefully and began applying her limber tongue along the blonde's pouting pussy lips. Kelly was feeling quite unsure of matters as Witch Hazel arranged her on the couch, she kept feeling that there was something about what was going on that she would normally protest about but her brain seemed to keep telling her to relax and enjoy it. She thought about it for a bit as the other woman paused to smell her pussy and she thought it had something to do with cocks but she couldn't pin it down any more than that. Then the woman began running her tongue along Kelly's sensitive pussy lips and Kelly lost herself in the pleasurable sensations that were being created by that action. She pushed her hips up towards the brunette's warm, wet mouth and was rewarded by having the other woman's tongue enter her damp slit. Kelly began a low moaning, registering her pleasure about what the other woman was doing to her.

Witch Hazel spent a few minutes energetically lapping at Kelly's cunt, pleased with the noises Kelly was increasingly making as she groaned out her approval. She sensed that the blonde was nearing an orgasm and she thought about whether or not she wanted to force that issue. Since she had never been with the other woman before, she had to calculate if Kelly would still respond well to stimulus after her first orgasm; some women tended to be like men and just wanted to sleep after they came but she sensed that the blonde would still be very eager to perform. Therefore, she intensified her efforts and pushed Kelly into her climax. Kelly bucked wildly and broke away from Hazel as she thrashed around in the throes of her orgasm; Kelly didn't usually climax when men fucked her and most of her orgasms had been of her own doing with the help of a vibrator or her fingers. She wasn't used to there being someone else in bed beside her when she climaxed and she wasn't used to being careful about where she lashed out. Witch Hazel managed to back out of range after being hit by one flailing arm and watched the other woman with interest. She knew that Kelly required more training on the matters of getting her pussy eaten; luckily, she thought, she was more than prepared to take on the pleasant task. But having seen that the blonde was obviously not cognizant in the matters of lesbian sex, she determined that it would be of little use to try to teach her to reciprocate right then. Therefore, rather than have Kelly try to eat her pussy, Witch Hazel decided to begin the other woman's training in the joys of pain.

She left the bed and began gathering her tools as Kelly enjoyed the bliss of the aftermath of her orgasm. The witch hummed a joyful little tune as she accumulated the items she needed; she piled a group of different coloured candles, her lighter, a quirt, a flogger, a large needle and a short stout vibrator. She fondled a buttplug and thought about adding it to the group but decided that might be pushing the other woman too far for the moment. She smiled to herself as she thought about how she would use it on Kelly sometime in the future. The key tonight, she reasoned, was to get the blonde introduced to what her future held for her but not to create too much fear and pain. She just wanted Kelly to start to understand what her role in matters would be going forward.

She gathered up her implements and went over to the couch where the blonde was still lying there, slightly dazed; she flipped up the permanently attached restraints and began to fasten Kelly down, beginning with her arms. Kelly offered no resistance and in fact started giggling when her arms were lifted above her head and tightened down. She had a strange trust in this woman and she tried hard to puzzle out why in her mind; she had a nagging feeling that she should be more worried about what was happening to her than she was. Soon Witch Hazel had her completely fastened by her arms and legs to the sturdy inclined couch and she took off her clothing so that she was naked as well. She climbed onto Kelly and sat down on her hips so that her damp pussy rubbed against Kelly's lower belly right above the blonde's slit. She wiggled her ass vigorously to get comfortable causing Kelly a bit of discomfort as she ground her weight against Kelly's well-padded hips. She'd placed her things on a table she had brought over near the couch and now reached over to select a purple candle that appeared to be in the shape of a nude woman reaching up towards the sky, imploring the gods or whatever to assist her. She carefully lit this candle and placed it on a brightly patterned holding dish before closing her eyes and reciting something to herself under her breath. Kelly watched her with interest, unsure about what was going on but again, strangely calm. Witch Hazel leaned forward and kissed Kelly hard on the lips, smearing both of their lipsticks before grabbing the blonde's plump lower lip in her sharp teeth. Witch Hazel bit down hard enough to draw blood from Kelly's abused lip; Kelly had to restrain herself hard to keep from trying to pull her head back, knowing that she would lose part of her lip if she did so. Kelly could feel tears leaking down her cheeks as a trickle of blood ran down her throat. Witch Hazel carefully sucked some of Kelly's blood into her own mouth and then said, quite eerily "With this blood I do consecrate this sacrifice. With my will and wish I do desire that my spell hold true. With my belief in my benefactor I believe my bidding to come true. With my continued obedience to my craft I will be held bound to do my worship's work. With my continued life I will do as I must to hold everything I believe in to happen. On this most holy of days I demand that this occur." Kelly felt that the room grew gradually colder and darker as the witch said her speech and couldn't help but feel that there was another presence in the room even though she couldn't see anyone. Witch Hazel wasn't finished; she once again waved her slim hands in front of Kelly's face in an intricate pattern before stating "This creature before me shall walk the days with a fur coat and brilliant, shining eyes only to become human again as she joins me in my bed. When I have taken as much pleasure from her as I desire, I will dismiss her and she will once again take her familiars form." Kelly felt a sharp pain behind her eyes as Witch Hazel's grey eyes seemed to bore into her blue ones.

Then the brunette took another candle from the group on the table, this one a long straight red one and lit it from the flame of the purple figurine. She held it, lit and dripping, over Kelly's plump white breasts; the hot wax burned as it struck her flesh and Kelly gave some startled yips of pain before moaning about her rough treatment. "Your pain and desire will give power to the spell" the witch hissed. "Make all the noise you want. I won't stop and no one will bother to rescue you." Kelly gave some thought to yelling out for help but was surprised when her mind began to shut that thought down. She was amazed that she began to enjoy the feeling of the hot wax dripping onto her; she could feel her cunt tingle and her clitoris twitch beneath Witch Hazel's hips. Witch Hazel grinned quite evilly as she recognized what was happening to the blonde; she reached over and retrieved the squat vibrator which she guided beneath her hips and into Kelly's wet, willing cunt. It took her six hard thrusts with it to embed it all the way into the blonde cunt and Kelly grunted encouragement with each thrust. Witch Hazel knew that the blonde was now lost in her enchantments and her own desires; she would crave being treated in an extremely rough manner as regular sex would no longer satisfy her lusts. Once the brown vibrator was seated, Witch Hazel turned it on and its powerful motor hummed merrily in its fleshy cocoon; Kelly bucked her hips upwards as the motor inside her drove her wild and gave a strangled shriek of pleasure. Witch Hazel slammed her weight down onto the blonde's hips to get her back into the proper position; she could feel the buzzing motor working in the other woman even as she did so. They spent a few minutes fighting with their hips until Kelly finally succumbed with a piercing whine of discomfort tinged with happiness. Witch Hazel spent a moment or so, checking to see that the fight had left the blonde and she was going to accept what was happening to her; she knew that Kelly was enjoying the vibrator because she could feel a huge damp area underneath her ass as the blonde pumped out liquids. When she was satisfied, she took the flogger and spent a few minutes slapping its soft leather strands all over the blonde's tits and torso; Kelly thrashed around a bit as she enjoyed the vibrator inside her and the warmth developing on her skin from the abuse. After a while of this, Witch Hazel returned to lighting candles and dripping wax down onto Kelly's unprotected tits. She could see that the blonde was so lost in her own mind that her eyes had nearly rolled up into the back of her head.

She applied a fair coating of wax in six different colours and sat there for a moment, admiring the almost artistic display they created; Kelly was moaning and twitching somewhat below her. She liked how the blonde's arousal had hardened her nipples as the wax had coated them and she reached out with her hands, broke the wax away from them and used her thumb and forefinger to roll the other woman's long, chunky nipples. Kelly made noises that she took to be approval. After a few minutes, Witch Hazel decided that it was time to remove the wax; something was needed to break it up so that chunks could easily be broken free of the soft flesh below it and she had just the thing at hand. She rocked her hips hard against the reclining woman, enjoying the rapid buzzing still going on deep in the fleshy cocoon, and reached out to grab the quirt. She slipped herself back down into position and then struck the waxy breasts hard about three times each with the leather whip. Kelly squirmed, cried out and thrust her chest up as the whip came down on her; she registered both pain and excitement from the actions. Witch Hazel ground her hips down onto the restrained woman, retrieved the needle and began picking chunks of wax from the soft breasts, humming happily as she did so. She was quite careless with how she was doing her task and made sure to nick the skin of the blonde, causing some light bleeding from the scratches created. When she'd removed a lot of the coating wax, she stuck the pointed end of the needle against the base of Kelly's left nipple and pushed it through until the point was out the other side. Kelly screamed at the pain that this caused but then settled back down in wonder as it drove her over the edge and she climaxed. Witch Hazel thought that she was riding a bucking bronc as Kelly writhed around under her as she orgasmed.

Witch Hazel looked over longingly at the flogger again but decided that it would be overkill for today; she was immensely pleased at how Kelly had performed and decided that she'd suffered enough for that day.

As the other woman was settling back down, in the aftermath of her second climax, Witch Hazel removed the needle and the vibrator before releasing the bonds. She repositioned the blonde and brushed some more wax particles from her skin. She tilted Kelly's head and looked deep into her dazed eyes. "I am done with you for now" she commanded and Kelly gave her a bemused grin. Then Kelly thought, deep in her mind, wait, what was it that the witch had said about fur coat and dazzling eyes. She could feel that something was happening to her; it felt like something was growing out of her cheek. She reached up and felt something like a set of whiskers there. Wait, Nooooo!

THE PUNISHMENT GAME: FIGGING

Lorilei was standing in the bathroom, looking at her reflection in the mirror; she was concerned about the crowsfeet forming on her thirty-seven year old face. She already had to dye her dark hair to hide the gray in it. Avoiding looking too closely at her flaws, she documented her good features; her large rack was still outstanding, her tummy was acceptable and her ass well-padded but toned nicely. She considered her legs to be too short but had received compliments on them as recently as two weeks ago at work. She steeled her nerve and went out into the club to where she was supposed to wait with the other three women until they were to be introduced to the members of the club. She had been complaining about a need for money to some of the other women at work and then one of them invited her for a drink after work. The woman had asked Lorilei how desperate she was to reduce her credit card debt and what she'd be willing to do to accomplish that. Lorilei had looked her carefully in the eyes and told her that she'd be willing to screw men or women in order to obtain the money, providing that the price was right. She'd heard some rumors about this woman and the types of things she was involved in. The woman had laughed and said that she wasn't suggesting anything quite that mundane and personal but that there might be something Lorilei would be willing to do that would earn her more than enough money to pay off those credit vultures. Lorilei had asked for more details and the woman explained; Lorilei was appalled by what was being asked of her and therefore asked for time to think about it. The woman was happy to let her have all the time she needed. They both left after that single drink.

Two weeks went by and Lorilei was in even worse financial shape; the mechanic told her that she needed to pay for a lot of work on her car. She thought about what she'd been offered and decided that she could do it; she phoned the woman from work and asked her to set it a meeting for her. She met with the executive members of the club, who asked her to strip down and pose for them as they asked their questions, and concluded a satisfactory meeting with them. They answered her questions fully and she felt that they were being very honest with her and she gave them the same courtesy, knowing that it would make things go better. They all left the meeting with the executive giving her as much time as she needed before making the decision; there was a rotating schedule that ran every fifteen days so she could have a choice of dates. It took her less than twenty-four hours to decide to do it and she called and arranged a date that would work for her.

Now Lorilei was standing before a raucous crowd in her short black dress, displaying an incredible amount of her cleavage and thighs while perched on the highest heels she'd ever attempted to wear. Her heart was thumping terrifically hard behind her massive chest and felt to her like a scared rabbit trying to break free. She looked around at the other women on the stage and couldn't believe how calm they looked. She didn't realize that the other women felt the same as her and couldn't believe how calm she was. She tried to smile invitingly and friendly to the people in the noisy crowd as they jostled around to get better looks at the frightened women. She'd been told that there was an incredible amount of gambling that went on at this club and that was a part of the draw. Of course, the main feature was watching naked women writhing in pain. She'd been told that the women would have to pose there in front of the crowd for ten minutes so that all of the people had a chance to examine them and place their wagers and she felt like it had already been an eternity. She wished that she could have a drink of water to soothe her parched throat but had been cautioned that she might want to avoid drinking too much liquids before the activity. There was plenty of opportunity for accidents and the less messy they were, the better.

Finally, she could see the younger helper women for the women on the stage beginning to make their way through the audience. There was a lot of hooting and hollering as the pretty, naked women wiggled through the mass of onlookers. Lorilei looked into the face of the slim blonde who stopped before her; the girl wasn't paying her any attention but was waving to the crowd and acknowledging their comments. The hostess rang the crystal bell to get everyone's attention and the skinny blonde began helping Lorilei out of the tight black dress; she wasn't wearing any underwear underneath it, per instructions, but had to wiggle her body quite a bit to get it up over her head. That had been the intention of making her wear the garment. The noise level increased as all of the people watching got to observe the four women fighting to get their exceedingly small, tight dresses off their lush bodies. Lorilei could see that two of the other women had fairly large tits, not as big as hers of course, and the one who didn't, still had a legitimately perky pair. Lorilei also noticed that all of the four women were quite heavy in the rear ends and assumed that because of what was about to happen to them, that it was a feature that the executive looked for. She took a deep breath for courage and noticed some women about halfway back looking at her with a good deal of interest as her chest swelled. She gave them a tentative smile because she was still very nervous.

The chime sounded again and the blonde led her over to the small piece of furniture that she would be fastened to for the rest of the contest. It was kind of like a low slung set of stocks and Lorilei was aware that it would arch her back and cause her to push her plump ass out. There were a set of angled mirrors a couple of feet in front of it so that the audience could see the expressions on her face as she went through her ordeal. The blonde woman fastened Lorilei into the small, heavy stocks, strapped braces to her knees so she wouldn't be able to bend them and did up ankle restraints that would prevent her from moving them too much. The audience wanted to see her ass jiggle as she went through her suffering, not her dancing her feet around.

Once Lorilei was secured in place, the blonde woman took a tube of KY jelly and squeezed a large dollop right onto her exposed rosebud; Lorelei wiggled her ass because of the cool temperature of the stuff on her warm skin. The other woman squeezed a bit more onto her fingers and then began deftly working it into Lorilei's anus. Lorilei found it to be very erotic and pleasurable and she gave some low moans of approval; she felt very embarrassed and exposed until she heard the other women doing the exact same thing. The blonde deftly applied even more and worked it up Lorilei's asshole as deep as she could; the young woman knew that Lorilei would appreciate all of the lubricant once it became time to insert the huge buttplug into her tight hole. She had done this to several women before. She gave Lorilei a light slap on her ass to indicate that she was done and they were just waiting for the other three to get finished. Lorilei took another deep breath, trying desperately to calm herself before being put to the test. She avoided looking at the massive buttplug that lay on a low table beside her. She didn't know how she was going to be able to take that up her asshole.

The crystal bell sounded again and the blonde took up the other item that lay beside the huge buttplug; a rather large suppository that had a core of fresh shaved ginger root and had layers of cayenne pepper, wasabi mustard and hot pepper sauce wrapped in layers of dissolvable wax. The suppository would melt under body heat, releasing its contents deep in the anus of the girl it was put into; she would suffer from the effects of the contents while the audience relished her pain. The contest would go on until only one woman remained in it and she would be given the grand prize. Just for entering the contest, Lorilei would receive a fairly substantial amount to put towards her debts, winning it would wipe them out completely and give her a small amount for saving. Lorilei knew that it would hurt but she intended on winning the contest. Rumour also had it that the winner and any interesting participants would be invited back to a tournament of champions for substantially bigger prizes and she intended to find out if that was true. The crystal bell rang again and the helper forced the suppository up into Lorilei's asshole, making sure not to damage it and start the process early. Then young blonde began forcing home the buttplug. The small top half entered Lorilei easily enough but she could feel when the bottom half started stretching her sensitive asshole. The girl wiggled the plug while pushing it in to get Lorilei to stretch more and had it to within an inch of full insertion when Lorilei clamped down her anus muscles. The blonde stroked her exposed asshole and wiggled the plug even harder as she strained to get it in the tight hole. Lorilei knew that she had to allow it into her or be disqualified so she let out a shriek and relaxed her anus as much as she could. The buttplug went in with an audible popping sound and Lorilei moaned with relief. The meaty part of the plug was beyond her rosebud that was now clamped around a smaller shaft further back; the plug effectively sealed off her asshole while it was in place.

A few minutes went past while she listened abstractly to the people watching and she began to feel a warming sensation deep in her bowels. Oh no, she thought wildly, my body heat is melting the wax and I'm beginning to feel the hot pepper sauce. She gave a moan of frustration and was surprised to hear the other women making noises too as they started feeling the hot sauce. She wiggled her butt about hoping to get a little relief from the sensations in her ass but was just rewarded with some catcalls from the audience. The warmth inside her intensified and she groaned in pain, knowing that things were only going to get worse. She tried to focus her eyes on a spot on the floor in front of her so that she could meditate and ignore the pain that way but the heat was too distracting. She cast her eyes about, hoping that something would occupy her attention but was unsuccessful. Then she felt a stronger heat and recognized that the next layer of the suppository was gone. She assumed that what she was feeling now was a result of the cayenne pepper, but maybe it was the wasabi; either way, she wasn't happy about it. It appeared that the other women were also disgruntled about what was happening to them and she could hear one of them shrieking her pain.

Lorilei screwed up her eyes in concentration and focused her mind on what she planned to do with the money. She was groaning from the painful sensations in her ass but was able to partially distract her attention from the agony. She did notice that people were attending to the shrieking woman now and she was being relieved with having her buttplug pulled and getting a cold milk enema. Lorilei wondered if maybe being given a forceful enema in front of a crowd of strangers might be more embarrassing than having to endure the figging. She knew that even if she won, she would have to undergo the same treatment so it wouldn't really matter if it was. She recognized quite quickly that thoughts of being humiliated by the enema was actually working to distract her and help her with controlling the effects of her pain. She thought more about different types of enemas that she could be forced to undergo and was actually moved to laughter about the thought of a champagne enema. Everyone notice her chortling, even her opponents who were becoming totally disheartened by the fact that she could laugh about matters. Suddenly there was still more intensity in the heat in her ass and she bit her lip to muffle her cries of pain. One of the other women was now begging for relief while the other one was groaning quite loudly. Lorilei calculated that if she could hold on for three or four minutes more, she would win this contest. Sweat poured off her hot face and even broke out across her bare ass.

She wiggled her ass and tried to pick up her feet but the restraints held them in place. She moaned out her pain and wondered how much time had passed. She grew quite worried because she could not hear the other woman's suffering, not realizing that her own noises were covering the sounds. She could hear the audience urging the two of them to continue and she tried to comply. She was just on the verge of surrendering when the buttplug was pulled roughly out and a tube that delivered cool, soothing liquid was shoved inside her. She sighed mightily with relief as the burning pain in her asshole was diminished. She knew that she had won the contest because she had never spoken the words to give in. She relished the relief and began making plans for the money that would be left over once she had paid off her debts.

SHEILA CUCKOLDS BARRY

Barry and Sheila had a good marriage; it had lasted over ten years and produced two wonderful children, both girls. They had gone through some rough times together but many more happy times than that. Barry felt that Sheila was still one of the sexiest women that he'd ever met and she'd gotten most of her figure back after the two pregnancies; Barry was of the opinion now that the extra weight and size she now carried made her even more attractive than when he'd first met her when she was quite skinny. They had sex with each other every day, quite often more than once, unless one of them was sick. Barry was aware that he had to do his part in all of the household duties from washing dishes, to sweeping and dusting, to taking care of the two girls if he expected for Sheila to have the energy and ambition to screw him. He tended to all of these duties with a positive attitude, knowing what the reward was going to be. Sheila was aware from discussions with other married women, how much of a treasure Barry was; the other women complained that their husbands did nothing around the house and then expected to fuck their wives hard in bed that night. Lately though, Sheila had been feeling a little restless; something seemed to be missing in her life and she couldn't figure out quite what it was. It had been going on for a couple of months. Barry had noticed her distraction but left it to her as to when they would talk about it; he wanted her to feel very comfortable talking about her problems with him.

Sheila was having a frustrating morning, the girls had made quite a mess of the house and she was having to straighten up the chaos. She could feel her anger and frustration rise and had to remind herself that the girls were just children and were actually very well behaved most of the time. She paused in what she was doing to glance out of the window; it was a very opportune time because one of the young men who lived down the street went biking past in his tight, short shorts and muscle shirt. Sheila stared intently at him, relishing the wonderful sight until he was too far away to see; she suddenly realised that she was drooling, both from her mouth and her heated pussy. She recognized what she thought she was missing from her life and felt an incredible amount of shame. She wanted to be fucked hard by other men; that was incredibly unfair to her husband and children to be so selfish, she thought despondently. She cleaned up the mess and scolded herself silently as she worked. She did a thorough cleaning of the whole house as punishment for her disobedient thoughts but it did nothing to lessen them.

Barry came home from work in a fairly good mood to a spic and span house and a thoroughly grumpy wife. He asked Sheila "Why did you decide to clean the house today, honey? Are we expecting some guests?"

"No" she replied, snarling at him. "It was just time for it to be cleaned. I got tired of living in a pig sty and decided I needed to do something about it." Barry looked around the house with a bit of wonder, it had looked fine to him when he'd left for work that morning, certainly no worse than usual. He took a closer look at Sheila and determined that something was troubling her. He thought about telling her that she should have waited a couple of days so that he could've helped her on the weekend but eventually decided that none of this was about the cleanliness of the house, so he refrained. He decided that he'd give her until bedtime to approach him to talk about what was bothering her and if she hadn't done it by then, he'd bring it up. They spent a rather tense evening together without her initiating discussion of the matter upsetting her.

When she was involved with undressing for bed that evening, Barry scrutinized her very closely; he knew that something was bothering her and it upset him that she wouldn't share it with him. He spent a moment reviewing in his own mind, his own actions of the past couple of weeks to determine if he might have done something to infuriate her but came up with a blank. He knew that he'd done some things that she hadn't been overly fond of but nothing that should cause her to hold back her feelings and telling him about what was upsetting her. Still, maybe he'd missed something, he thought and decided to simply ask her. "Honey, have I done something to upset you?" he asked with a concerned look on his face.

She glanced up at him and saw his look, it just made her feel more miserable about herself so she lowered her head again and stared at her feet. "No, you haven't" she muttered quietly.

"Then can we talk about what is bothering you?" he asked softly as he went and sat by her on the bed. He reached out and began massaging her neck for her, something she usually liked very much. She raised her arms and stopped him, she wasn't in the mood for that. "I've always believed that we could talk about and solve any problem if we work together on it" he intoned softly as he put his hands back in his lap. He was surprised when she just burst out sobbing. He ached to put his arms around her and pull her into his body to comfort her but he was too afraid that she'd push her away from her. "Oh, honey" he stated sorrowfully. "How can I help make things right if you won't tell me what's wrong?"

After a few more minutes went by, the silence broken only by her choked sobs, she finally ventured to speak. "You're going to hate me. I've done something incredibly wrong and I can't get it out of my mind."

Barry looked her over carefully as thoughts of what she might have done raced through his head and he opened his arms to her. She threw herself into his loving embrace and they hugged quietly for a moment. He broke the silence by quietly asking "What did you do that's bothering you so much? You know that I can forgive you almost anything. It may take a little time but we'll get through this."

She took a further moment and then quietly replied "I've had lustful thoughts about being fucked by another man."

He pulled away from her slightly so that he could see her tearstained face. "And?" he asked, puzzled.

She frowned at him and replied "And nothing. Just imagined what it might feel like to have someone else screwing me."

"Honey" he stated, slightly exasperated with her. "I've told you that I think about other women occasionally and even sometimes when I'm in the middle of fucking you. It's normal and nothing to be ashamed about. I'm actually surprised that you haven't had those ideas before. Why are you making such a big deal about it? It's nothing." He pulled her back against his body, incredibly relieved.

"Yes" she stated, slightly muffled. "But you're a man and it's okay for you to think like that. It's how you're built. I'm a woman, a wife and a mother. I'm not supposed to have those thoughts. I'm supposed to be happy with what I have." She began silently crying again.

"Oh, bullshit" he exclaimed. "Who says you're not supposed to have those thoughts. The same people who believe that a man should sit idly by as his wife cooks supper rather than grabbing some potatoes and peeling them to help out. You know that I don't agree with those people. I think you can have any thoughts that you want." He held her in his arms and rocked her for a couple of moments, enjoying the feeling of her soft body as he did so. Then he stated "I love you, honey, and you can have all of those types of thoughts that you want. If it makes you feel better, you can even tell me about them. I'm not going to get mad about it and you might even turn me on with them." He parted from her again so that he could lock eyes with her and asked "Do you want to make love or would you rather just go to sleep?"

Sheila looked up at her husband through some still unshed tears and realized how much she loved him; he was a very good man, kind and understanding. She felt a bit tired from her tumultuous day and would have preferred to sleep but then, she thought, maybe an half hour or so of getting lovingly fucked would do them both a world of good. "I'm yours for whatever you want to do to me, big man" she simpered at her husband. "Maybe I should be spanked for my naughtiness" she suggested.

Barry looked at her, she usually didn't offer spanking as an option, and he seriously considered it but then he thought that she'd take it as a punishment for her feelings and he truly believed that she deserved no punishment. "I'll hold you to the spanking another night" he promised as he reached out to help her out of her remaining clothing. "Tonight I think it'll just be a little arousal, maybe a bit of oral and a whole lot of hard banging. I want you to see stars before I'm finished with you."

Sheila felt some jolts of electricity from excitement shoot down her spine as she started getting incredibly aroused. "Oh, big man" she cooed as she helped him work off her clothes. "Don't make promises you have no hope of keeping. I'm not that easy a girl." Barry growled at her playfully as his cock began to stiffen and tent his loose boxers. As soon as she was completely nude, he whipped off his own underwear and jumped onto the bed beside her. He began kissing her mouth while he worked his left hand in between her plump thighs. He inserted his index finger about an inch inside her vagina and started stroking up and down her slit causing her to ooh and ahh as she enjoyed the feeling. He traced her slightly extended inner lips knowing that such action caused her to become quite aroused and slowly flicked her stiffening clit hood with his thumb. She sighed in contentment and started massaging her own breasts with her hands, squeezing on the nipple and pulling it slightly outward from her body. Barry looked into her somewhat dazed eyes and grinned joyfully at her; he liked seeing her so relaxed and yet tense from arousal. He knew that she needed some time and generous foreplay in order to have a hope at an orgasm and he was intent on giving her that opportunity every time he fucked her. He felt that she deserved it and knew that he could literally get off in less than five minutes if he ignored her needs and just paid attention to his own. But that wasn't fair to her and she was his partner and his reason for living so he put her happiness at the top of his list. He'd done this for her for so long, he could do it while his mind was occupied with other matters and tonight he thought about what she'd told him. He examined his feelings about watching another man screwing her and was amazed that he was extremely turned on by the thought. He actually had to shy away from the mental image because he was in danger of prematurely ejaculating on her. Hmmm, he thought, that's something that I never thought would interest me, I wonder if I can talk her into pursuing it so I can see if it makes me as hot as the thought of it does.

He recognized that she was quite wet and therefore ready for the next step. He moved his mouth down to her left breast and greedily sucked on the erect nub while forcing two of his fingers through the soft folds of her plump cunt. She stroked his hair with her left hand while her right still fondled her right tit and she began making some noises to show her approval and arousal. He loved both the feel of her somewhat fleshy body and the intimate sounds she was making. He felt his cock getting incredibly stiff and realized that he had to distract himself somewhat before he blew his load. He was surprised that he was acting this way because he usually could handle himself quite well; he wondered if the thought of her being penetrated by another cock was solely responsible and decided that it was only part of it. He determined that he should pursue these thoughts at another time and began to plan his morning for the next day; that always occupied him enough so that he could last the required amount of time. After a few more minutes, he could tell by the change in the tone of her moans that she was ready for the next step and he shifted down her body so that his mouth was now on her sodden pussy, he teased her with his tongue, enjoying the thrilled sounds she was making. He thought about their lovemaking and began to feel like maybe they'd gotten into too much of a routine, he enjoyed the fact that he knew exactly how to set her off but rued that they really didn't try too much different anymore. He chortled as he thought about the one time that she'd tried to reciprocate after he gave her oral and the astounded look on her face as he'd shot his load extremely quickly into her mouth. He glanced up and could see that she was wondering what he was laughing about down there so he got his mind back on his business and tongue lashed her quite thoroughly.

Now that he was satisfied that he'd gotten her as close to her orgasm as he could, he climbed on top of her, conscious of the fact that she didn't like him to make her bear too much of his weight, and entered her pussy with his cock. He spent a few moments on rapid insertions and withdrawals, never penetrating her too far; he was aware that this built up a tremendous need in her to feel him fully inserted into her. He noted that she was drooling liquids from her pussy a little more than usual and wondered briefly if she was imagining that he was a different man. He gave a little smile at the thought and decided that he'd try to convince her to fuck another man while he watched. But for now, he thought, I've got to do my best to make her cum before her tight wet pussy makes me cum. He started to drive deep into her hips, ensuring that he contacted her hips hard, knowing that she liked that. He spent about three minutes energetically thrusting his prick in and out of her squishy pussy, desperately trying to distract himself as he withheld his orgasm, in order to attempt to get her to climax.

He could feel his control slipping away fast and he whined intensely, both to relieve his own feelings and to warn her that he was about to come. He couldn't tell if he'd done enough to get her to orgasm but he was beyond his control not to unload into her wet cunt and he gave a loud shout of triumph as he spurted a jet of cum into her. His balls began aching rather pleasantly as he emptied their load and he realized that he'd been holding his breath and was feeling a bit oxygen starved. He panted furiously as he attempted to regain his control over his body and his mind whirled in its sea of endorphins; he felt a tremendous feeling of accomplishment, like he always did when he orgasmed. He was aware that it was a rather petty achievement but it was one that he enjoyed so much. He became aware that he'd collapsed his weight onto Sheila and that she was now bucking hard against his heavy body as she fought through the throes of her own climax. He felt a loving, approving sensation that he'd managed to make her cum; he really adored the feeling of her hips slamming against him because he knew that he'd accomplished what he'd wanted. He focused on her sweaty face with its closed eyes and open, panting mouth as she writhed beneath him and was intensely happy that she was enjoying herself so much. He knew that it would take a few minutes for her to subside and recover from the intensity of her orgasm so he just lay on top of her relishing all of the feelings that swam through his addled mind.

As he started to recover his wits, he moved off of her, aware that she didn't like to have to bear his weight for too long because she said that it hurt her back. He registered the warm sweaty stickiness that coated his lower belly, crotch and upper thighs and wondered for the umpteenth time why sex had to be so messy. He went off to the bathroom and got a facecloth, ran it under warm water and cleaned himself off. He squeezed it clean and took it out so that he could begin cleaning her up. As he was just finishing up, he could sense that she was almost back in control of her mind and he looked at her to see that she was regarding him lovingly. He leaned down and gave her a tender kiss on the lips. "Thank you for letting me be your husband and enjoy fucking you" he whispered in her ear.

"Thank you for being my husband, fucking me well and taking care of my needs" she replied. He pulled his head back so that he could see her face and that she was grinning happily at him so he returned that same grin; he was aware that they both had very deep feelings for each other but he felt that it was important that they express those feelings often to remind themselves of them. Early on in their relationship, she had been very embarrassed about expressing her feelings to him, especially right after sex, but she'd learned to do so and it made both of them feel closer.

She was preparing to drift off to sleep when he decided that he needed to talk to her about one more thing. He looked into her exhausted face and asked softly "I would like to see you fucking another man like your fantasy you told me about. Would you consider doing that for me? Don't answer now. Just think about it, would you? Good night, love." He rolled over to his side of the bed and was soon asleep.

As they were clearing the breakfast dishes in the morning, she glanced around to make sure that the girls were out of earshot and asked "Do you want to fuck another woman?"

He gave her a careful, measured look and asked back "Would you like to see me fucking another woman?"

She considered it momentarily and then sighed, stating "No. I think that I'd feel very jealous about that and somewhat betrayed. Are you quite sure that you wouldn't feel that way? I'm very afraid that once the genie is out of the bottle, we can't put it back in again and I'd hate to do anything to ruin our happy marriage." She watched his face closely.

"I am quite sure about it" he stated firmly. "But I leave it in your hands to decide if you wish to do it. I won't ever bring it up again but will wait for you to make a decision. Take as much time as you need." He checked his watch and said "I have to get off to work now. I'll see you tonight." He gave her a firm kiss and headed off.

It was over two weeks later as they were once again preparing for bed that she brought the matter back up. "We need to talk" she said as she removed her bra and sat on the bed in only her panties.

"Sure" he replied, clad only in his boxers. He went over and sat beside her and reached out to hold her hand. "What do we need to talk about?"

She took a deep breath to steady herself and he couldn't help himself, he watched her chest swell with lust and pride. She noticed where his attention had been drawn to, and instead of being insulted, she was complimented; it was nice to know he was still so interested in her body. "Were you completely serious when you said you'd like to watch another man fuck me?" she asked, slightly tremulous.

He reached out both hands and began massaging the base of her neck, he could tell how much asking that question was stressing her by the tightness he found there. "Of course I was, honey" he replied evenly. "If it is something you would like to do, I believe that I'd find it incredibly arousing. I think we should make no commitment right now about more than a single time so we can adequately assess our feelings after it happens. You have my complete blessing to try this and I promise to never hold it against you in our life together." He looked her solemnly in the eyes and then gave her a very passionate kiss.

When they'd finished the kiss, she looked into her lap and stated "I've kinda chosen the man that I'd like for it to be." She looked up quickly to gauge his reaction, surprised when he just nodded and gave a half shrug. "Do you have any objections to that?" He just shook his head negatively and waited for her to continue. After a moment of studying him, she said "He's a young man that lives down the street. I've seen him jog by in his shorts and he does something for me. I don't feel right in approaching him by myself and wonder if we'd overwhelm him by doing it together." She looked at him very wistfully and asked "Do you think that you could go talk to him on your own and outline to him what we want from him?" I know that it is a lot to ask. Making a man go ask another man to fuck his wife, but ..." she trailed off as she watched him nervously.

Barry gave her another deep kiss before saying "I'll be happy to approach him and see if he is interested." He grinned at her and stated "I think that you have made an excellent choice. He looks like he could fuck you very hard. Now let's fuck so I can prove to you how much I love you." They screwed each other hard and fell asleep exhausted.

The next morning, Barry gave some consideration as to the best way to approach Tommy, the man Sheila wanted and someone he knew very casually. Did one just walk up to another man and ask if he'd like to fuck your wife while you watched, he wondered and the thought made him smile so he thought that it was probably not the right method. He took over a week, making plans and discarding them to decide what he was going to do; Sheila never mentioned it to him, letting him make his move under his own conditions. Their sex life continued as normal with each of them enjoying it.

Barry was out in the yard on a Saturday evening, rolling up the watering hose when Tommy jogged by, heading back to his house after his run. Barry impulsively called out to him "Hey, Tommy. Got time for a beer."

Tommy stopped, turned around and headed over to him. He was panting a bit from his exertions but didn't look too tired. As he walked over, glowing with a light sweat coating, Barry could understand very well why Sheila was attracted to him. He was muscular in a lean way, had a handsome face and if the bulge in his tight shorts was genuine, he had a fair package on him. Tommy waited to speak until he was just a couple of yards away, saying "Sure, neighbour. I'm always up for a beer." He stuck out his hand and confessed "I can't remember your name offhand, sorry."

"It's Barry" Barry replied as he shook the proffered hand. "Just give me a moment. Is Bud okay?" When Tommy nodded, Barry went into the garage and pulled a cold beer out of the fridge and brought it back to Tommy. Tommy popped the top and took a long swig of the cold elixir.

"Not a huge Bud fan" he confessed. "But any cold beer hits the spot right now. Is there something I can do for you?"

Barry looked at him and decided to be quite forward about matters. "I was wondering if you've noticed my wife?" he asked quietly, thinking that he'd see if he was even interested in Sheila before proceeding.

Tommy immediately held up his hands and stretched them out before him while taking a half-step away from Barry. "Hey, sorry man. You know how it is. You see a pretty woman wearing something skimpy as you go by, you just got to have a look at it. I didn't mean any harm by it and if I offended you or her, I apologize profusely." He met Barry's eyes and said "I'll just head home and will try to keep my eyes to myself in the future." He started to move away, keeping an eye on Barry.

Barry was very astounded by the turn of events and was momentarily shocked into silence. He recovered his wits as he recognized that Tommy was leaving and he didn't want this opportunity to get away from him. "No, no" he protested. "You're taking this all wrong. I hadn't even realized that you'd been looking at her as you went by." He smiled as friendly as he could to Tommy and said "I know that she's been looking at you and she likes what she sees. She's asked me to talk to you." Although he'd said that quite quietly, he looked around and then continued "Maybe we should talk about this in a more private location. Come on into the garage." He turned and walked into the garage, hoping that Tommy would follow. It took a couple of moments for Tommy to decide to at least enter the doorway. He peeked in to where Barry had set up a couple of lawn chairs and was sitting in one of them. He noticed that the empty lawn chair was near the door and a ways away from Barry. He decided that he was probably safe to enter and was quite intrigued about what Barry might want from him. Never venture, never gain, he thought as he sat in the chair.

Barry spent about ten minutes talking to Tommy, convincing him that he was glad that Tommy had noticed Sheila and that he was okay with the fact. He even outright asked Tommy if he was interested in fucking Sheila, omitting the fact that he wanted to watch for the moment and Tommy sidestepped the question, figuring that it might be a trap. Barry spent time trying to convince the reluctant man that he was fine with Tommy fucking Sheila. After the ten minutes, Tommy left with the half promise to think about it and Barry went back into the house.

Tommy thought matters over and found that he couldn't get the thought of fucking the plump, pretty blonde Sheila out of his mind. For a full week, she invaded his night time fantasies and he woke up, hoping to find her beside him for real. He was cautious about the fact that her husband had brought the matter up to him but was, nonetheless, extremely intrigued. On the next Saturday afternoon, he screwed up his courage, put on some nice clothes and went to knock on their door. Sheila answered the door. She had been scrubbing the kitchen floor, dressed in a tank top and cutoffs and she was sweating extremely noticeably. He could see from the look on her face that she was surprised to see him at the door and was mortified by her own appearance. He liked the way the sweat glistened off the tops of her plump breasts and the look of her somewhat soft thighs. He caught a good whiff of her smell and thought that it was quite intoxicating; he could feel his cock swelling and had to quickly adjust himself. Sheila noticed what he was doing and gave him a heart-warming smile. She could feel her nipples perking and her pussy tingling. "Hi" she said, breathily. "Come on in."

Once he was in and the door closed, he looked her in the eyes and said "Your husband asked me about something last week and I thought I might like to talk with you guys about the matter." He intensified his gaze. "That is if you are both still interested in it." He was hesitant about spelling it out in case she didn't know anything about it.

"Oh yes" she said, nodding vigorously. "We wanted to know if you'd be interested in fucking me." She paused and gave him a slightly coy smile. "Barry mentioned that you'd been looking at me. I'm happy that I can still draw some interest." Then she remembered what she currently looked like and was deeply embarrassed as her face flushed. "I'll just get Barry up here to entertain you while I clean up and put on something presentable." She went over to the basement door, opened it and yelled "Barry." She came back to keep him company while Barry came up and still blushed furiously.

"Please" he said protesting. "Don't get into something different on my account. I like the way you look." He gave her a lecherous grin before stating "And I love the way you smell." She gave him a very quizzical look and then Barry arrived and interrupted them.

Barry held out his hand and the two men shook hands. "Tommy, glad that you came over. I assume that this is because of what we'd talked about." He half turned to Sheila and continued "I'm not sure that you've ever been introduced to my wife. This is Sheila. I've told her that you've been watching her, the same as she's been watching you."

Tommy reached out and took her proffered hand, turning it and bending forward to give it a soft kiss on the back of the hand. He kept one eye on Barry to judge his reaction and was surprised to see him smile widely at his gesture. Sheila was flattered and flustered, still thinking about his comment on what she smelled like; she could feel her arousal increase. Barry waved them into the living room and gestured for Tommy to take the couch as he sat in the chair a bit away from it. Sheila went to sit on the arm of Barry's chair but Barry shooed her to go over and sit by Tommy. Tommy saw this and patted the area close to him to indicate to her that he'd like her to be beside him since it seemed that Barry truly didn't mind. She sat near him and he put his hand on her slightly sweaty, bare thigh; she was thrilled to feel his gentle touch and gave him a big smile. Barry hid his own grin as he watched how his wife arched her back to push her tits out so that Tommy could notice them better; he knew that she was quite aroused and was showing it to them both.

He gave them a moment or two to get adjusted and then asked Tommy "I assume that you're here to talk about fucking Sheila. Am I right? Do you have any questions or conditions that you want to put on that? I know that Sheila and I have discussed this and we have some conditions but I don't think that you'll find them intolerable." He paused and looked at Tommy, waiting for him to answer.

Tommy dragged his eyes away from Sheila's plump inviting chest, feeling his cock twitch in anticipation and met Barry's eyes. "Yes, I decided to come over here to tell both of you that I might be interested in doing this. I wanted to make sure that Sheila here was a willing participant and not just doing it for you, Barry." He gave a half shrug of apology. "No offense but I just had to be sure." He ran a bold eye over Sheila and said "I can see that she's quite anxious to do it so that concern is taken care of. I'm not prepared to commit to it being a regular thing if that is what you're looking for and I'm not prepared to father a child if that's what you want either. Other than that, I think that we can work things out." He gave Sheila a broad smile and she grinned back.

"We're looking at a one time thing right now. You won't be allowed to hurt Sheila. We're not looking to get her pregnant. She's on the pill but if you want to wear a condom, you'll get no objections from us. Nobody will take any pictures of the sex but I want to watch. Of course, we all want to keep quiet about this so nobody has to avoid any neighbours." He looked at Tommy seriously and asked "Is that fine for you?"

Tommy looked a little uneasy. "I'm not sure about you watching and I'd like to discuss what is considered hurting her. I tend to like things a bit rough and may get somewhat rowdy when I get going with her so we should be clear about what is acceptable before it happens."

Sheila gave him a look of alarm and asked "What do you mean by a little rowdy? What is it that you like to do?" She was concerned that he liked to see women crying out in pain and wasn't prepared to do that. She was having serious second thoughts about the whole matter. Barry could see that she was preparing to pull out and wasn't happy about it but he couldn't see getting her to agree to something she didn't want to do.

Tommy sighed. "I've been told that I like to slap a woman's tits and ass while I'm screwing them. I'm not really aware that I'm doing it because I'm too caught up in the fucking. I also like to bite. Not hard enough to leave any marks but enough that the woman feels it. I just want you to be aware of that."

Sheila smiled broadly; she could accept that type of action and even enjoyed it. "If that is all we're talking about, I don't have a problem. But you didn't want Barry to watch. That is a major reason why we are doing this. Can I ask why you're objecting to that?"

"I'm afraid that he'll change his mind once the action starts and get involved by trying to break it up. Especially since, unless I'm mistaken, you've never done this before." He waited for their nods. "If he remains in the room to watch, I would like him to wear some restraints for the safety of all of us."

Sheila was about to protest but Barry waved her into silence and he examined Tommy. Satisfied by whatever he saw there, he stated "I'm willing to wear some restraints if that will make you feel safer. I don't have a problem with that." He turned to Sheila who still had a disgruntled look on her face and said softly "He's not about to hurt you or me. He lives just down the street from us and we're the ones who picked him out and asked him to do this for us. A person who meant to harm us would hardly wait for such an opportunity, he'd push us towards his plan. It's up to you but I say we should go for it." He gave her a reassuring look.

Sheila looked over at Tommy and asked "What's your plan for this sexual encounter? What would you like to do to me?"

"I'm assuming that we can have an evening together. I'd like for you not to shower before I come over. It's okay if you shower in the morning but I'd like for you to ripen with your natural scent for the day. That means no perfume and I'd prefer no makeup either. I want you to do some exercising and yoga poses in front of me for about a half hour. Then I want about half an hour to lick the sweat and juices from your body and cunt. I'll eat you out to hopefully an orgasm. This is generally when I'll do some light smacking of your ass and tits, I promise no marks that conservative clothing wouldn't cover. Then I'll put you on your hands and knees on the bed and take you from behind. Depending on how excited you get me, I should last about ten minutes. After I orgasm, I'd like ten minutes to recover and then another half hour doing as I please with you. That could include watching you exercise some more, masturbate or I might want to eat you out once more. Does that sound acceptable?"

Sheila looked at him, lust shining brightly in her blue eyes and replied breathily "Ummm, yeah. That sounds great. I'm sure I'm going to enjoy that." Then she remembered her husband and looked over at him, asking "What do you think, honey?"

He'd been watching her and could tell by her fidgeting that she had grown very excited as Tommy described what he wanted to do to her. He was quite intrigued that Tommy wanted Sheila to be unwashed, he'd assumed that the younger man would want her to be as pristine as possible. Barry knew that he enjoyed Sheila's natural scent even though she thought it to be offensive. He smiled at her and then at Tommy and replied "I think that sounds quite stimulating and I look forward to watching it. Now we just have to set up a day and time. I think that we should see if we can get someone to take the girls for the night, don't you, Sheila?" Sheila nodded thoughtfully and began running possible candidates through her head; she was about to get off the couch and go call to see who might be available when Barry stopped her. "I'm sure you'll have plenty of time to do that later. Is it all right if we call you with a time, Tommy? Are you pretty free over the next while?" Tommy nodded and then he started to get off the couch. "Hold up there, too, if you would, Tommy. You wanted to lick the sweat off Sheila's tits and she's still pretty sweaty right now. Would you like a sample of what she tastes like?"

Tommy looked Sheila in the eyes to gauge her acceptance and was heartened when she gave him a hesitant grin; Sheila was reluctant only because she didn't feel sexy at all, sweaty with her hair in rats nests. Tommy looked over at Barry and said

"I'd appreciate it if you remain in your chair there where I can keep an eye on you while I do this." Barry nodded his acceptance of the request. Tommy positioned Sheila so that he could see Barry over her shoulder and grabbed the bottom of her tank top and pulled it up over her head. Sheila had lifted her arms to help him and was mortified to remember that she hadn't shaved her armpits for more than a week. Now that she thought about it, although her legs were fairly recently shaved, her bush was quite unkempt. Tommy stopped to admire her partially undressed form; he was amused that she was wearing a rather plain white bra that was obviously more for comfort than appearance. Sheila followed his gaze and blushed as she recognized that she was wearing her household chores bra that firmly supported and restrained her tits. She was about to apologize when Tommy silenced her and pulled her forward against him so that he could unhook the bra. Sheila felt the release and her tits slumped somewhat towards her feet. Tommy quickly cupped their heavy weight in his big hands, marvelling at their size and plumpness; he thought that she probably had the biggest tits he'd seen in real life. He massaged her large aureoles and her nipples popped out; she had nipples that were over a half inch long and about a quarter inch across. He spent some time rolling them with his thumbs and fingers as she moaned her approval over his treatment of them. He could feel his cock stiffening and was regretting that he wouldn't be fucking her that night. He checked to see that Barry was still in his chair and began to work his tongue along the top of her right tit; there were still beads of sweat on them and he sucked them down eagerly, savouring the salty taste. He moved to nuzzle her large nipple and raked his teeth lightly across the sensitive nub. When he did that she stopped her noises and jumped away from him somewhat in surprise. He straightened up to see what she thought about what he'd done and also to check on Barry. He could see that she was considering her feelings about him raking his teeth over her nipples; he was very pleased when she moved back towards him proffering her large tit to him.

He applied his mouth to it again, sucking the large pink nipple into his mouth and probing at it with his tongue; Sheila moaned continuously in delight and he found those noises to be very stimulating. He could smell that she was very wet and he wondered if he should feel her pussy; he freed himself from her, eliciting a grunt of protest, to look at Barry. Barry smiled widely at him and made a motion that he took as permission to go farther. He bent back to her tit, applying his mouth to it again and slid his hand onto her soft inner thigh near her crotch. He could feel her stiffen slightly in surprise but then she put her hand down and pulled his slightly closer to her wet pussy. He took that as consent to feel her up. He pushed his hand up the wide, short leg of her cutoffs, maneuvered around her tight panties and pushed a finger into her warm, squishy cunt. He marveled slightly at how thick her bush had been as he went through it. He worked his finger lightly in and out of her as she gasped in arousal and delight. He seriously contemplated working her wet cunt over until she came but then decided that he was already taking things too far. He didn't want to upset Barry too much at this stage, so he removed his finger and gave it a quick lick to taste her juices. Sheila gasped in disappointment when he removed his finger from her pussy and gave a whine of frustration, trying to entice him back. He just backed away from her slightly and gave her a friendly smile. He could see that she was revved up and ready to go but decided that it would be best to leave her for Barry to take care of. He'd get the chance to go farther with her at the later date.

Barry was quite shocked when Tommy backed away from the aroused Sheila; he realized that Tommy was excited by her and would have loved to take her but he was trying to be a gentleman. Barry could feel his own prick hardening even further as he recognized that he would have to be the one to satisfy Sheila's desire. When Tommy looked his way, he gave the younger man a small salute of approval and understanding, along with a big smile. Sheila groaned again as she realized that Tommy wasn't going to go any farther with her today; she needed relief from the pressures that Tommy had built within her and if Tommy was unwilling to do the deed, Barry would have to. She decided that they needed to get rid of Tommy immediately so that Barry could satisfy her urgent need.

"Thank you for coming over and I'll be in touch with you when I have some possible dates" she said quickly to Tommy as she stood up hoping to get him to take the hint to leave. Tommy stood up cooperatively, grinning broadly at her, and let her guide him to the front door and out of it. When she had closed the door, she did a quick check on the girls and rushed back down to find Barry. Barry grinned wildly at her when she returned because he saw that she didn't even realize that she had just gone to the front door, topless. He went up to her and stroked her bare tits softly. She made a startled O with her mouth, mortified by what she had just done; she hoped that none of the neighbours had been watching and had gotten a good peek at her tits. Barry's hands went immediately to her waistband and he quickly got her out of the cutoffs while she was still contemplating matters. He slid her soaking panties down and guided her backwards onto the couch. He climbed on top of her while sliding his own shorts and underwear down and entered her pussy with his erect cock firmly. He wasted no time going about matters, knowing how stimulated she was and she was very grateful to him. She was quickly on the verge of her orgasm and he strained a bit to hold back his own so that she could cum. She gave a yell as she came and he rode her a bit longer before he came himself. She lay beneath him, smiling happily up at him and he settled his body on her warmth while searching for a kiss. After cuddling for a bit, Sheila realized that she hadn't checked on the girls in a while so she separated herself from Barry to go take care of that. They were fine.

Sheila arranged for the girls to stay over at one of the neighbours for Saturday night and confirmed with Tommy that he was free that night, so the date was set for when he was going to screw her. She spent the week cleaning the bedroom so that she wouldn't look like a slob; Barry laughed and told her that Tommy would be like any other man and wouldn't notice or care what the bedroom looked like but the cleaning made her feel better. She also shaved her legs three times to ensure that they would be silky smooth for him; she'd noted that he seemed to like her armpit and crotch hair so she left that alone but she decided that her legs had to be well taken care of. She tried out many outfits to see which one she felt that she could get away with wearing the best. She got quite pissed off at Barry because he was no help to her in deciding; he liked them all. She felt her anticipation growing all week; Barry loved it because she wanted to be fucked all the time and he was certainly willing. Sex with Barry during the week was pleasurable but didn't scratch the itch that she needed taken care of.

Finally Saturday arrived and even though Tommy wanted her to be in a state of not total cleanliness when he arrived, she spent a long time in the shower making sure that she at least started the day absolutely clean. She checked her pussy hair over a number of times, clipping any hairs that seemed to stick up too much and seriously contemplated shaving her hairy arm pits. She finally decided that she was as ready as she could be, having left her pits hairy and emerged from the bathroom. Barry was being an absolute dear, she thought lovingly, haven woken and fed the kids while she was occupied with getting ready to fuck another man. When she went out to join her family, dressed in loose sweats for comfort, she kissed her husband thoroughly to the delight of their young children. Each girl also wanted a kiss from her so she indulged them and let them also talk about their week, even though they'd already told her about events during the week. Now was the time for her to appreciate her family and what it truly meant to her. She loved being a mother and wife, she realized, and no amount of great sex would ever come close to replacing that. She also recognized what a risk Barry was taking with allowing her to indulge in her fantasy and she loved him even more for trusting and understanding her.

As the time grew closer, Barry took the two girls over to where they were going to stay for the night and got them settled in, while Sheila fussed about in the bedroom ensuring that everything was in place. She also started putting on her outfit for the night. She'd decided that she'd wear her little black cocktail dress with stockings and garter belt; it had a nice lacy top to it that partially exposed her big tits. She knew that Barry liked seeing her in it, even though she usually wore a lacy bra under it and wouldn't be that night, so she assumed that Tommy would enjoy the same outfit. It was quite short on her thighs and even had a small slit up them to expose even more of her plump legs. She hesitated momentarily while she looked at how her legs looked in the dress; she was dismayed that her thighs looked too fat but then reasoned that they were going to look that way no matter what she wore. She hoped that the lacy tops of her stockings would distract from how heavy her thighs were. She was always surprised when Barry gave her compliments on her legs because she felt that they were a huge flaw in her appearance even though Barry seemed to like them so much. She lifted her dress to wrap the garter belt around the top of her hips; she knew it would have been easier to have put it on before the dress or to take the dress off but she figured she'd put up with the inconvenience. She gave an excited smile as she fussed with getting the belt tightened and positioned just right, enjoying the feeling of power that it gave her. She felt tremendously sexy and could feel her pussy getting damp from her arousal. She knew that it was too soon for that but she couldn't help herself; besides, she reasoned, Tommy asked for her to be natural, not cleaned up, when he arrived. She once again admired herself in the mirror and again gave some thought to changing her outfit. She knew that she was being too picky about her appearance but she couldn't help herself.

To distract her mind from worrying over her looks, she picked up her fancy black silk stockings and rolled them up so she could put them on easier. These stockings had been a gift from Barry for their anniversary and she'd been hesitant about wearing them; she had cheaper nylon ones that she could have worn and had initially tried out the outfit with the cheaper stockings. Barry had noticed and insisted that she wear the expensive ones, knowing that she liked the feel of them so much better. She once again felt the stab of love for her husband. She pointed the toes of her left foot, inserted it into the cup of the rolled stocking and smoothed it up her foot and leg, enjoying the sensation of the fine silk on her skin. She spent a moment adjusting the lacy top and then fastened the straps firmly to the eyelets and tightened them firmly. She repeated her procedure with her right leg and once again enjoyed a rush of arousal. She loved how her body responded so well when she knew that she was getting ready to get fucked; she had to earnestly consider wearing panties until Tommy was about to arrive she thought because she was in danger of drooling over everything unless she regained some of her control over her emotions. As she thought about it, she gave a quick sigh, and dug out a pair of plain white cotton panties and slid them on over the stockings; she'd take them off about fifteen minutes before Tommy's arrival. She then went over to sit at her makeup table so that she could properly prepare her face. She'd gone fairly heavy on the makeup earlier in the week to get Barry's opinion and he'd convinced her that she should use the minimum she felt was necessary because Tommy had already seen her without any makeup and had been very interested. She knew that she still needed some makeup on her face to keep from feeling too exposed; this young man was coming to fuck her and she needed to look near her very best for him.

She applied a light layer of powder blue eye shadow, darkened her eyebrows a bit and highlighted her cheekbones with some rouge. She'd tried out several lipstick colours, once again Barry had liked most of them, and decided that, even though she had too wide a mouth for it to look extremely good on her, that she would go with a very bold, bright red. She worked the lipstick around her lips, enjoying the greasy feel of it as it went on, and grinned at herself in her mirror. She decided that it looked okay and might appear sexy and wanton to the younger man; a look she was definitely aiming for. She figured that she'd leave everything else alone, even though she gave a critical check on her crowsfeet and her slight double chin, and would leave off using her light scented perfume until closer to the time of arrival. She gave a quick check of the bedroom clock and was amazed that it was much later than she'd thought. She hadn't realized how much time had actually passed as she was busy getting ready. It was just an hour until Tommy was supposed to arrive. She frowned as she thought that Barry must have been home from dropping off the kids for quite a while and she wondered what he was up to; she decided that she had to go find out.

Barry was sitting quietly in the living room, reading a book; he looked up at her and smiled as she entered. She went over to him, needing him to hold her to calm her nerves about what was going to happen later and he put out his arms and guided her into his lap. He lightly stroked her thigh as he hugged her close to him and she nuzzled her face into his neck. He held her for a few minutes and then asked "Are you okay with this still? We can call it off if you wish. You've seemed fairly excited all week and I've enjoyed watching and fucking you because of it. But if you're having second thoughts about it, then I have no problem with you putting it off."

She raised her head to look at him and asked "Would you like for me to call it off?"

He shook his head. "No, I would like for you to go ahead with it. But only if you are ready. If it's not today, then maybe some other time. Or not at all, if that is truly what you want. You just seem a bit down right now when you were so excited as late as this morning. I don't want you to be concerned about what you are doing. I just want you to have fun doing it." He gave her a warm smile.

She smiled back and said "I'll be fine. It's just that the waiting is kinda getting to me. I'm so glad that you're so supportive of me. I love you."

"I love you, too. And I always will. Remember that." They sat cuddling for more than ten minutes without saying anything more to each other. Then Sheila decided that she had to get ready for Tommy so she disengaged from Barry, stood up and then reached up under her dress to pull her panties down. Barry gave her a strange look.

Sheila blushed a bit and said quietly "I was so excited that I was afraid of drooling all over everything so I put on panties." Barry just grinned at her in response. She went back to the bedroom to make a final check on her makeup and outfit and to get rid of the panties. It took her a few minutes to determine that everything was fine and she didn't need to touch anything up. She then went downstairs where Barry was now in the kitchen, drinking a cup of coffee. He offered her a cup but she waved him off, too nervous to try to drink anything. They spent a few minutes waiting in the kitchen with Sheila too nervous to do anything, even talk, and Barry appearing to be completely at ease with everything.

Then the doorbell rang and Sheila jumped up to go answer it, Barry laughed and said "Sheila, maybe it would be better if I answer it. It may not be Tommy and could be one of the neighbour children collecting for school or something. The way you're dressed and how frazzled you are, you're liable to shock them into premature puberty." He grinned at her to take any implied criticism out of his words as she slowly came back and stood by her chair. She gave him a very faint smile in return.

However, it was Tommy at the door and he was dressed casually but nice in a newer pair of black jeans and a red silk shirt, open across his chest. Barry greeted him warmly as he thought how much Sheila was going to enjoy running her hands through his chest hair because Barry was almost hairless in comparison with what Tommy was showing. Barry could feel the twinge of anticipation start to spark up his prick at the thought of this younger man fucking Sheila hard. Tommy was a tiny bit nervous, especially with Barry answering the door, but he smiled at Barry and was relieved when the man smiled back. Once he was inside, Barry led him down to where they had set up things in their bedroom, confident that Sheila would have made her way there while he was answering the door. Sheila had some misgivings about them using the bed they slept and fucked in but Barry assured her that it would be fine and besides, did she want to do it in one of the children's beds.

Sheila was waiting for them in the bedroom and she'd tried to drape herself casually on the bed but she leapt up as soon as they entered, ruining the effect entirely. Barry had to stifle a laugh, not wanting to embarrass her, as she stood there, wanting to run up to Tommy and press herself against him but a little cowed about doing that with him there. Barry went over to the heavy easy chair that he'd moved into the bedroom; Tommy should be able to effortlessly secure him to it. He'd laid out a number of restraints that he'd bought over the years to spice up his sex life with Sheila a bit; she only allowed him to use them on her occasionally, when she was in the mood for that sort of thing. As he was settling himself into the chair, Sheila worked up enough courage to go up and hug Tommy and he'd responded by pulling her soft body tight against him so she could feel the beginnings of his erection through his tight pants. Barry watched, amused, as Sheila rubbed her body against Tommy's crotch, enjoying his hardness. Tommy enjoyed Sheila's antics for a while and then decided that he better go over and secure Barry. He fastened Barry to the chair, making sure that nothing was so tight that it would cut off circulation but not too loose so that it could be slipped out of. Barry was impressed by the job that Tommy did on him and began to wonder if he would be able to convince Sheila of letting Tommy restrain her in the future.

Tommy went back to Sheila and they spent a few more minutes of kissing and caressing while still fully dressed; Tommy didn't seem to be in too much of a hurry to start fucking Sheila, giving her time to build up her arousal. Barry was impressed by his performance and thought that Tommy must have had a very experienced woman in his past sexual history that taught him how to handle women. Barry had learned from a friend of his mother when he'd been younger and wasn't involved with Sheila; he'd enjoyed his time with her and had learned a tremendous amount before she broke it off as she pursued another conquest. Tommy raised Sheila's dress and began rubbing her large ass, relishing its soft plumpness. Sheila got a case of the giggles both from the feeling of what he was doing and his obvious delight of it. While she was busy trying to stifle her laughter, Tommy took advantage and removed her dress entirely.

He began rubbing her large chest, saying "Here, I'll help you take care of that problem."

"I'm not sure that's helping all that much" she replied dryly as his large hands crushed her soft tits.

"So you want me to stop then."

"Oh no, don't you dare. You started this and I expect for you to finish it" Sheila purred as she enjoyed his rough treatment of her plump tits. "I want you to suck and bite them as well."

"Later" Tommy growled as he busied himself with rolling her nipples so they became totally erect. Sheila moaned softly in her pleasure as he did that and he liked how her noises increased his arousal. He could feel his cock straining at his pants but he wanted to keep it restrained while he brought her closer to where she might orgasm. He knew that if he took it out and she touched and played with it, he would be in danger of climaxing before she was anywhere near ready. He decided that he would test to see how much pain she would enjoy so he gave her nipples a hard twist. Sheila gasped loudly and moaned in pain and pleasure as she pushed him away from her. Tommy let her force him back from her and remained where he was so that he could discover what her response would be after she got over her surprise about what he had done. He was incredibly pleased when she almost immediately threw herself back at him.

"Oh, do that again" she begged. "It felt incredible. I can feel my clit twitching hard." She moaned and said "Tell me that you're going to do that to me some more."

Tommy laughed, almost meanly, as he gave her ass a solid thwack and said "Oh, baby, we're going to do that and more. I'm going to make you plead and cry tonight." He realized that he might have taken things a little too far when she pushed back from him a bit and looked him in the eyes, showing a little fear in her eyes and face. He pulled her back into him and stated reassuringly "But only in a good way that you'll enjoy." He was pleased that some of the tenseness left her body.

"Thank you" she murmured softly as she pressed her soft body against him. "I'd like to whine and cry a little but I don't want to be hurt." Tommy checked on how Barry was taking all of this and was reassured to see that the other man had no issue with what was happening. Tommy once again began teasing Sheila's long, large nipples out and this time he began a light twisting of them almost immediately as soon as they were erect; Sheila made a lot of noises as he did that but pressed herself firmly against him to encourage him to do even more. As she wrapped her thick thighs around his right leg, he could feel her starting to create a wet spot against it from how wet her cunt was becoming. He could smell her natural scent and the sharp acrid scent of her increasing arousal under her light perfume and he enjoyed it tremendously. Tommy gave some consideration to moving on to deal with her cunt but he was having too much fun with her large tits; he figured that she would still perform well if he made her orgasm before he finished playing with her. He could feel a remarkable jolt of arousal at the thought of her writhing from multiple orgasms.

He grabbed a large chunk of her soft left breast and squeezed it hard and she whined sharply. He was about to lessen his grip of her flesh when he saw her nod gently to indicate she was okay with what he was doing so he changed his movement into a more kneading motion and she moaned with pleasure. He shifted his hand over about an inch and repeated his gesture and she made a guttural sound as the arousal hit her. He chuckled a bit at her reaction because it startled him slightly and then did that three more times before he decided to move onto something else. He was a bit surprised at how hard she was panting and decided to check on how aroused she actually was. He reached down between her legs and pushed his index finger into her fleshy, sopping cunt; there was a definite squelching sound and his finger came out of her dripping from her desire. Hmmm, he thought to himself, she is certainly about to orgasm real soon; it won't take too much to push her over the edge. The question is, is it too soon. She's an experienced woman so she should be able to cum and still want more, he thought. I'm going to make her climax and then see how hard it is to bring her back to the edge.

He pushed her rather roughly onto the bed, surprising her with his insistence, and lifted her legs to force her to lay on her back with her hips right at the side of the bed. He knelt down and pushed his mouth up against her wet cunt; she gave a wild high-pitched shriek as his tongue lashed out at her pussy lips and ran up and down them. He noticed a sharper smell emitting from her and determined that she was almost completely there. He plunged his tongue into her cunt as deep as he could go, his nose actually brushed against her aroused clitoris as he did so. She shrieked again and bucked her hips up against his face as she released her orgasm. His face was coated with her cum but he continued to tongue her hard and she writhed and bucked with desire. Her whines of pleasure drove him wild and he sought hard to make her orgasm a second time. After a few more minutes of this action, she had a smaller, less explosive orgasm and he released her and sat up to observe her. He could see that her desire had muddled her mind and her eyes were completely unfocused. He gave her a gentle pat on the belly and swung her legs around so that she was more comfortably on the bed.

He looked over to Barry, who was grinning broadly at him. Barry said "She'll need a few minutes to recover but she should return looking for even more from you. It's been a while since I've managed to ring her bell twice in a row and she's going to want to show you her appreciation. You might want to help yourself to a drink while you wait. I don't think she'd mind too much if you want to play with her tits. You really seem to like them."

Barry nodded and decided to do as he'd directed but first he asked "Do you need anything?" Barry shook his head negatively and relaxed back in his chair; he was aroused but didn't need to do anything to relieve it. Sheila would take care of him once Tommy had left.

Nearly ten minutes passed and even Tommy was growing a bit weary of fondling Sheila's large tits before Sheila began to stir and rouse herself back to complete consciousness. She sat up and gave Tommy a fantastically wet French kiss before saying "Thank you so very much. That was incredible." She then looked at him a little coyly and asked "What would you like to do now?"

Tommy knew exactly what he wanted to do. He wanted to fuck her as hard as he could for as long as he could before he burst. "I want you to kneel on the bed so that I can get behind you and fuck your cunt for all I'm worth" he told her, his voice thick with his desire.

"Would you like me to lick your cock a little for you first?"

He shook his head and said "No. I'm so hard that I might climax if you did that and I want to feel your warm flesh completely surrounding me as soon as possible." So she got into the position that he wanted and he pushed himself firmly into her. She compared the feel of his cock in her to what Barry generally felt like and determined that there wasn't too much difference physically between them. But she had a delicious feeling of wantonness from knowing that it was a man who was not her husband deep inside her hips. She gave him a minute or so to establish the rhythm of his thrusts into her before she started to push her ass back towards him as he thrust forward. He gasped a bit in surprise the first time she did that but found it to be very stimulating. Knowing that she liked things a bit rough, he slapped her ass when she did that; she gave him a growl of appreciation when he did that. They only groaned and moaned as they fucked each other as hard as they could, neither one of them daring to spend any breath talking to the other. Both of them were coated with a sheen of sweat and were gasping for breath as they both felt the imminent feelings of their climax. Tommy felt his balls clench tightly as he spurted his hot cum into her well-lubricated cunt and she whined in delight as she felt his cum soak her. Tommy stopped and focused on his pleasure as he sent a second spurt into her; she bucked her hips hard against him and then had her third orgasm of the evening. Tommy felt incredibly exhausted and wanted to collapse onto her but felt it would be bad manners to do so until she'd finished her climax. When she appeared to be finished, he pushed her totally down onto the bed and sank down onto her soft form, feeling tired but absolutely satisfied; she continued to buck a bit underneath him in the aftermath of her third orgasm but he just ignored it.

Barry was entirely aroused and very concerned that he was going to pop off; the sight of Tommy fucking Sheila as hard as he could was unbelievably arousing to him. He knew that if he wasn't so well restrained, he would have been over there encouraging Sheila as she climaxed and wanting to taste what she was like in the heat of being screwed. He wasn't too sure how Tommy would've handled that so he was kind of glad that Tommy had insisted on him being restrained. He examined his feelings to determine if he felt any jealousy for the younger man but found that he didn't; he was just extremely happy that Sheila had seemed to enjoy the encounter so much. He decided that he wouldn't ask Sheila for details of differences between Tommy and him unless she brought it up but was determined to see if she would let him do some of the things to her that Tommy had done, such as slapping her ass while riding her. He figured that it would be about fifteen minutes before the couple on the bed bothered to stir so he figured that he'd relive some of the best parts of their action in his mind. He couldn't wait to try to talk Sheila into letting it happen to her again.

BARON AND BARONESS TAKE A PLANE RIDE

Paloma Jackson hummed to herself as she got herself ready in the morning to go to work; she was to be the stewardess on the private flight for the Baron and Baroness to an exclusive resort on an island not far from Bermuda. She was a taller brunette with a fairly full figure and toned legs and ass that she worked hard to maintain. She knew that she had an okay, not beautiful face, with a wide mouth and thick lips over a small overbite. She recognized that she had not been chosen by the Baroness for her beauty but rather because she worked hard at being good at sex with both the Baroness and her husband. Paloma had been quite willing to do things that the other prettier women had balked at and therefore she held the position as personal stewardess to the Baron and Baroness. Her job wasn't overly demanding because the Baron and his wife didn't fly more than three times a month and usually less; and, if they were going away for more than a couple of days, they usually gave Paloma the option of inviting her family to join her on the excursion. Of course, her husband and two daughters would have to fly commercial rather than on the fabulous private plane she would be on with the Baron and Baroness but the Baron had no problem with paying their way and could command seats on even a sold out flight without any problem. Paloma understood why her family couldn't be on the private plane; it wouldn't be right for them to see the Baron and Baroness rejoining the mile high club with her as their escort, now would it, she thought.

She got herself out of the steaming shower and carefully rubbed the body lotion that the Baroness had bought her, knowing that her husband liked the smell and feel of it on Paloma's lush body. She could feel her nipples perk as she thought about how the Baron's strong hands liked to crush her nice sized tits; it had been nearly three weeks since the last flight and she kind of missed screwing the Baron. She gave some thought to Baroness Molly and recognized that, although she really liked men, the redhead could force Paloma to cum hard by putting the dildo to her slick cunt and making her ride it vigorously. The Baroness was also a fan of watching Paloma eating the wet cunts of their large female entourage; the only real downside to a longer flight, thought Paloma, was that she often felt like she had lockjaw afterwards. Still the money and perks were fantastic and there was no way in hell that Paloma was going to let a little thing like that dissuade her from performing to her utmost for the Baron and Baroness. Paloma went into the bedroom where her husband was still sleeping, thinking that the poor man must be feeling exhausted from the effort of fucking her so hard the previous night. She liked how jealous he got, knowing that she was off to fuck the Baron and she always made sure to let him know that she really liked how the Baron fucked her so he would keep on top of his game. She loved her husband but he wasn't the best in bed and never would be; she was content with the rest of her life with him and the fact that she got screwed by one of the best men she'd ever slept with in her life on a fairly regular basis made her husband's bed performance acceptable. She quietly gathered the parts of her uniform and began donning them. She smiled to herself as she thought about how different this clothing was to the uniform she'd had to wear when she worked for a major airline. Her outfit had been specially chosen by the Baroness and was tight enough to fit her like a second skin. Now that she thought about it, she realized that it was a little too tight across her stomach; time to spend some more time in the gym, she thought a little despondently.

Soon she had all of her clothing on and was examining herself in the full length mirror; she decided that she could get away with the tightness of her uniform for now. She would hate to have to go to the Baroness to ask if she could be refitted for a new uniform; she figured that the Baroness would understand but, Paloma herself, would be terribly disappointed. She grabbed her high heels in her hand so she wouldn't make too much noise as she left and left the bedroom. She checked her nine year old daughter's bedroom and found her older child awake; she smiled at her and bid her good morning. The girl got out of bed and followed her, realizing that she was preparing to leave and wanting to have breakfast with her mother. Paloma checked on her younger daughter and discovered that she was still sleeping so she quickly and quietly withdrew to let her continue snoozing. She went into the kitchen in her stocking feet to join her daughter who had already seated herself at the table and was pouring a bowl of cereal.

She started a cup of coffee brewing and found her low calorie cereal in the cupboard; she took the cereal over to the table and poured a serving into the bowl that her daughter had thoughtfully set for her. She smiled at her daughter as she prepared her breakfast and asked "What's up, little one? Why have you chosen to get up at this time in the morning? It's a little early for you."

Her daughter smiled slightly and then solemnly replied "I wanted to have breakfast with you since you're going to be off on a trip this morning."

"You, your father and sister are all going to be flying to join me in a few days for more than a week" she told the girl, slightly concerned that her daughter seemed upset about the insignificant separation. "We'll be spending that time in a fabulous tropical resort. I understand that the weather is supposed to be very nice so it will give us lots of time to lie on the beach and swim in the warm ocean. There is supposed to be a great set of pools at this resort and even a waterslide. You two kids should enjoy yourselves greatly. Is something worrying you?"

The young girl hemmed and hawed for a bit before replying "Not really, Mama. I just wished that we could travel together for once. I'd feel safer on the plane with you with us."

Paloma got up and fetched her coffee to give herself some time to think. It was obvious to her that her daughter wasn't really afraid of flying without her but that she didn't want Paloma to fly with the Baron and Baroness. She wondered how much the young girl understood about what her mother was doing with them. She knew that she'd found out about what happened in bedrooms at night between adults at about the age her daughter was now at; she gave a small grimace as she remembered how wrong what had been relayed to her at that age had turned out to be. She wondered if she should spend the time to tell her daughter the truth about sex and then recognized that she really didn't have time to take care of the matter in the manner that it deserved at the moment. She knew that she had to set the young girl's mind at rest though so she said quietly "I've told you before that I can't. It is part of my duties to travel with the Baron and Baroness and they can't be disturbed by you and your sister. I know that you would try to be quiet and respectful but you are children, so you would likely forget. You know that the Baroness always remembers your birthdays with gifts along with her Christmas presents. Her generosity with my pay also allows us to live as well as we do. It is important to the whole family that they are happy with the job that I do and that we not disturb them." She gave her daughter an imploring look, wanting her to simply accept the circumstances as undeniable facts. Her daughter sighed as she recognized that her mother didn't really want to talk about the matter at the current time and the two of them finished their meal in a slightly uncomfortable silence.

Paloma was marking off the supplies that had been loaded for the flight and she was humming a happy little tune, determined to put her daughter's concerns aside until she had time to deal with them. She decided that it would be best to wait until the entire trip was over and they could spend the time it took to allay the girl's concerns. She knew that she was never going to give up her job because it caused her such joy but she could definitely make the girl understand why she did as she did. She recognized that there was likely some talk going around at the private school that her daughters attended and that her older daughter was probably upset by what she might have heard. She would have to inform her daughter that she needed to learn to ignore such talk; it was no one's business, outside of the family, about what she did for the Baron and Baroness. As she was thinking about this and concentrating on her task, a slim hand slipped up under her short skirt and pinched her ass.

She jumped, slightly startled, but turned with a smile to receive a wet kiss from the Baroness. She gave a breathy gasp as the other woman shifted her hand to stroke Paloma between her legs as she pushed Paloma back against the open cabinets. The two women kissed for over a moment as the Baroness let her hands wander all over the other woman's lush body. Baroness Molly forced her tongue into the Paloma's warm, willing mouth and wriggled it around. Paloma moaned her excitement into the redhead's mouth but she broke the kiss after just over a minute. She knew that she needed to make the preparations for takeoff and dallying with the Baroness was not getting her work done. "Oh Baroness" she said in a husky moan. "I'd love to let you play with me further but I need to get ready so that we can leave. I can't do that while you are distracting me. I promise that once we are at cruising altitude, I will come and find you so that we can continue with this wonderful action." Baroness Molly just smirked at her, she'd known that this would be Paloma's reaction; she knew that the stewardess had to get the plane prepared but by exciting the other woman and giving her time to think about it would make Paloma even more aroused by the time that she could allow the Baroness to take pleasure of her. Baroness Molly left the area to go find her seat near the Baron to prepare for takeoff.

The Baron had been aware of where his wife had been headed and also knew what the result would be; Baroness Molly would be as anxious as any of them to get underway and would return, rather than delay preparations for takeoff. He'd settled himself in one of the very comfortable seats towards the back of the plane. Normally he would have chosen one of the four well-appointed single seats near the front like he expected his wife to do but he'd had an ulterior motive in his mind for his actions. He'd grabbed the hand of the new blonde that they had added to their staff and led her back here. He was busily acquainting himself fully with her large, heavy tits, much to her obvious delight. He looked up to see his wife give him an encouraging smile before taking her seat and then bent back over to continue to nibble on the blonde's perky nipples. He knew that he'd be forced to give up his efforts in a few minutes when they had to prepare for the takeoff so he decided to enjoy himself as much as he could. He wondered if he'd have enough strength to induct the new blonde into the mile high club or not; he was aware that tradition dictated that he renew his membership with Paloma and was looking forward to that but a little variety was also nice. He figured that he might just be able to pull it off, given the length of the flight.

A few minutes later, Paloma made her way back into the passenger compartment to prepare them for takeoff; she was a little disconcerted not to see the Baron in his normal seat. She wondered briefly if this was going to be a complete lesbian flight and felt a twinge of disappointment but then she caught sight of the back of the Baron's head. She smiled as she realized what he was doing and then extended that smile over to the Baroness, who was perusing a magazine while waiting in her seat. The Baroness noticed Paloma's smile and shrugged her shoulders in response. Boys will be boys, she thought, knowing that her husband liked a new set of tits to play with and a new cunt to stretch over his dick. She'd hired the blonde knowing that her husband would soon avail himself of her bountiful assets and she wasn't jealous about that fact. In fact, the blonde had performed very well at licking the Baroness's cunt and she'd been monopolizing the girl for the past week. She'd calculated that the Baron would probably make this move and thought that if she kept the girl away from him, it would enhance his desire for her. She knew that her husband recognized what she was doing and enthusiastically played along. They could anticipate each other quite well and worked at causing the other to have to work at obtaining their desired reward; it was a wonderful game between the two of them.

Paloma made her way back to where the Baron was seated and said sweetly "Baron, I know that you are pleasantly occupied at the moment but I am going to have to get you to sit back and fasten your seatbelt so that we can takeoff. You can return to your task once the Captain has turned off the seatbelt sign." She looked at the blonde's big, wet tits, letting her glance linger on them for a moment before focusing on her face. She grinned knowingly and said "Miss, I'm going to have to ask you to also fasten your seatbelt." She resisted the urge to reach out and stroke those wonderful breasts. The two of them complied, the blonde smiled invitingly at her and she headed back to her seat to let the Captain know that they were ready.

As they taxied down the runway, she looked over the passengers; she noticed that it was the usual household group with the new blonde replacing the housekeeper who was usually a part of this group. She wondered if the change was permanent and why it might have occurred. She'd enjoyed the few times that she'd been screwed by the other woman and had thought that the Baroness had enjoyed her as well. She wondered if she should ask after the other woman or just let things slide. She pushed that thought from her mind as they began to level off and she prepared herself to perform her duties when the Captain turned off the seatbelt sign.

Her first duties were to ensure that all the passengers were delivered the refreshments that they required for the start of the trip; they were good at helping themselves when she was tied up with the Baron and Baroness at later points in the trip. She cracked the bottle of the Baroness's favourite champagne and poured it out into the special glasses that the Baroness had made. The Baroness had heard about how glasses had been made in the shape of a French noblewoman's breast and thought that she liked the idea of her and her guests drinking from glasses designed to resemble her own tits so she had these glasses specially commissioned. Paloma really enjoyed the look of them and the story behind them titillated her fancy. Of course, she served the first glass on her tray to the redhead so that she could give her approval for the others to receive theirs. She kept focus on the redhead's bright green eyes as she offered the tray of drinks, knowing what was about to happen. As usual, the Baroness took the champagne glass in her left hand while her right hand slipped up between Paloma's thighs. The Baroness quickly parted Paloma's engorged pussy lips and slid two fingers up inside of Paloma, who murmured her approval as she felt those fingers being pushed up into her. The Baroness made a huge show of sampling the champagne, rolling it around her mouth before letting small sips slide down her throat as she worked over Paloma's damp pussy. The women around the Baroness enjoyed the show as they usually did and waited very patiently for the Baroness to decide that she'd had enough so that Paloma could serve them next. Finally, the Baroness was satisfied and she popped her wet fingers out of Paloma's pussy so that the girl now kneeling beside her could lick them clean for her; it always impressed Paloma about how eager these women were to sample her juices. Paloma quickly served all of the other women their champagne and headed back to serve the final four passengers. She noted that the Baron had returned to licking and playing with the blonde's tits while the other two women back there watched on excitedly. She placed the Baron's glass by his seat and offered the glasses to the watching women, who took them almost absentmindedly. She then proffered the remaining glass on the tray to the blonde.

"Would you like some champagne, dear?" she trilled, sweetly. "I can get you anything else if you would prefer it."

"No, the champagne sounds wonderful" the blonde lisped in a clear young voice. Paloma hid a grin as she realized that the reason for the blonde's lisp was the two new tongue studs she had in her mouth. Paloma recognized the Baroness's handiwork in that; she knew that the Baron didn't kiss women other than his wife more than perfunctorily and although he enjoyed the occasional blowjob, he didn't care if the woman's tongue was studded or not. So Paloma grinned at her and offered the last glass. She then went to arrange the small snacks so that she would be finished with her duties and able to join the Baroness.

Paloma brought back the snacks that everyone liked and arranged them for easy access before she slipped out of her uniform and into the Baroness's lap, nude but for her stockings and heels. She wiggled her plump bum against the Baroness, getting herself comfortable and kissed the redhead deeply. Baroness Molly was expecting her and stuck her wet tongue down Paloma's throat while reaching out and kneading her heavy breasts. Paloma was very wet with desire and her juices were dripping down her thighs onto the Baroness's skirt. While they were busy with each other, the four women around the Baroness undressed each other until they also were only in their stockings and heels. Although Paloma didn't bother to look, she knew that the two women with the Baron and the blonde would be performing the same maneuver. This was typically how the flights with the Baron and Baroness went.

Paloma and the Baroness spent a few minutes enjoying their actions before the Baroness gently pushed Paloma off her lap and guided her down onto the rug before the solo seats. She arranged Paloma on her hands and knees on the rug before reaching into the leather bag that one of the women had opened up, exposing the sex toys inside. Another of the women assisted the Baroness out of her clothing and into a strap-on harness as the Baroness selected a long, thick dildo to attach to it. Paloma gave a long, low moan of delight as she recognized her favourite dildo to ride and the redhead grinned wickedly at her, aroused by her excitement. Baroness Molly assisted Paloma in impaling herself on the large toy and once she had breached Paloma's wet pussy, shoved it home as deep as she could. Paloma grunted loudly as the toy slid up into her, rocking her hips to accept as much of it as she could. She gave a delighted squeal as the tip hit her cervix. The Baroness was aware that many women didn't like being penetrated that deeply, finding pain rather than pleasure, but Paloma wasn't one of those women. She loved the totally filled and breached feeling that the large toy created in her and she eagerly pushed her hips back hard against the Baroness's thrusts. It didn't take very long for Paloma to achieve her first orgasm and the Baroness quickly worked the large, slick toy out of her as she wriggled around, gasping from its effects. The Baroness knew that the Baron would want to use Paloma also so she didn't bother to push the lush woman any further.

Once the Baroness removed the toy, she knelt over the woman and applied her tongue to the woman's squishy, gaping pussy, sucking up some of her sweet juices. She didn't spend very long doing that before giving up her position so that the other women could sample Paloma. She liked the taste but recognized that her women loved the taste of each other so she was willing to oblige them. She selected one of the four women and led her back to her seat where she sat, leaning back and swiveled the seat so that the woman could drape herself over the Baroness. That way the woman's mouth could service the Baroness's pussy while her own pussy was available for the Baroness to play with, being right by her left shoulder. The Baroness was aware that a lot of women couldn't hold this pose for long but her own women were used to it and their practice of yoga each morning gave them the strength and flexibility to do it. She gave a brief thought to the blonde and wondered how long it would take to train her to do that maneuver; she hoped the girl would be able to perform it very soon. Then she wondered how the Baron was making out with her and if he'd be able to fuck her after being with Paloma; she was pretty sure that he was going to give it his best shot. She gave a small smile and shifted to give the woman draped over her better access to her wet cunt; she played with the woman's breasts.

A few minutes later, the other three women had all sampled Paloma so the Baroness allowed the woman she was with to go get her taste. She called Desdemona over to finish the job of eating her pussy out to orgasm. She knew that Desdemona could fit herself into the position that the other woman had held, even though she was a little short to do so comfortably, but the Baroness decided she just wanted to orgasm so she made Desdemona kneel in front of her and draped her long legs over the other woman's back. It only took a few minutes for Desdemona's talented tongue to push the Baroness to orgasm and she enjoyed the earth shattering sensations of her climax. When she was in the bliss of her aftermath, she was pleased to see that Paloma was now sitting up, almost fully recovered from her own orgasm. She knew that the Baron would be over shortly to claim his reward from the lush woman and she smiled.

About five minutes later, the Baron had joined Paloma, he was nude and his dick was wet and hard; the Baroness wondered briefly if the new blonde had been sucking on his dick or if he'd had one of the other women do it. It really didn't matter, she thought as she quickly dismissed it from her head. She gave some thought about going back to try out the new blonde herself but decided that she wanted to watch her husband fucking Paloma; there was lots of time for the blonde later. Then she thought about how much fun it would be if she and the Baron put the new blonde girl into a three way and decided that that was a definitely delicious plan. She glanced around to where the other women were busy teasing and playing with one another as the Baron helped Paloma get into position on her hands and knees. She contemplated ordering one of them over to entertain her but decided that she just wanted to watch the fucking without any other distraction. She really liked watching the Baron with other women because it gave her a chance to critique his performance. Then, when he was fucking her, she could give him some pointers that would assist him in screwing her better. She was glad that he didn't take those pointers as criticism but took them simply as they were meant, as ways to improve. The Baron told her whenever he felt that she could improve her performance as did her regular girlfriends; the Baroness was always willing to try things that might make sex better or more interesting and her partners knew it. Molly was aware that she was a pretty good fuck but she strived to become the very best she could be; she smiled as she idly thought about what sort of award should be given for such a feat. Maybe she should hold a ceremony each year and give out Mollies, she thought wickedly.

The Baron was up inside Paloma now and using his hands to guide her broad hips back towards him so that she would accept all of his long cock. The Baroness knew that his cock wasn't quite as long or thick as the toy that she'd forced Paloma to accept earlier but it was still a fairly magnificent prick. Paloma was looking back at the Baron under her left armpit and from the contortions of the woman's face, the

Baroness could tell that she was enjoying the fucking. Once the Baron had begun bottoming out in Paloma's willing, wet cunt, he took a few leisurely strokes to ensure that he was well lubricated and then stepped up the pace of his thrusts. There weren't a lot of women who liked the hard rough pace that he set but he knew that Paloma was one of them; that tended to be why he enjoyed fucking the plump woman so much. The Baroness and some of the other women would tolerate that style occasionally to please him but he always used it with Paloma. He was busy enjoying the pounding he was giving her and he started to feel the clench as his balls started to release their load. It wouldn't be too long until he spurted, he thought as he fought for breath. He could see Paloma gasping underneath him and was pleased by the sight. He knew that he wouldn't be able to get her to orgasm, given his pace but wasn't worried about the fact. One of the pleasures of having so many willing women around was that they were quite agreeable about taking over for him and getting Paloma to her orgasm. This was one of the few times that the Baron was selfish enough to achieve his own climax without worrying if his partner was also achieving theirs. The Baron could feel the cum spurt out of him and he drove his cock as hard as he could up into Paloma's quivering cunt. Both of them groaned in approval as he emptied his hot load into her. The Baron slumped a bit, feeling a bit exhausted after his efforts and waited for his dick to deflate enough to slide out of her on its own. When that happened a moment later, one of the women pushed him gently out of the way so that she could apply her tongue to Paloma's pulsating pussy and bring her to climax. The Baron moved out of the way graciously and then got to his feet to go back to sit by his wife.

The Baroness smiled at him as he approached and he could tell that she'd enjoyed his performance once again. He thought about how lucky he was to have her as his wife and again was pleased with her willingness to allow him to entertain himself with other women without becoming jealous about the fact. He knew that he enjoyed watching her perform with other partners of both sexes. He settled himself in his seat so that he could recover and accepted the glass of champagne from the woman who brought him one. As he sipped the bubbly wine, he thought about whether or not he'd recover enough to fuck that new blonde this trip. He could feel his dick twitch at the thought and decided that he probably could.

GROUP SEX PARTY

Merryanne looked at her reflection in the full length mirror in their bedroom nervously; she unconsciously smoothed down the sides of the short skirt of her little black dress as she contemplated all that was planned for tonight. She'd drawn the duties of hosting their first get together and she'd planned out everything for over a week and had some backup items in case the original ones she had intended were not well received. Her husband had assured her less than two minutes ago that she looked extremely sexy and smart, that her dress didn't make her ass look too big and that her lipstick was just the right shade of red for her colouring. But she didn't trust him to tell her the truth. She knew that he'd say just about anything in order to get her to agree to fuck him and even though she most likely wouldn't be fucking him until much later tonight, he'd want to remain on her good side. She grimaced at how her light brown hair looked, she'd tried to put in some reddish highlights but they really didn't seem to make her hair sparkle the way it looked on the box. Her eyes looked a muddy brown and her cheekbones didn't accentuate the way she'd hoped for when she'd applied her blusher. And, damn that horny son of a bitch she thought angrily, her lipstick did not highlight her curvy lips or match her colouring at all. She was prepared to wash off all of her makeup and start again; while she was at it, she reasoned, she might as well choose some different underwear and a new dress, this one wasn't working for her at all. Suddenly the doorbell rang downstairs and she didn't have time to change anything at all, their guests had begun to arrive. She looked at her watch and saw that they were fifteen minutes early; damn them, she cursed to herself, why couldn't people arrive on time.

She rushed down to join her husband, who was waiting patiently for her before answering the door, knowing that it was important to her to be there to greet the arrivals. He gave her a bright smile and a slow stare going over her figure with approval; she frowned disapproval at him and considered snapping at him waspishly but decided instead to ignore him. She grabbed his arm, put on a bright happy smile and walked him to the door to answer it.

They opened the door and there was Barb and her husband, Frank; Barb was her best friend and the main one that had helped her with her arrangements for the evening. Merryanne examined the two of them as they stood there; they were both blonde with Barb being a good deal lighter in colour than her husband. Merryanne knew that Barb was a natural blonde but used some hair colouration to make it lighter. Barb looked fairly composed but had an undercurrent of excitement racing through her and Merryanne felt a stab of hate for her rush through her even though she knew that it was totally unfair of her. Frank just looked as casual as he ever did, just like he was coming over for a barbeque but Merryanne could see that he was dressed much better than usual. Undoubtedly the work of Barb, she thought as she glanced over at her own husband, who was wearing the outfit that she'd insisted on. The two men greeted each other easily and friendly, shaking hands loosely and grinning excitedly at each other. Merryanne ushered them in and they were about to walk down to the living room when she stopped them with a fake cough. They both turned to look at her and she pointed to the small side table just inside the door that had a number of items on it.

"Have you forgotten that you're supposed to pick a card to get your number for this evening" she admonished them a touch stridently, her nerves getting the best of her. She grabbed the six pink cards and held them out to Barb, face down. "Here, Barb, pick one." Barb quickly took the one on the far left and turned it for all to see; it was the two. Merryane put those cards back on the table and held out the blue ones to Frank. He chose one of the center ones and got a four. Merryanne gave a small smile of relief, afraid that he'd get the two; it wouldn't do much for her party if husband and wife got the same numbers she thought. She noted a small smile of satisfaction on Barb's face and realized that she was thinking the same thing. Then she looked at the faces of the two men and realized that all of them were thinking the exact same thing. She almost snickered as she thought about how naughty they were all being. She reached out and took Barb by the arm and began guiding her towards the kitchen. "You can give me a hand to put out the snacks and things, Barb." She called back over her shoulder to the two men "You guys can make yourself scarce for ten minutes or so."

Merryanne's husband, Bob, blew a sigh of relief; Merryanne had been driving him crazy with her fussing about things all day. He understood that it was a very big thing for all of them and she was concerned about getting everything right but did it really matter that he got Cheddar cheese when she'd asked him to get Gouda. Cheese was cheese and nobody would care what type of cheese was available tonight; not with the activities that they had planned. He noticed the look of reprieve on Frank's face and grinned at him. "Thanks for bringing Barb over early to distract Merryanne from her fussing. You've no idea how crazy she's been driving me."

Frank grinned back at him. "I have some idea. Barb's been ready for over a half hour. I thought that she was going to wear a trench in the front hallway with her heels because of her impatient pacing. This gets me out of a lot of grief too."

"Well, I've got the game on the TV down in the rec room. We can watch it for a few minutes while we wait for the others to show up. I'll just have to keep an ear out for the doorbell. Can I offer you a beer or anything?" Frank asked as he led the way downstairs.

"No, thank you" Frank replied as he followed. "Considering what might happen tonight, I'm going to hold off on the alcohol until later. Feel free to have one yourself, if you want to. It won't bother me."

"No, I better hold off too." The two men watched the game for nearly five minutes before the doorbell rang again. Bob quickly ran up the stairs to join Merryanne in answering the door; she gave him an appreciative smile as he bounded up the stairs. At the door were two couples, Callie and Ed and Yvonne and Mike; Merryanne invited them in and had them pick their cards. Callie picked three, Ed picked five, Yvonne picked four and Mike chose one. Merryanne smiled as she realized that there was already one chosen couple for the night, Yvonne and Frank, although neither of them knew about it yet. She calculated that the other two couples would probably arrive very shortly so she guided the two new couples into the living room where Barb was putting out the last few things and told Bob to go get Frank. She played hostess and asked what everyone was drinking; Mike chose a beer and the other three asked just for coffee. She could tell that all of them were excited, nervous and anxious to get started. The lack of alcohol consumption let her know how serious they all were taking things and she smiled gladly. They engaged in some small talk for about two minutes before the doorbell rang once more.

Bob escorted Merryanne to the door and there was a couple waiting outside, Laura and Ken. They were brought in and Laura picked one while Ken got three. Merryanne led them down to the living room where they were greeted warmly by the rest of their friends. Now they were just waiting for the last couple to arrive and it was still five minutes before the hour. Everyone chattered animatedly while they waited and there were a number of old jokes and digs passed between them; they had all been friendly with each other for a while and were normally quite comfortable in one another's company. Every couple had hosted all of the other couples at regular dinner parties before and the group as a whole had met a number of times for special occasions. Now they were getting together for a different reason.

Just before the hour occurred, the doorbell rang for its final time that evening. Merryanne and Bob greeted Jill and Sid and Sid explained that Jill had delayed them because she'd decided she needed to give last minute instructions to the babysitter. Since all of the children of the six couples were over at Jill and Sid's house being watched over for the evening, Merryanne could see no reason to be upset that Jill had ensured that everything was being taken care of before coming over to join them. Jill chose a six and Merryanne flipped over the final pink card to see that she had the five. Sid chose a two and Merryanne handed the six over to Bob. The four of them headed into the living room and greetings were exchanged while all of them sought out their opposite number.

Merryanne asked them to go sit by the person who had their number and it worked out like this: Laura with Mike, Barb with Sid, Callie with Ken, Yvonne with Frank, her with Ed and Jill with Bob. They all smiled at their pairing and looked to Merryanne to tell them what was going to happen next. The women knew what was going to happen because they had carefully negotiated matters between them; the husbands had just been told that they would be having a group sex party with an exchange of partners and they had no problems with that.

Merryanne brought out a small board that she had drawn up and on it was a list of sexual activities It read:

1. Heavy Petting and Kissing for 10 minutes minimum
2. Handjob
3. Cock Sucking
4. Pussy Eating
5. Vaginal Sex
6. Anal Sex

She knew that the women wouldn't bother reading it because they would be too busy watching both their temporary partners and their husbands to determine their reaction to the list. She herself looked first at Bob, saw him nodding in acceptance and approval, and then at Ed, who, it seemed to her, was busy frowning at something on the list. She remembered the hassle that the women had endured as they decided on what should be on the list. She had insisted that there be six items for what she had planned to work and at one point it looked like they were going to have to put something as innocuous as nipple licking on the list to fill it out. She and Barb had hammered away at the two most reluctant participants to get them to agree for more than a couple of weeks. The first four items on the list, everyone had agreed to without much discussion; the fifth item had required a fair amount of conversation until all of them agreed on it. The sixth item was the one that almost sunk the whole prospect as three of the women had said no way immediately; they managed to talk the reluctant ones around. Even now she was unsure if Laura would agree to perform anal sex in front of the others or not, if she should be chosen to.

She spoke, mainly for the benefit of the men "You've all had a chance to look at this board so I will explain to you the rules of this game tonight. We've all agreed that we want to spice up our sex lives. We've drawn numbers so that we can match up for tonight only; there will be no carryover. If we decide to do this again, the hostess will decide what goes on the board and how she wishes to match people up. Us women will be the ones deciding if we ever do anything like this again so it any of you men have objections, tell your wife to withdraw you from the group." She paused and looked around the room to see if any of the men were objecting to what she had said. They all looked back at her with varying degrees of interest from quite to intense. "I am going to roll this six sided die. The number that comes up first will designate which couple will be charged with performing the public sex act. A roll of this other die will select which item on the list that the couple will perform." Once again she paused to let that sink in and to see if anyone had any questions. Frank raised his hand hesitantly and she nodded to him.

"You're serious that if a six is rolled as the item chosen, the couple is going to have anal sex right here in front of everyone?" he asked with an astonished look on his face.

"Yes!" Merryane and Barb chorused back at him. They looked at each other briefly before Barb motioned for Merryanne to go on. "Everyone has to commit to doing what is on this board or we will all just go home. And we won't bother to arrange any other of this type of date. I'll just give everyone five minutes to discuss it with their partner for tonight and their wife." She prepared to go over to talk with Ed and then she'd check in with Bob so that she could be sure that he was game with it.

Before she could do that, Sid spoke up. "Excuse me for interrupting but before we do that, can I ask what the other five couples will be doing tonight?" He gave a broad smile and said lightly "Besides being treated to one hell of a show, that is."

Merryanne moved back to her spot and said "Okay, it has been decided that once it is determined what the public activity is going to be, the other five couples will get some time alone in the bedroom. The woman is going to perform up to the rolled activity but not beyond it. So if the activity rolled is a one, all you guys only get to kiss and caress your temporary partner. Your bad luck tonight. However, if the roll is a five, the woman will decide how far up the chart she is willing to go. She can decide that she will only do a blowjob on you and you men have to accept that. No matter what goes on in the bedroom between you and your temporary partner, we want no discussion afterwards about it. Do you understand?" She was met with a bunch of nods from everyone.

She went over to talk to Ed. "You're actually okay that if our number is drawn and the number on the list is anal sex, with me screwing your ass?" he asked incredulous. He peered anxiously at her face while waiting for her to answer.

"Yes, I am" she stated firmly. "And all the other women here better be prepared to do the same. Is there anything else you'd like to talk to me about right now?" She looked at him until he shook his head negatively a moment later. "Then I'm going to go over and check on Bob." She walked over to Bob and Jill; Bob had been holding Jill's hand while talking softly with her, he saw Merryanne coming over towards them and dropped Jill's hand like a hot potato. He smiled up at her guiltily.

She smiled at him and told him "It's okay, dear. I'm fine with you touching her, same as I will be fine if she chooses to let you fuck her tonight. I don't want to know about it and I won't be telling you what I'm going to allow Frank to do to me. So unless either of us has to do it in public, we won't know what happened." Jill excused herself to go have a quick chat with Sid. Bob just held his wife's hand and smiled a trifle excitedly at her; she could tell that he and most of the men were thrilled by what their wives had planned.

After a few more minutes, she went over and got Ed, taking him up to in front of the rest of the group; Ed now had a beer in his hand and was taking sips of it to steady his slightly frazzled nerves. She made sure everyone's attention was on her and she picked up a somewhat oversized black die and rolled it onto the coffee table. It bounced and spun before settling down to read three. She looked over at Callie and Ken, who held those numbers and would be doing the public sex act that night. Callie looked smug and immensely pleased with what had happened; Ken looked a little startled and then fairly aroused. He did give a quick glance over to Laura, who was relieved that her number hadn't come up, and then to Ed to try to gauge their reactions. Laura gave him a small smile of encouragement and Ed just gave him a small shrug; Ed understood that Ken would do what the women wanted him to do and that he'd get a chance to do the same or something similar with another man's wife, namely Merryanne. Merryanne paused for a moment to let everyone look at Callie and Ken; she could tell that the men were quite excited that they were going to see Callie nude and in action tonight. Callie was a little plump, the result of giving birth to two girls and a boy, but was in reasonable shape with a well-defined rack and a wide set of hips. She had a pretty oval face with a generous mouth and intelligent brown eyes. She discovered that she liked the attention that the others were now directing her way and shook her head elegantly, causing her long dangling earrings to sway just under her jawline.

Merryanne took the oversized white die and handed it over to Callie so that she would be responsible for her own fate. Callie dropped the die and all eyes watched it spin; it landed on a three. Laura let out a very noisy gasp of relief while Yvonne and Jill made smaller noises. Barb, Callie and Merryanne showed small signs of disappointment while two of the men showed some relief in the results and the remainder just looked noncommittal.

"Well, that's that taken care of" Merryanne said neutrally as she gathered up the dice and other materials to move them out of the way. Callie gave Ken a small, sexy smile and Ken grinned broadly back at her. "Now we have a choice to make. Does the couple perform the public sex first followed by each couple making their trip to the bedroom or should we go in order of number drawn and therefore the public sex is more in the middle of the rest. What does everyone prefer?" There was a small discussion about this point.

Laura said forcefully "Since I am number one and I'd like to get my task over with as soon as possible before I chicken out, I'd like to go in order of number drawn." She looked over at Mike and said quietly "Sorry Mike, it's no reflection on you. I'm just a bit of a bundle of nerves." Then she looked over to Callie with her eyes pleading "Do you have any objection to that, Callie?" Callie shrugged her shoulders slightly and shook her head negatively. The rest of the women chimed in that it was fine with them.

Laura quickly grabbed Mike's hand and led him down to the master bedroom; the remainder of the group sat, chatted and snacked on the refreshments while they waited. The women grouped over to one end of the living room while the men sat a small distance away. No mention was made regarding what might be happening in the bedroom or what might happen to them later in the evening. Everyone was trying to be extremely mature about the whole thing but Merryanne could tell that most of the men were incredibly excited by the prospect that they were most likely going to get a blowjob by a woman not their wife. She felt a little aroused herself; since she'd married Bob there had been very little sexual contact with other men. She and Bob did try a couple of times a year to allow her some sexual interaction with other men while he watched but it had been hard to find partners who were willing and she felt so sleazy about doing it with total strangers. She looked over at Barb, who'd been the main one to help her convince the other women in the group to do this and to help her organize matters for tonight, and examined her quite closely; she could tell that the other woman was turned on because her quite prominent nipples were poking hard against her dress. Barb noticed Merryanne observing her and blew her a kiss before raising her eyebrows and giving her a wide smile.

After nearly ten minutes, Mike came back into the living room to join them; he looked quite smug and exceedingly satisfied; he carefully avoided looking Ken's direction. He told them that Laura was just taking care of a few minor matters and would be rejoining them shortly. The men kept a close eye on Ken to see how he reacted but he seemed to be fine with matters. After nearly five minutes, Laura rejoined them and looked very guiltily in Ken's direction. He got up off the couch he'd been sitting on and walked over to her slowly. He put his arms around her and drew her into him. He bent to kiss her and she avoided his attempt, extremely aware of where her mouth had just been. He took a firm hold of her face and planted a wet kiss on her mouth. Laura was shocked but then felt her heart gladden; apparently Ken was going to be fine with her and she felt her love grow for her understanding husband. The watching women broke out in a smattering of applause for their performance and the men nodded their approval. Merryanne felt that the group had just crossed a significant first hurdle and was heartened that the rest of the evening would probably go well.

Barb tossed her blonde hair, smiled at Frank and held out her hand for Sid, leading him back to the bedroom. It took just over ten minutes for them to do as they wanted and both of them came back together. Barb glanced shyly at Frank to see if he was going to welcome her back like Ken had done for Laura. He walked up, hugged and kissed her on the mouth. Merryanne could see him whisper something in Barb's ear and she nodded her head and smiled a bit at him. While this was going on, Jill looked over at Bob, got a nod from him and joined Sid to give him a small hug before going back to sit by Bob. Merryanne was a bit worried that Jill might be jealous of Barb and decided to keep an eye out for that during the rest of the evening. Now it was time for the public performance but Merryanne figured it was a good time to make sure that everyone had a drink and any snacks they might want before the show.

As she was making sure everyone had refreshments, Callie approached Merryanne and said softly but firmly "For God's sake, Merryanne, will you stop with all your fussing and delaying. I've got to suck a man's dick in front of everyone, including his wife and my husband. I've got a bad case of stage fright right now and I'm afraid that if I don't get started right away, I'll chicken out. As it is, I'm liable to toss my cookies when he cums in my mouth and that'll look very bad to him. Can I please get started?" Merryanne gave her a slight hug of understanding and pity and quickly got everyone ready.

Merryanne led her over to a low-slung hassock and Ken quickly came over to join them. Callie hiked her dress up so that she could easily raise it above her waist while seated and plopped her rear end down on the soft cushion, she motioned for Ken to come over to stand near her. She used both of her hands to undo his belt and pants and pulled the pants down to his ankles. Ken was wearing a fairly loose fitting pair of green striped boxers and he was definitely showing signs of how big his cock was because he was starting to tent them. Callie took a moment to admire him standing there and adjusted her dress up so that she could fondle herself while performing the blowjob. Once she was satisfied with all that, she reached out and pulled Ken's boxers down quickly and smiled as his long, thick cock flopped out; it was almost fully erect. Callie knew exactly how to make it stand fully erect. With her left hand, she stroked it lightly for a moment or two and then bent forward to take the head of it in her warm, wet mouth; Ken gave a loud groan of pleasure when she did this. The people watching could see that he was fighting to keep from putting his hands on the brunette's head to hold her mouth up against his cock. He figured that she would object if he did that and he didn't want her to pause or stop what she was doing. He looked down and realized that she was looking up at him and he felt that the eye contact was quite erotic. The few times that Laura performed a blowjob on him, she preferred to close her eyes and concentrate on her task. Ken felt that Callie was definitely more into giving blowjobs than Laura and he was grateful that she was doing this. She began using her tongue, swirling it around over his sensitive, circumcised head; Ken gave a few grunts of happiness and pushed his hips forward at her. She reached out with her left hand and pushed back against his thigh, indicating that she didn't want him to do that. She slipped her left hand down into her own panties and stroked her damp pussy while continuing to tease the end of his prick with her mouth and tongue.

Ken became aware that most of the men and some of the women were making noises of arousal as Callie worked the tip of his cock and it turned him own even more to have this happening to him in front of them. He was surprised by that fact because he'd always assumed that he'd feel inadequate and get stage fright in front of an audience. From the noises that Callie was making with her mouth full, he presumed she was also excited to be doing this in front of their friends. Since he'd gone back to remaining motionless for her, she brought her left hand back and began lightly massaging his heavy balls. It felt fantastic and Ken moaned loudly in pleasure; Laura had never done that for him before. Callie let go of him with her mouth and looked up into his screwed up face; Ken gave a whine of frustration that she'd stopped but she just smiled broadly at him as she let him suffer somewhat. He was almost ready to plead with her to continue when she took hold of him and reapplied her mouth to his cock. He sighed a moan of relief and enjoyed the sensations again. She took him a little further into her warm mouth and used the base of her tongue to push against the delicate tip of his cock. Ken once again made noises of approval. She engulfed his cock entirely and he could feel it bang against the soft back of her throat; she pulled her mouth off of him and gagged a couple of times before she swallowed him once again. Ken was now keeping up a steady whining as he vocalized his pleasure and his struggle to keep from popping off in her mouth too soon. He clenched his muscles in his groin because he didn't want this to end too soon. Callie realized that he was very close to orgasm, she could end the performance real quick if she just pushed him a little more but she liked the attention so she removed her mouth from his shaft, lifted it and began licking his ball sack. She quickly discovered that what she was doing was a mistake; Ken had never experienced such action before and was incredibly turned on by it. She gave a heartfelt sigh and moved over to kiss and nibble his inner thigh for a bit while he calmed himself down. The watching group gave her some noises of approval for her actions, knowing that she was drawing out the blowjob for their entertainment.

After a few minutes to recover himself, Ken offered Callie the end of his cock once more and she sucked it vigorously, bringing him back to fully erect. She then spent a couple of moments licking up and down his shaft, murmuring her enjoyment of the process. She could hear the women muttering their own approval and a few groans of enjoyment from the men. She stroked the loose skin along the shaft a few easy times and then took it back into her mouth where she swirled her tongue against the head and tried to stick the point of it down the small slit in the top. Ken was groaning with pleasure and fighting to keep from holding her head against his crotch. She cupped and stroked his balls in their loose sack and then pressed her index finger hard against the base of his prick. Ken gave a grunt of surprise and his erect cock began to deflate; he was flabbergasted by what she had done to him; how could she do that to him, he thought angrily. Callie never moved her mouth off of his cock and continued to work him over eagerly; Ken soon realized that he was once again starting to harden and he was relieved as he recognized that she'd just done that to extend out his performance. Less than a minute later, he was straining to hold back his orgasm and he could tell by the ache in his balls that it was going to be a huge one.

"Ummm, Callie" he grunted out somewhat harshly. "I'm about to blow my load. It's likely to be big and if you don't want it in your mouth, you might want to move it." His face screwed up big time from his efforts to withhold his cum. Callie just murmured something that sounded like acceptance and kept working his hot cock over with her warm, flexible tongue. She could taste the bitterness of his pre-cum and was preparing herself for the warm, acrid mouthful she expected to follow. Ken gave a loud groan of triumph and unloaded his cum deep into her mouth. Callie choked slightly as the warm gooey mass filled her throat but she gamely swallowed the spurt and got ready for the second emission. Ken moaned something that sounded like 'Oh my God' and sent a second load down her willing throat. Ken had never experienced a blow job as good as this one before and he was extremely pleased about the whole experience. He felt that he'd been drained of all fluids and his cock began deflating rapidly even though Callie kept it in her warm mouth. Callie gradually became aware that he was finished and she was mouthing a dead horse so she delicately removed her mouth and began cleaning up the remaining cum on his cock. She then took her hand out of her panties and straightened out her clothing before standing up. She was heading to the bathroom to wash out her mouth when Ed intercepted her and gave her a deep, hard kiss; she was shocked that he would do that considering her mouth had just been on another man's cock. She felt an immense stab of pride and love for her understanding husband and paused to lengthen out the kiss. The women all applauded Ed's actions while some of the men nodded their approval. Callie blushed in satisfaction and then broke away from Ed to make her way down to the bathroom.

Merryanne looked around the crowd of her friends, they were excited and bubbling with joy; it looked as though her hosting of the night had been a tremendous success and she was ecstatic. She looked forward to later in the night when she'd have to fulfill her obligation to Ed and suck his cock. She also looked forward to the coffee meeting the women would be holding the next day to discuss what had happened here and whether or not they wanted to continue with such parties. Merryanne looked over and smiled widely at Barb, who returned it with equal pleasure; she was willing to bet everything that tomorrow all of the women would unhesitatingly vote for sex parties to continue. She began to think up some changes that she'd like to see happen at the next one she hosted.

THE EXPECTANT BRIDE

Francine was busy looking over the book that showed bridesmaid dresses while waiting for Jenny to come out and show her one of her selections for her wedding dress. The tall, pleasant looking brunette was scowling at what the dressmakers thought made a good dress for those who weren't the bride; everything seemed to be blocky and clunky looking. She was sure that whenever she chose to get married, she would insist on going to a dress shop where they understood that the bride would be quite radiant on her own for her special day and she didn't need for her best friends to look poor and dowdy in comparison to her. She sighed in exasperation, obviously Jenny didn't feel that same way; not that she was overly surprised because Jenny had always been very self-centered and narcissistic. She gave some thought about how Jenny had dragged her down here when she really didn't want too much to do with the beautiful blonde's wedding; Jenny insisted that they had to have lunch together so that they could discuss something extremely important, although she left out what it was, and then had contended that she stop at the dress shop first. Francine could feel her stomach rumbling because she had assumed that they would be at the restaurant and eating by now, rather than looking at frippery that Jenny wore much better than her. She once again wondered why she remained the blonde's friend rather than go her own way; she felt that she was a strong enough person to do that but something about how Jenny looked at her when she wanted something caused Francine to give in to her. She sighed loudly again and stuck her tongue out at the book; of course, that was the exact moment that Jenny and the salesgirl helping her chose to return.

"What are you doing, Francine?" Jenny asked with a frown creasing her pretty face. The dirty blonde haired salesgirl also gave Francine a perplexed look and Francine felt like she had when she'd been in Grade Two and Jenny had talked her into making a rude gesture behind the teacher's back and who had immediately caught Francine doing it. She blushed a deep red colour as they looked at her and just gesticulated mutely, hoping that they would drop the matter and go on with what they were doing. Of course Jenny would do no such thing and she said to the salesgirl "I have to apologize for my friend. She's always doing something to embarrass herself and me. You wouldn't believe some of the things she used to do in school and still sometimes does in bars." She looked quite sweetly at Francine and asked "You haven't been drinking, have you? It's still quite early in the day for you to be hammered." Francine was furious, thinking Jenny knew quite well that she hadn't had anything to drink and the reason that she was always doing stupid things was that Jenny insisted that she do them. She tried to defend herself but nothing made its way out of her mouth; she just sat there gaping slightly. Jenny smiled sweetly at her before turning back to the salesgirl. "I want you to keep this dress for me while I make up my mind" she commanded.

The salesgirl sighed and went to tell her that she couldn't do that; all dresses were supposed to be sold on a first come basis, no holdbacks. Of course the salesgirl was fully aware that Jenny had six other dresses being held while she made up her mind. "Of course, I'll be happy to do that" was what came out of her mouth.

Jenny turned back to Francine and said "Well, Francine, are you ready to go get something to eat. I'm starving but I have to watch my figure so that I can fit into my wedding dress. We need to order only some salads." Francine nodded, as her heart sank, she'd been looking forward to a good burger and some fries but Jenny insisted that if she was eating salad, Francine would be too. They went out and Jenny drove them to the restaurant in her little red sports car.

When they entered, the lunch rush was finished and there were plenty of tables. Jenny asked the hostess for a more secluded table away from everyone else and the girl led them over to a back table in the corner. Jenny told her that it would do fine and proceeded to seat herself; Francine also sat down. "Just water for both of us" Jenny commanded the girl.

While they waited for the water and for the waitress to come take their order, Jenny chatted merrily about how hard it was to arrange everything for the wedding while Francine just sat and nodded agreement. Francine knew that Jenny would make snide remarks at her if she chose to interrupt so she just kept her place and nodded sympathetically on cue. The waitress arrived with the water and noted that they hadn't looked at the menu yet. She went to recite the lunch special still available and to ask if they needed time to decide when Jenny announced "Just two small garden salads with French dressing on the side." The waitress glanced at Francine but Francine refused to meet her eyes; she knew that she would be eating salad even though she still wanted that burger. It was easier if she just did as Jenny wanted, she thought to herself miserably. She resisted sighing, knowing that Jenny would take it as a slight and tear into her; Jenny was still running her life like she had in high school. The waitress left and Jenny returned to telling Francine how hard it was to find a caterer who'd agree to provide wonderful food for her budget. Francine let her mind drift a bit as she listened absent mindedly to the cheerful prattle.

The waitress was back very shortly with their order and wished them a good meal. Francine poured the French dressing over her salad, even though she really preferred Ranch, and dug in ravenously. Jenny just dipped a few pieces of lettuce into her dressing and ate them delicately. She waited until Francine was about half way done her salad and then purred "So, Francine, I understand that you've been keeping a secret from me all of these years." Francine choked on her salad, wondering how Jenny had found out about her; she was sure that she'd been so careful.

"What do you mean?" she squeaked out through her tight throat and then reached for her water.

"You've been eating pussy" Jenny replied brutally.

"I-I-I" Francine sputtered as she coloured and cast her eyes around the room frantically. Thank God, there was no one nearby, she thought desperately. She wondered how Jenny had found out about her after all of these years and what she was going to do about it. Francine could picture Jenny crowing that information to all of her friends and Francine being snubbed because of it.

"Oh, don't bother denying it or trying to explain it" Jenny told her with a superior smile. "I have access to some rather erotic pictures of you doing it. I've spent a little money making sure that I have the only copies on your behalf and I plan on recouping my investment from you." She stabbed a small piece of tomato with her fork, dipped it and slid it into her mouth as she watched Francine's florid face.

"Of course I'll pay you back the money" Francine said frantically. "But, can we keep this a secret between us, please. I'll be ruined if it gets out" she begged.

"Oh, I plan to collect more than just the money from you, you sniveling little dyke" Jenny hissed as she gave Francine a withering look. "You're going to make sure that I am kept extremely happy if you don't want me exposing you. I've been worried about how I was going to remain faithful to Paul once I married him. Now, I realize that I really don't have to. I'm going to let him know what you are. He'll agree that you'll make a wonderful pet for both of us." Francine gave her a look filled with horror as she realized what Jenny was saying. "You're going to let Paul do anything he wants to you and then he'll get to watch while you work at satisfying me. What better wedding present can you give the man you love." Jenny let Francine ponder the matter in silence for a few minutes as she ate a few more bites of her salad; she knew that Francine would give in to her because she always did. She kept the fact that she didn't actually have the pictures, because there were none that she knew of, to herself, confident that Francine would never ask her to prove the fact. She began to hum a bit of a show tune as she waited for Francine to say something.

"I'll do whatever you want with you" Francine said humbly. "But please don't ask me to allow Paul to fuck me."

"Oh, no, I can't agree to that" Jenny said with a cruel smile. "You're my gift to him so that he will allow me to do what I want while we are married. Besides, I know that men have fucked you before. They tell me that you're not a bad lay, even if they have to do most of the work. They also say that you're much better with your mouth than your pussy." She expanded her smile to a grin and continued "I don't much like to have a cock in my mouth but Paul, like most men, likes to have his cock sucked so you're going to be my little bitch and do it." She paused and looked thoughtful. "Maybe if you milk his balls enough with your pretty mouth, he'll not want to fuck you." Then she continued, mock sadly "But Paul is pretty energetic and I'm pretty sure that he'll make sure that he fucks you often. He's expressed a desire to screw my ass but I'm not sure that I want that. Maybe after watching him in your ass twenty or thirty times, I might see if I like it." She noted the horror creep back into Francine's face and flashed her cruel smile again. "Oh, are you an anal virgin?" she asked, sweetly. "Well we'll soon remedy that." Then she paused once again as a thought struck her. "Maybe Paul can gift rides of you to his wedding party. It would be much more memorable than a tie tack or cufflinks like most men give out. Don't you think?" She didn't really mean it but the more she thought about it, the better that she liked it. Then another wonderful inspiration came to her. "In fact, if you're as good with your pretty tongue as I've heard, I think I'll let you eat the pussies of my wedding party at the bachelorette party. Oh, they're sure to enjoy that." She saw Francine looking miserably at her and commanded "Cheer up, you little dyke. I insist that you always be smiling when you're around me or I'll give you something to make you miserable." Then she shook her head sorrowfully, "If you'd told me about your little secret when we were younger, think about how much fun we could have been having. Instead, I have to hear about it from other people. Oh, by the way, you won't have to worry about wearing a bridesmaid dress. I know that you hate them. You're not going to be at my wedding. Instead you're going to be tied to a bed with a vibrator in your ass and another in your cunt, getting ready to provide us with some real fun for the wedding night." She noticed that Francine had stopped eating and said, in a commiserating tone "Lost your appetite, have you. Well, if you're finished, then we can go. I booked a room at one of those motels that you sneak away to so we can see how well you perform with me." She signalled for the waitress so that they could leave.

Francine spent the time until they arrived at the motel room thinking about how she could get out of this and could not come up with anything that she thought would work for her. About the only way, she could be free from Jenny, she thought wildly, would be to kill her and she contemplated that but realized that she wouldn't have the guts to do that. Still, it had been fairly satisfying, thinking about Jenny's eyes bugging out as she strangled her. When they entered the room, Jenny turned to her and said, snidely "You've been awful quiet. I hope that the cat hasn't gotten your tongue. I so dearly want to feel it against my clit. Now get all your clothes off so that I can look at you." Francine hesitated about doing that so Jenny gave her a smack across the face. "Oh dear" she said menacingly. "Do I have to start the harsh discipline so early. Get your fucking clothes off!" Francine hurried to obey; she'd noticed that Jenny had brought in a small suitcase with her and was not anxious to find out what she had in it.

Jenny stood by Francine, watching her undress; Francine quickly stripped down to just her panties before she hesitated, her hands at her sides, hesitant to remove that lacy item. Jenny, seeing her hesitation, reached out and smacked Francine's plump right tit hard enough to leave a hand impression on it. Francine jumped and cried out but rapidly removed her panties. Jenny placed Francine's hands behind her back before sliding her hand between the nude woman's thighs to make her open her legs up more so that she could better see her cunt lips. She gave Francine a quick brush with her fingers, enjoying the other woman's flinch. She was happy that she was correct about how pliable Francine would be for her and contemplated how far she should force the other woman to go that first time; she'd packed her little bag for all sorts of eventualities but decided to keep things fairly simple this first time. There would be lots of time to make Francine do other things like she had threatened earlier.

"Come sit over here beside me on the bed" she commanded as she retrieved a small egg shaped vibrator from her case. Once she had sat down with Francine beside her, she made the other woman lift her left leg up onto the bed to give her better access to her cunt. She let the brunette lean against her, enjoying the feel of the plump tits being pushed against her side. "Lick this" she directed, holding up the vibrator near Francine's mouth. She smiled as the woman complied, knowing that she hadn't bothered to clean it since the last time she'd used it on herself. She wondered if Francine could still taste her on it. "Get it good and wet" she commanded. "It's going up inside you. I want to watch you cum for me before you eat me out."

Francine obediently ran her tongue over the toy, she suspected that Jenny was going to be rough with her and she wanted as much lubrication on it as she could get. After a minute, Jenny snatched it back from her and then pushed it up against her cunt lips. Francine felt it go up inside her and then Jenny pushed it as hard as she could up into the brunette; Francine moaned in pain as the firm egg went rapidly up her cunt. As soon as it was up as far as it could go, Jenny turned the toy on at its highest speed; Francine could swear that the fillings in her teeth were being shaken loose. She wondered how powerful the motor was; she wasn't aware that Jenny had gotten the most powerful one she could get. Once she got used to how hard it was vibrating in her, Francine began to enjoy the feeling it was generating in her. She could feel her cunt muscles starting to squeeze down on it and her juices began to flow. Jenny started grabbing and stretching Francine's nipples and Francine brought her arms forward to block her. Jenny slapped her face once again and pushed her arms back behind her. "Do you want to be cuffed?" Jenny threatened. Francine shook her head and tried to comply with Jenny's wishes. Jenny slid her hand in between Francine's thighs and captured her clitoris in between her fingers; she squeezed and pulled on it. Francine let out a small squeal of pleasure at that treatment. Jenny slapped her across her face and said disgustedly "You like that, don't you. You little dyke." Francine could feel her face grow hot from the shame she felt. She was confused about what Jenny wanted from her; if she was so disgusted by her, why fondle her like she was, Francine wondered. In spite of that, Francine could feel her orgasm building from the toy inside her as well as the humiliation Jenny was making her feel. She began to fidget as the pressures in her increased and she realized that Jenny was watching her raptly. She cringed a bit at the naked interest in the other woman's eyes; she wasn't used to being made to orgasm before a woman who appeared to hate her. She was surprised to find that she really wanted to show off before the blonde.

Soon Francine lay down on her side onto the bed, her legs were beginning to shake as she began to cum and she writhed her body. Jenny pulled the vibrator out of her quite roughly and Francine spurted a small amount of liquid out onto her inner thighs. Jenny ran her fingers through it and pushed them into Francine's mouth; Francine eagerly licked her juices from the other woman's fingers. She'd tasted her own juices often and enjoyed them. Jenny slammed her wet hand across Francine's face and snapped "Nasty little dyke." She then stood up and removed her panties, putting the sopping underwear over Francine's head like a hat. Francine could smell how aroused the blonde was and realized that she was tremendously looking forward to tasting her. Jenny pulled her head up under her dress so that Francine's face was against her damp pussy. Francine pushed her face against the other woman's short blonde fringe, breathing her sweet aroma in deeply, before sliding her tongue up between the swollen cunt lips. Jenny gave a few moans of pleasure as she felt Francine probing her aroused pussy; it felt good and Jenny could feel an electric spark being generated deep inside her hips. She possessively grasped the back of Francine's head and rocked her hips against the other woman's face as her orgasm built. Francine licked the drooling slit franticly for about two minutes as Jenny moaned and writhed against her, enjoying what was being done to her. Then Francine moved up and found the blonde's swollen clit and lightly ran her teeth against the sensitive organ. Jenny shrieked and grabbed the back of the brunette's head even tighter. Francine was worried that Jenny would push her away but instead the blonde pulled Francine even tighter against her. Francine licked and sucked rapidly as Jenny bucked her pussy hard against her face; Jenny pretty much coated Francine's face with her juices as the brunette tried hard to force her into orgasm.

This felt so much better than the often painful act of riding a hard cock, Jenny thought. She pondered how nice it was going to be to have this soft tongue up inside her on a daily basis as she felt herself nearing her climax. Jenny had never experienced an orgasm with a man inside her; her few climaxes had been achieved with her own fingers after an awful lot of work and here Francine's talented tongue pushed her over the edge in just a fairly short time. She knew that she was going to have to make sure to keep the brunette fearful and compliant so she could always enjoy her.

Francine, for her part, was also enjoying the sex act; Jenny's cunt was sweet, aromatic and responsive. She was enjoying hearing the moans of the blonde as she pumped liquids from her pussy. Francine really liked eating another woman's pussy and recognized that she would have no problems with doing that to Jenny repeatedly. It had been one of her fantasies when they were growing up together but she had been too chicken to act on it. She'd been afraid of what Jenny would say or do to her and now that the blonde knew, Francine realized that Jenny would be harsh with her and it really turned her on. Francine was only beginning to realize how much she enjoyed being humiliated by another woman, especially one as bitchy as Jenny. As Jenny shrieked as she orgasmed, Francine dreamed about how wonderful it would be to eat this woman a couple of times a day. She was apprehensive about all the other things that Jenny threatened to do to her, especially the bit about letting men screw her, but she knew that she loved this part of what they were doing. She hoped that Jenny would let her cuddle her as she recovered from her climax; she felt that act gave real feeling to her efforts.

SPRING SUNDAY AFTERNOON OUTDOOR FUN

Jan was busy stretching her long, powerful thigh muscles; Carrie was bent over, providing her back as a base for Jan to stretch on. Mickey and Donna looked on with Mickey watching Jan's legs with rapt interest; she liked how the tall girl's muscles bunched and stretched as she went through her warmup routine. Mickey wished that she had Jan's height and slimness although she got a fair amount of compliments about her shorter, plumper form. A number of guys had told her that they preferred her to Jan and she wondered if they were just leading her on but enough of them chose her over the chance to fuck Jan that she was beginning to establish some belief in their words. The four girls had no problems attracting suitors and rather had to turn down lots of offers. They were out here on this Sunday so they could enjoy one of their favourite activities, namely an outdoor orgy.

With the four pretty, fit college girls were eight men who'd been invited to participate in the afternoon's activity; three of them were doing some warmup activities while the other five were standing around, loaded down with supplies for the picnic. They were at the parking lot at the base of the path that wound through the foothills. About five miles up the path was a nice clearing in the woods that the group was headed for; it was a pleasant walk that stretched out their muscles wonderfully. The four girls were aware that there were a lot of people who gathered in the woods to watch them having sex with the guys in the clearing and they were excited about it. As long as the watchers stayed out of the clearing and didn't interfere in any other way, they were welcome to watch as far as the girls were concerned. In fact, some of the people who the girls assumed would be watching were gathered a distance away, waiting for the group to get started; there were a number of men and a few women in the other group.

Jan lifted her leg from Carrie's back and then bent over to place her palms on the ground in front of her; her short, tight shorts rode up high into her crotch as her leg muscles popped against her skin. Mickey watched and gave a low moan of appreciation as the dirty blonde haired woman did this; Carrie and Donna exchanged grins, knowing the arousal that Jan was creating in Mickey. They'd both enjoyed Mickey's active tongue previously but were aware that Jan had never availed herself of it. Jan was aware that Mickey wanted her as much as any man but she was unwilling to sample that lesbian activity even though she was aware that the other three had gotten together. Jan did enjoy teasing Mickey though and made sure that she did so at every chance. She knew that Mickey enjoyed men almost as much as women and would get fucked by quite a few of them that afternoon. She considered herself the leader of the four of them and if she felt that they weren't performing as well as they should, she would replace them as quickly as she did any of the men. She was aware that there were a number of women anxious to be included in the afternoon activity. But Mickey had shown that she was always more than willing to fuck men until she was too tired to do so and it took a fair number of them to tire her out; she usually claimed the most of the four of them even though Carrie tried to challenge her most times. Jan usually only allowed three guys to fuck her.

Jan straightened up, turned and gave Mickey a seductive little smile, enjoying the feeling of power that it gave her; she was happy to see that most of the men had also been watching her display. "Well" she called to the group. "I think that we're about ready to get started." The group quickly muttered their agreement and they all set out down the path. After a few steps, Jan broke into her starting trot and began to speed down the firm path. "Whoever catches me gets their choice of who they want to fuck first" she called challengingly over her shoulder. This was a constant because this activity had been started to give Jan some hard exercise; she had the long, lean body of a distance runner and that was what she was. She knew that the men were faster and stronger than her but she loved pitting herself against them; the effort of trying to outrun them gave her a great deal of arousal and forced her to perform wonderfully. The three men that would be chasing her grinned at the group as they waited for her to reach the lone pine tree near the turn in the path about two hundred feet away. They knew the rules of the game; Jan had to be given a head start so that she wouldn't be caught until just before where the clearing was. It gave her a good run. If any of them broke those rules, none of the women would fuck them and that was their goal for the afternoon because catching Jan first only gave them bragging rights amongst themselves. They pretty much had their choice amongst the four girls anyways but it was fun to be the one to catch Jan.

As Jan speedily turned the corner, the three men sprinted after her as the rest of the group walked in a more leisurely manner. It would take the fit young people about forty-five minutes or so to reach the clearing. It was about ten in the morning so they would be there between ten thirty and eleven; enough time for the girls to fuck all of the men at least once before they sat down for lunch. Carrie, Donna and

Mickey each had small light packs containing extra clothes for all four women and light blankets to protect them from the ground. The five men walking with them had the heavier items distributed amongst them including food and water for the girl's to wash off the worst of the mess that the men would spatter them with.

It's a little nippy out here" Carrie complained. Donna glanced over at her, noticing that the brunette's large nipples were pushing prominently at her light top. None of the three women bothered to wear bras even though both Carrie and Mickey were really too large to comfortably be without their support. Jan had the smallest tits of the foursome and she wore a very supportive sports bra so that she wouldn't develop nipple rash from her running.

"Oh, quit whining" Donna said teasingly. "You love how the colder air makes the men stare at you." Carrie grinned at her and looked around at the men to make sure that they were all aware of her tits. The men grinned back at her, aware that she wanted them to look at her without any shame in the fact; it made a very pleasant change from having to sneak glances at a hot woman like they usually had to do. About three of them were busy watching the enticing bounce of Mickey's magnificent tits and she was busily rolling her shoulders to give them even more movement. The men could feel their dicks begin to stiffen and more than one of them wondered if they would be able to last until the clearing. They were aware that the girls wouldn't do anything to relieve their arousal until they reached the clearing.

The women walked along the path enjoying the attention and the cool but still pleasant morning. They enjoyed throwing suggestive glances at the men, knowing that it revved them up; they were pleased if they could get at least one of them hurry on ahead, afraid that he was going to climax in his pants before the clearing. The girls set a strong pace that they knew the men could easily maintain with their longer legs so that Jan and her pursuers wouldn't have too long a wait. They chattered easily with the men and each other about all sorts of different topics; since all of them were in college they had a healthy curiosity about all sorts of things. When they'd gone about a third of the way to the clearing, Mickey turned to survey the size of the group following them. She was pleased to see almost twenty people in that group and excitedly told the others about it. Carrie and Donna took the news in a blasé fashion, they really didn't care how many there were that would be watching them. Mickey was a little miffed at their attitude because she liked to know there was a large group watching; she could feel her nipples perking and her pussy leaking slightly from her arousal.

Carrie noticed because she knew Mickey the best of them and teasingly asked "Do we have to stop so I can lick your wet pussy for you?" Mickey blushed slightly and a few of the men gulped at that image in their minds and then hurried forward towards the clearing as they felt their control slipping. Carrie laughed in uproarious fashion at the chaos she had caused in their little group. She knew that Mickey wouldn't take her up on the offer, preferring to wait until a man could put his dick into her at the clearing but she would have gone through with it if it had been accepted. Although Mickey was the most lesbian of the four, Carrie wasn't very far behind her on that path. Donna just watched them indulgently, somewhat amazed that the pair of them were the most sexually active with either sex of the foursome. She knew that the other two young women were growing more excited the closer they got to the clearing and she could feel her own desire building towards its peak. She found these little excursions tremendously helpful in relieving the tensions that had built up over the week.

They had an enjoyable but otherwise unremarkable remainder of a walk to the turnoff where they left the path to go to the clearing. Mickey wanted to wait for the following group so that they wouldn't miss the turnoff but Donna quickly pointed out the fact that it was now a fairly obvious path up to the clearing from all of the feet that had trod on it. Besides, she told Mickey, most of the followers had probably been there before and could find the clearing in the dark if they had to. Mickey allowed herself to be coaxed along. When they entered the clearing, Jan and six men were waiting for them. Jan had gotten a towel from the pack that one of the men had carried and was wiping down her bare breasts, having discarded her sweaty sports bra. She also had one of the sprinters kneeling on his hands and knees so that she could use him for a seat. Mickey, Donna and Carrie knew instantly that this was the man who'd caught Jan and could have his pick of any of them.

"How far did you get?" Carrie called out, curious.

Jan scowled and replied "About a hundred and fifty yards from the turnoff." It had been one of her better runs so she was miffed that she'd been caught. She sighed and said "Steve, here, gets the honour of having the choice." Steve looked back at the three approaching girls with a gigantic grin; he knew which one he wanted, namely Donna.

The girls walked up and stood casually around Jan as one of the men who'd carried the packs brought over glasses of wine for them. Jan had an opened bottle of water that she sipped on, alternating it with the wine; she needed the hydration after her exercise. After a moment, with Jan wiggling her firm ass all over Steve's back, she got up off of him so that he could claim his prize. She kind of wanted the honour of being chosen to be hers but wasn't too terribly surprised that it was Donna. She'd known that Steve would like to have a more intense relationship with Donna but Donna had no interest in limiting herself to one man.

So Donna led him over to where the blankets were stacked, grabbed the top one and led him over to her favourite side of the clearing. She handed Steve the blanket to shake out and arrange while she whipped off the little clothing that she wore. Steve was about to follow suit with his clothing once the blanket was in place but she stopped him so that she could have the pleasure of taking it off of him. Donna pulled up his shirt, exposing his hairy chest and ran her hands over his chest, enjoying the feel of it. She leaned into him and ran her tongue over his small nipples, enjoying the male taste of his sweat. She closed her teeth lightly on his nipple, relishing his small wince of pain and then proffered her own bare tits at him. He bent forward and traced her aureoles with his tongue, sucking in her nipples as they popped out. It felt extremely pleasant to have him sucking on her tits, she thought. He was still sucking them when she pushed her small hands down the front of his tight shorts to grab hold of his semi-erect dick. She smiled at him as she felt the cock quiver in her hands as it began to grow larger; she loved being able to handle a man's dick as it hardened, it made her feel superior to him, knowing that all his attention was now focused on that part of his body. She rubbed the soft velvety head of his prick with her fingers, enjoying his moans of ecstasy as she handled him. She thought very wickedly about causing him to cum in his shorts rather than in her but then decided that she wanted to feel him spurt inside her. She realized that he was fairly close to his climax and that she would have to work fast. She let go of his cock, pulled her hands out so that she could grasp the sides of his shorts and pulled them quickly down to his ankles. She could see a small bead of his pre-cum on the head of his cock and sighed slightly in exasperation. She'd pushed him too hard, too fast and now he wasn't going to be able to last any time inside her, she thought sadly. Well, there would be plenty of other men who would be available to fuck, she thought, feeling a little better about matters.

Still the less time wasted, the better, she thought and put her arms around his neck and hopped up onto his body. She wrapped her legs around his waist to hold herself there while he quickly guided his hard cock up into her wet pussy. She let herself slide down onto him and he started raising and lowering her so that she rode his cock. It took just over a minute for him to orgasm and she felt like she had barely had time to warm her cunt up. Still, she thanked him and held herself in place against him until his cock softened and fell out of her, trailing a thin stream of cum.

After Steve had made his choice, it was up to the three girls who they wanted to fuck; it was an unwritten agreement that the girls would make sure that all of the men attending would get fucked, usually as many times as they liked. Mickey and Carrie usually liked to see if they could handle all of the men each and Jan and Donna usually combined to fuck the eight men so most of the men were offered three rides and took advantage of it. Mickey wanted a man with a large cock to start with so she went over, grabbed the top blanket, and then the man standing nearby that she was familiar with, leading him over to her favourite spot near the entrance of the clearing. Mickey liked this spot because most of the watchers gathered there initially to start watching the proceedings. Mickey knew that she was an exhibitionist and was fine with that; she appreciated attention, clothed or naked and was attempting to become an actress in the college plays. As they headed to the spot, she handed the blanket to the man and stripped off her tight top so that the people gathered in the woods would get a good look at her big tits. She could see a number of them beginning to settle in and waved good-naturedly to them; which, of course, started her tits bouncing so many of them waved back to keep her at it. Mickey wasn't as dumb as she usually acted; she just found life worked better for her when other people underestimated her. When they arrived at the area, the man set out the blanket as Mickey stripped off her shorts and started fingering herself to get her juices flowing. She urged the man to undress quickly so that they could get started as she worked her cunt. He was out of his clothing quickly and showed her that he was eager by being fully erect. He was glad that Mickey had chosen him first because he hated the wait that being chosen second created; it was hell to sit there waiting with a stiff prick and erotic thoughts, trying not to ejaculate. He placed Mickey on her back, lifted her legs and checked how wet her pussy was; he decided that she was providing enough lubrication, so he entered her. He pushed himself in as hard as he could, knowing that she liked being penetrated like that. She easily took most of his shaft with a moan of approval; there was barely an inch of his long cock exposed. The man slowly began working his prick in and out of her cunt as she encouraged him in a slightly breathless tone as she relished the feeling of being fucked deep and hard. He concentrated on keeping his rhythm at a pace that wouldn't cause him to ejaculate too soon but that she would enjoy. He knew that he was in serious love with Mickey and had proposed to her a few times but she'd always turned him down, telling him that he was a good fuck and a nice man. She'd explained that she didn't want to settle down at the moment and wanted to continue to play the field. He'd been disappointed and was jealous when he saw the other men fucking her but he enjoyed their sex too much to leave the group. Everyone else was aware of his attraction to her and were fine with it as long as he didn't cause any problems. Finally the friction of riding her became too much for him to withstand and he felt his balls clenching in preparation for his climax. Mickey was panting and thrusting her hips up to meet him but he knew that she wouldn't be orgasming before he climaxed. "Sorry, sweetheart" he whispered to her as he came with a heartfelt groan. Mickey hadn't really expected him to last long enough to push her into orgasm because most men couldn't but she wasn't displeased with his performance. He'd done quite well and she told him so as he pumped his cum into her.

Carrie chose her man next and led him over to about ten feet away from Mickey and her man; she just pointed him out and walked over there, leaving him to get the blanket. When he arrived, she took the blanket and held it against her, asking him to strip so that she could look him over. This wasn't so that she could make any sort of choice; she just liked looking at naked men. He quickly undressed, aware that Carrie was like that, and stood for her to examine him. Even though she'd seen him nude last week, Carrie took her time viewing his muscular body. In her opinion he bulged nicely in the right spots; she knew that the other girls didn't think that men had beautiful bodies but she liked the male figure. She beckoned him over and handed him the blanket to shake out and arrange as she watched his nude body as he did that. Then she indicated that he should kneel on it. She was aware that he was erect and needed some fairly quick attention but if he came before she was ready for him, that was his problem in her mind. She didn't care too much if he lost his load, he would have to make sure that she was being taken care of first. There were other men that would be fucking her so if one creamed himself without entering her, so be it. She walked up to him and pulled his head down to her crotch. He knew what she wanted so he used his teeth to pull down her shorts and started licking her. She smelt of arousal and sweat, a heavenly aroma, in his opinion and he could feel the pressure on his balls. He anxiously licked at her as he tried to ensure that she would let him into her before he exploded. She decided that he'd tried well enough and took pity on him, making him lie down on his back. She straddled his hips and fit his hard cock up into her before pushing her hips down onto him. He slid easily inside her and she used her weight to push him fully up into her cunt. She put her hands on his muscular chest and rocked her hips, raising them slightly as she rocked forward and lowering them on her backward stroke. He groaned his enjoyment of what she was doing and she set a fairly steady pace, wondering how long he could maintain his control. She knew he wouldn't last long enough to make her orgasm but hoped that he would at least be able to start her process enough that the third man she fucked would be able to make her cum. Frequently, she only came with the fifth or sixth man; that was one of the reasons that she indulged so many of them. But it looked as though this man was going to come too early, judging by his moans and the contortions of his face. Why was it that men always made such funny faces as they were about to orgasm, she wondered, as she pumped her hips against him. Then she felt the hot spurt up inside her and settled her weight on him to receive his load into her; she knew from experience with men that there was no sense in riding them any further, they tended to deflate fairly rapidly once they had shot off. It was like trying to push a rope up inside you when they weren't hard any more, she thought, disgusted. When he was done, she wiggled her hips to dislodge his soft cock from her pussy and dripped some of his cum back down onto his hips before sliding up him so that she could expel some cum onto his belly. She liked to think of that as her way of marking him as her man, knowing that he'd likely be fucking some of the other girls. She giggled slightly as she did this, very pleased with herself. The man was aware that she usually did this and didn't bother to protest; he'd eat his own cum out of her if that was what she wanted.

Jan chose one of the other runners, grabbed one of the blankets from the pile that held extra for later and took the man over to an area beyond the other three girls, farther away from the onlookers. She didn't really like them watching, feeling that it inhibited her, but recognized that there was no way of preventing them. She lay on her back and pulled down her shorts to her ankles, not bothering to try to take them off over her running shoes. The man stripped his own clothing off and quickly got down by her legs. He lifted her feet and squeezed between her legs, entering her as he rested his weight on her. With Jan, it was strict missionary position with minimal talk or extraneous movement. She wanted to get fucked fast without any of the fuss that the other women put up with. In her opinion, sex was needed to keep her body happy and healthy but it didn't have to be more enjoyable than the exercise she put her body through. The men admired her muscular body but found the other three girls to be more enjoyable lays. They were aware that she was the main reason that they were all here so tried to make sure that she got what she wanted out of the sex but felt that it was purely mechanical with her. A few minutes of hard pumping and the man came inside of her. She bucked him with her hips, signalling him to get off her almost before he'd finished ejaculating in her. The man sighed as he followed her wishes but carefully tried to hide his disappointment from her; not that it mattered, she dismissed him from her mind as soon as he was off her. Once he was disentangled from her, she pulled up her shorts once more and went over to wait for the others to finish. She'd sit out the next round; she went over to the pack that held her belongings, dug out a tshirt and her text book. She pulled the shirt on and went over and sat cross-legged near the small fire the men had built, cracked her text book and started studying.

Carrie finished the first of the other three young women and she went and sat on the communal blanket to wait for the other two to finish. She didn't bother to talk to Jan, knowing that she was wrapped up in her studying, but just sat there sipping her wine. The girls had decided a protocol long ago and it stated that since Donna had been chosen, not given the opportunity to choose, she would get the choice of the remaining four men for the second go around. Carrie knew that Donna would be willing to participate in the second sex session but would likely sit out some of the later rounds while she and Mickey fucked the men. If Jan had been chosen, then the girls would be able to choose in any manner since Jan never participated in the second round even if she was chosen. Not many of the men chose Jan, she reflected, because she was really a bit of a cold fish, sexually. Donna finished up next and joined her, greeting her enthusiastically and plopping down beside her to lean against her. Carrie smiled and gave the other woman a quick kiss. When they had finished, Donna said "I think I'll wait until Mickey is finished even though I know who I am choosing." Carrie shrugged her shoulders and nodded, not caring when she'd be fucking her second man. The desperate urge to be fucked had left her so now she could just enjoy the sex. Mickey finished a few minutes later and came over, eager to get on with matters. Donna chose her man and led him over to her blanket while Mickey indicated for Carrie to proceed; she'd take one of the two men left.

Donna led the blonde, somewhat stocky man over to her blanket and assisted him in undressing. He wanted to caress her tits so she let him do that for a while, enjoying the sensations it caused in her mind. After about a minute and a half, she decided that they needed to get on with matters and pulled him down on top of her. He arranged himself on top of her and then let her take his weight as he reached down and fitted his stiff prick up against her pussy entrance. He pushed himself gently but firmly up inside her and she relished the feel of him filling her. Once he was inside, he nuzzled and kissed her neck, letting her get used to feeling him in her pussy; she knew that this was his way and refrained from pointing out to him that she was nicely stretched out by the man who'd already fucked her and could handle him easily. He began a slow pumping into her and she just relaxed to let him do all of the work. He was a good but not magnificent lover she thought and then it struck her that she might be doing him a favour by introducing him to a friend who wanted a monogamous relationship. He was too caring a man to compete well with the other guys, she thought, as he continued his slow, gentle fucking of her. She began to think about how to plan her week ahead as he stroked evenly in and out of her cunt. She tried to remember to at least mutter her appreciation every once in a while because she knew that he was trying and needed the encouragement. He was a somewhat interesting change from the others but he'd only been invited for the past three weeks at her insistence. She figured that the others were going to insist on his replacement soon. After some time she could sense from his noises and the clenching of his muscles that he was on the verge of his orgasm so she bucked her hips against him to help him finish. He grunted slightly as she made contact with him and increased the speed of his thrusting a little bit. She gave him an encouraging smile as he came in her; she barely felt his spurt of cum inside her. Once he was done, she quickly encouraged him to get off her so that they could go back and join the others.

Carrie led her dark-haired fellow over to the blanket and sat comfortably on it, indicating to him that he should strip for her. He grinned at her and took off his clothes in a slightly teasing manner before standing nude in front of her, stroking his cock. She smiled good-naturedly at him, aware that he had a fairly average cock but was proud of it. He was another man who'd only been invited during the last month or so and would probably find himself not being asked back. It wasn't that there was anything particularly wrong with him but there was nothing spectacular about him either. And the competition was fierce amongst the men willing to join them. The girls knew that most of the men in the university would give anything to join them and they sometimes chose to exploit that. She motioned for him to lie down and straddled him. She fucked him hard and steady until he came and then marked him in her usual fashion. She studied his face as she rubbed her wet pussy against his belly, wondering if he even realized that she and likely Mickey would be insisting on his replacement after today. He was a choice by Jan and she wondered if Jan had even fucked him before inviting him to join the group. It was her turn to choose a man next and she'd definitely be holding a competition this week between the four or five she thought might be worthy in order to make her choice. Still, there was no need to be rude, she thought so she helped him to his feet and kissed his cheek very lightly before leading him back to the group.

Mickey was a bit surprised that the other two girls had chosen two men with quite average size cocks rather than the guy of the four remaining men with a nice big prick. Sure, she thought, he's a bit rougher than the other men and he really only likes to enter you from behind but his cock is bigger and he can rock your pussy better than the guys with average pricks. She gave him a smile and he quickly came over to follow her towards her blanket. Knowing his preferences she knelt down, facing the onlookers and he rapidly knelt behind her. He pushed her feet farther out so that she spread a little more and put his hands on her shoulders pushing her down so that her chest rested on the blanket. He didn't waste any of his time ensuring that she was prepared for him because he firmly believed that it was the woman's responsibility to ensure she was ready to be fucked. Besides, he thought dismissively, the blonde, big titted bitch had already been fucked and was undoubtedly sloppy from that. He was very careful not to let the girls know his true feelings about them, the whores that they were, because he wanted to continue taking advantage of them. He'd be as ingratiating as these other bastards so that he could fuck the lot of them, he thought nastily. He rammed his cock up into her well used cunt as hard as he could, feeling the cheeks of her plump ass smack against his hips. He was fairly proud of the sound that resulted and her grunt of effort from taking him so hard. He had to make sure not to look over her to see the watchers because they tended to inhibit his performance, making him unsure of himself. He had a small twinge of hatred for the fat blonde making him feel that way and he punished her by thrusting against her as hard as he could. She grunted as he pushed her forward about six inches as he slammed into her. She didn't realize his true feelings towards her and would have told him to go fuck himself if she knew. She thought that he just liked doing it hard and she was about the only one of the four that would let him have his way completely with her. He concentrated on holding back his climax for as long as he could as he smacked against her ass noisily, hoping to enjoy the sensation of her warm cunt for as long as he could. But he didn't last more than three minutes before he spurted inside her. She was panting a bit from holding herself back against him and gave him a small moan of appreciation even though he hadn't done too much to push her along her path to orgasming. When he was done, he quickly pulled his still stiff prick out of her and went back to the group so that he could get a towel to wipe her juices from his cock. She just shrugged her shoulders and stood so that the watchers could admire her for a bit before she rejoined the others.

Donna was just arriving back at the communal blanket as Mickey walked up and the pair of them sat down to wait for Carrie to finish with her second man. Mickey politely enquired if Donna was going to join Carrie and her in giving a third session before lunch or if she was going to sit it out like Jan. Donna occasionally did fuck a third man before lunch but today she wasn't feeling in the mood to do that. So Mickey knew that Carrie would take the final unfucked man while she would choose one of the men who'd already fucked one of the other women. She decided that she would choose Steve, who'd been the first man with Donna; he deserved the honour since he had caught Jan and she did like to fuck him, she thought. Carrie finally joined them and shot Mickey an inquiring look; Mickey nodded toward the only man not fucked and Carrie nodded her head in understanding.

Carrie took the man over to her area and mounted him; he gratefully accepted her offering and they had a pleasant fuck. She recognized that she was beginning to tire a bit and would need to rest for a while but they would be stopping to have lunch. She would be able to recover over that time period but would have to pace herself a little more so that she would be able to fuck all of the men. She really didn't want to leave anyone disappointed.

Meanwhile, Mickey took Steve over to her blanket and lay on her back; she was willing to fuck in any position that he wanted but Steve first of all wanted to spend some time playing with her massive melons. He rubbed, sucked and kissed all over them for nearly five minutes, tremendously enjoying himself. Mickey also liked the attention; she was used to men treating her this way but it was still nice to feel them doing it to her. Steve then decided that he had to get on with matters and quickly kissed her down her plump belly before giving her damp, fragrant pussy a deep kiss and lick. She gave a small shiver of delight as he did this to her. Then he quickly climbed on top of her and entered her as she wrapped her legs around his hips to hold him in place. He started slow even though she easily took his full length into her cunt to give her time to build her arousal. He gradually increased his pace and soon the only sounds were the rhythmic slapping of his flat belly against her plump one and her moans of encouragement. But then he began to feel the pressure on his balls and the feeling of exhaustion from his effort and knew that he was going to climax soon. He was aware that she was currently nowhere near her orgasm point but that he had no hope of lasting until she reached it. So he just took his pleasure and came into her. Then as they both lay there recovering, he went back to playing with her tits.

When she got tired of that a few minutes later and decided that she was hungry, she urged him off of her and they went over to join the others. Some of the young men were busy roasting hot dogs over the small fire. They knew that only Mickey would eat a hot dog, the other girls had packed salads for themselves because they were very conscious of their weight. Mickey also had some salad for herself but enjoyed hot dogs as well; she knew that she was plump but she liked how she looked and didn't worry about others. They all sat together to eat. The three male runners had also brought along some salad and vegetables for themselves since they were also somewhat concerned about what they ate. The four girls drank wine and six of the men drank beer while the other two stuck to water. After they were all done, the men put out the fire while the girls gathered up the leftovers and packed them back away.

Mickey decided that she wanted some desert so she asked the men "Which of you would like a blowjob from me?" She gave them a big smile and all the men looked interested as they weighed the pleasure of a blowjob versus fucking her.

Carrie felt a little mischievous and since she tried to keep up with Mickey, she challenged the plump blonde "Why don't we each pick a man and blow him? The winner will be the one who gets her man to make the most noise. The others can decide which one it is." She shot a challenging grin at Mickey.

"What are the stakes?" Mickey asked, knowing that Carrie liked to compete with her but would tend to be vague about what they were contending for until she was sure that she was the winner.

"I need a paper written" Carrie admitted. "If you lose, you write it for me."

"And if I win?"

"I'll let you fuck me any way that you want."

Mickey studied Carrie carefully. It didn't sound like too fair a deal for her. She knew that she could write Carrie's paper easily enough and that she liked fucking Carrie but Carrie allowed her to do that on a fairly regular basis anyways. She was aware that the men were watching the two of them with extreme interest; they would be thrilled to watch the two of them have sex together. She mulled insisting that Carrie agree to being fucked by her in front of them but decided that she wasn't particularly interested in fulfilling their fantasies any more than she already did. They hadn't done anything to deserve it, she thought, I'll save that for some time when I want something from them. "If I win, you wear the tit squeezer and I get twenty swats on your behind before fucking you" she stated. The men made some noise as they contemplated the image of that but the girls ignored them.

"Agreed" Carrie said, reluctantly. She liked being fucked occasionally by Mickey but didn't like it when the blonde wanted to inflict pain on her. But she needed Mickey to write that paper for you. "Why don't we do it with these two" she said, indicating two of the men with more average size cocks. No sense wasting a man with a big cock that would feel better in her pussy rather than her mouth, she thought. "Did you have a preference?"

Mickey studied the two men. One of them had fucked Donna and the other had fucked her. She decided that it really didn't matter between the two of them so she chose the one that she hadn't already been with. Carrie nodded in agreement with her choice and the two women dropped to their knees and beckoned the men over to them. The men gave grins to the other men and then walked over to the women. Mickey took the stiff prick offered to her and spent some time licking the sensitive head while Carrie swallowed as much of her man's shaft as she could. She knew that she'd get used to it being in her mouth enough to be able to engulf the whole shaft which was something Mickey was reluctant to do. Mickey liked sucking cock but was not comfortable with trying to deep throat them because of her gag reflex. She had a soft but active tongue and used it. The men moaned as they each enjoyed the two girl's different styles and it didn't take too long before they spurted. Each groaned enthusiastically as they climaxed. A couple of the group put forward that Carrie had won the contest but most of them sided with Mickey. Carrie accepted her defeat with graciousness; she knew that she could get Mickey to write her paper for her; she would just have to offer enough to get the plump blonde to do it, she thought.

The girls spent the rest of the afternoon taking care of the needs of the men as they fucked them. Jan took on her three, Donna did five and Carrie and Mickey made sure that all of the men had sex with them. The girls were feeling pleasantly tired from their exertions and looked forward to getting back home to clean up. They did wash the worst of the jism from the men off them with the remaining water but it didn't leave them feeling especially clean. Mickey was looking forward to a nice hot bubble bath. The men were quite happy about the events of the afternoon and looked forward to next Sunday.

The group gathered their belongings and headed back to the parking lot so they could drive back to the college. They carefully took the items from the packs that they had carried and filled up the big car. Then the girls traveled back with Jan driving so that they could discuss the changes that they wanted to make before the next Sunday afternoon. They didn't finalize their decisions before they made it home and agreed to meet on Tuesday afternoon so that they could determine exactly what they were going to do.

BARONESS MOLLY LEARNS TO FUCK A SISSY BOY

Baroness Molly was nervous, she'd been married to the Baron for just over three months and was still learning how to handle the wild sexual lifestyle he led. She knew that she agreed before accepting his proposal to try anything and everything so that she could find out how she felt about it but today they were going to do something that she'd never imagined she'd be doing. She looked in the mirror and felt that she looked a little too drawn out and sighed. The Baron heard her and recognized that she was anxious; he went over and cuddled her warm fantastic body against hers, pushing his semi-erect cock against her nice, round ass. "Worried about today, Honeypie?" he asked softly.

The Baroness loved him cuddling her and feeling his nice cock up against her; for her, the sex between the two of them satisfied her greatly and she felt that she really didn't need any outside sex, but the Baron enjoyed it so she complied with his desires. She felt that she was still getting used to being a Baroness, living a rich, exotic lifestyle and adapting to living full time with a man to be bothered also learning how to be a dominatrix and learning alternative sex activities. But again, she had to accept that because the Baron had made it part of the proposal; he'd made it plain that he was prepared to move on from her unless she agreed to learn to be more exotic, sexually. She was aware that he got really turned on by watching her with other people in all sorts of situations that she'd never really imagined; she had to admit that she liked most of those situations herself. "Yes" she admitted softly. "I know that Helene will be there to help me and that these two men are supposed to be experienced in doing this but I can't help worry that I might screw things up."

"This is why we practice with people already experienced. They will help you learn how not to hurt your partner too much. Quite a bit of the more exotic sex has some pain involved and those who love it usually enjoy that bit of pain. You seem to enjoy being spanked and that involves some pain" he said quietly, looking to see what her reaction would be; he wondered occasionally if she was faking her enjoyment of being spanked.

She gave him a brilliant grin, knowing that he was probing her again to see if she'd refute her enjoyment of being spanked, tossing her hair back against him before addressing his reflection in the mirror "I do enjoy both you and Helene spanking me. I'll probably enjoy other people doing it to me as well. It makes me feel so vulnerable and at the same time so naughty. I really can't describe the sensations it creates in me. I know I cum long and hard after it is done to me. Helene is very similar but you don't get off having it done to you. I know that you get very hard when you do it to me or Helene."

"Yes" he admitted a little ruefully. "I never really got into being spanked myself. I don't really know why but it just does nothing for me." Then he grinned at her and continued "But having you or Helene, writhing around in my lap and crying makes me hard as rock. There's something very beautiful in seeing my red handprints on your pale plump asses; it's a work of art." She stuck her tongue out at him and went back to being concerned about how she looked. The Baron held her against him for a few minutes; both of them relishing the contact immensely.

Then she had to get dressed and made-up for the day ahead so she broke his embrace gently so that she could prepare her face. She cleansed her face before applying a light bit of foundation to it, she highlighted one eye with powder blue eye shadow and the other one with bright pink, knowing that it gave her a slightly other worldly look. She then applied her mascara and rouge before looking to see if she required any further enhancements; she'd learned that it was best to go fairly light on the makeup because with the energetic sexual activities, most of it just ended up on her partner. She decided that her purplish-red lipstick would be enough so she applied it to her plump lips. The Baron had stayed to watch her, even though it took her nearly ten minutes of concerted effort to apply it properly, and he gave her light applause approving it when she was finished. She scowled at him slightly, thinking that men really didn't understand how important it was for a woman to look her best and how hard it was to maintain that look. The Baron just grinned at her, thinking about the fact that he preferred her looks when she had no makeup on at all but he'd never been able to convince her of that fact. He admitted that her makeup was quite striking but it was gilding the lily as far as he was concerned.

She went out into the bedroom so that she could put her outfit on and he followed her, enjoying the rolling sway of her bare ass. They had separate bathrooms but he'd been in hers so that he could watch her prepare and lend her his moral support, knowing that she would be antsy. She went over to her bed where Desdemona had laid out her outfit for the day; normally the blonde stayed and helped her dress but the Baron had indicated that he wanted to help her that morning. So she had banished the girl, knowing that the other woman got jealous when she watched the Baron fondle her when he was supposed to be helping her. She found it curious that the blonde didn't seem to get jealous when they had threesomes and the Baron had his cock in her but she did over a simple matter of helping her dress. She figured that the blonde considered the duty to be hers alone. She dismissed the thought and picked up her lacy black body suit. She scrunched it up so that she could easily step into it and pulled the tight outfit up over her hips. It took a number of tugs before she was satisfied that it rode her as high as it could go. The Baron had tried to help but she pushed him away as he accidently, on purpose, squashed her tit as he reached around her. She growled at him for delaying her and he just gave her an oh so innocent grin; he knew that she'd recognized that he'd done that on purpose but it was fun teasing her. It also helped to distract her away from her worries. She pulled up the top of the body suit and there he really did help her, knowing that she had trouble doing it alone. He finished tightening her shoulder straps before lacing up the back. She looked marvelous there in that tight, black figure-hugging outfit. She got her black leather midriff girdle and began to place it. The Baron tightened it mercilessly, knowing that she wanted it that way. She gave a grunt of effort as he put his knee against her ass to pull it as tight as she wanted. The leather girdle pulled her nice soft stomach in and sucked up to her lower ribs. The Baron knew that it restricted her breathing but she liked being constrained like that and it made her look even better. Her somewhat broad hips jutted out even more from her now tiny waist. She then rolled her black silk stockings over her legs and the Baron helped her fasten the tops to the garters from the leather girdle. He liked how the garters crossed tightly across her pale ass exposed by the very high cut of the tight body suit. She then had him help her to step into her high black heels and he bent over to fasten them for her. If she bent over in those heels, she'd fall forward onto her head. Then she stood there, opening her legs slightly for him to admire her and he gave her a wolf whistle of approval. She coloured slightly, still slightly apprehensive about accepting his praise; she was used to displaying herself but not in receiving such vociferous approval.

"Helene is likely here by now" she stated, checking the clock to see that it was five minutes to the hour. "Why don't you go welcome her and the two young men that she is bringing. I'll be along in a couple of minutes. I just want to run a brush through my hair and check my makeup." She made a shooing motion at him with her hands but he just stood there and grinned suggestively at her. Then she realized that he wanted to watch her walk into the bathroom in those high heels before he left so she just shook her head good naturedly at him and then walked by him to the bathroom. She knew that her ass jiggled and swayed and she put a nice little wiggle in it as well for his amusement. He gave her a double wolf whistle as she reached the door and then left the room. She turned and smiled to herself as she watched him leave; she felt very happy and loved.

Around ten minutes later she entered the living room where Helene sat comfortably on a chair, dressed in a revealing short dress and stockings, with her legs crossed. Two young men stood near the center of the room; both were dressed in black wool pants and tight polo shirts. One of them was blonde and the other brunette; they were both an inch or two below six foot tall. The Baron was seated in a chair near Helene, chatting with her, as he looked the two men over; Helene studiously ignored them and concentrated on the Baron, she was aware that they both wanted her attention and she was denying them it. The Baroness smothered a smile as she recognized the technique Helene was using because she'd taught it to Molly quite early on in their relationship; Molly wasn't anywhere near as polished as Helene was but she was catching on. She thought about going and sitting on the Baron's lap but she noticed that the chair on the other side of Helene was moved up near her and the Baron; Helene had obviously directed the Baron to move it there and it indicated that she wanted Molly to sit there. So Molly obediently went over and sat on it, smiling pleasantly to Helene as she turned to look her over. Helene gave her a quirk of her eyebrow to show that she approved of Molly's outfit but she said nothing to her in front of the two young men. Molly refrained from telling Helene that she also liked her outfit because of that reaction; so she just broadened her grin. She was very fond of Helene and was learning a lot from her; Molly knew that she could trust the other woman because she was a long-time friend and lover of the Baron. Helene had been the one that ensured that the two of them got together in marriage, counselling both of them when they expressed doubts about living with each other and Molly was eternally grateful.

Although she desperately wanted to look over the two men like the Baron was unashamedly doing, she adopted Helene's attitude toward them and looked solely at Helene and the Baron. She smiled slightly as she caught Helene's small nod of approval. Helene beckoned her to lean forward and when she did, said quietly so the two young men couldn't hear "I'm going to get them to come over here and strip so that you can get up and examine them. Feel free to look them over thoroughly and feel them up as you want. The blonde is more experienced and probably better for you to learn on but if you have a strong preference for the brunette, feel free to take him." The Baroness smiled appreciatively and nodded her understanding and agreement. Helene sat back and commanded "Boys strip off your clothing and then come over here and stand in front of us so that the Baroness can get a good look at you." The two young men quickly complied.

As they stood there nude, legs slightly apart, in front of the three of them, the Baroness leisurely and gracefully got to her feet; she was ecstatic that she managed that because she was still getting used to the height of her heels. Helene had instructed her to wear higher heels to help emphasize her height and supposed dominance and so she wore them. She understood that the other woman was working hard to turn her into the perfect wife for the Baron so she followed Helene's instructions. It didn't mean that she found it easy but Helene also provided her with a sympathetic shoulder to cry on when she found matters too trying. She resisted looking immediately at the two men's cocks and instead, looked them in the face, examining their features. Both men were fairly handsome although the blonde was a bit better looking. Their upper bodies were nicely muscled as well. Baroness Molly walked behind them before dropping her gaze down to their waists; she looked over their taut buttocks with some interest because she was going to be more focused on their asses than their cocks. She still wanted to look at and hold their cocks but knew that she should look them over completely before doing that. She really couldn't see much difference between them; she knew that she could look at and appreciate small differences in women's asses but with men, they all looked much the same to her. But she spent some time looking them over because Helene had told her to do that; Helene had explained that it heightened the men's tension and their arousal if a dominant woman did that to them. She was quite amused to see the both of them flex their ass muscles for her approval. She reached out and caressed their ass cheeks before running her forefinger along the crack of their asses. Both young men pressed their asses back against her hand as she did that. She knew that she liked it when men did that to her and assumed that they got the same satisfaction out of it. She found it fairly pleasant to be the one in charge and felt her nipples pop out slightly and her pussy tingle wonderfully. She paused to assess her own level of arousal and noted with delight that her pause had caused both men to attempt a bit harder to attract her attention to them. She got a small rush of power and enjoyed it, looking past the two men over to her husband to see if he was watching her. He was and he grinned approvingly at her, further increasing her boldness and arousal.

She decided to be quite naughty and stepped up behind the brunette, butting his ass with her hips; he hadn't been expecting that and she pushed him forward somewhat. The embarrassed young man flushed about being taken unawares and she stepped back to deliver a smack on his ass. The hit didn't come anywhere close to hurting him in any way but it served to remind him of his mistake. She knew that the blonde would be ready for the same sort of maneuver so when she stepped behind him she reached around him and grabbed his semi-erect cock. He moaned in appreciation and pushed his hips back against hers. She fondled it for a moment, enjoying the size and his stiffening from her handling of him; she then felt a pang of guilt and looked quickly at the Baron. The Baron was laughing as he enjoyed watching her fondle another man and she realized once again that he truly did want to watch her perform with other men. It was a hard concept for her to grasp.

She decided that she would follow Helene's advice and led the blonde man by his cock over to one of the small mattresses in front of where the Baron was seated.

Helene smiled at her in a friendly fashion and pointed to the other mattress; the brunette man quickly walked over there. Baroness Molly guided the young blonde man down onto his hands and knees so that his ass faced the Baron; she reached between his spread legs and stroked his cock with her hand a few times. He moaned in appreciation and she could feel his cock stiffen even more. She smacked his ass with her free hand to inform him that his pleasure wasn't what was important here. He just wiggled his ass a little impudently and moaned louder. She knew that he was just trying to entice her into paying more attention to him and she was unsure of how to handle the situation. She looked over to Helene for guidance. Helene motioned for her to stop handling him and to smack him in the balls; so she did and the blonde man grunted in surprise as she hit him. Then he immediately assumed his position more erectly; he hadn't been expecting her to punish him so hard. The Baroness spread his ass cheeks to examine his asshole; he displayed signs of having been used hard recently but he looked clean and healthy, she thought. She looked over at Helene once more to see what she was doing. She was lubricating the other man's asshole in preparation for using it so the Baroness grabbed the tube of KY jelly and rubbed a liberal dose onto the man in front of her. She made sure that she forced a good dollop of it up his asshole.

Now that he was all prepared, she went over with her strap-on belt and a selection of dildos to where her husband was. She got him to help her fasten the leather belt around her and displayed the dildos to him so that he could choose which one she would use on the young man. He chose a shorter chunky one and helped her fit it to the belt. Helene joined them and the Baron helped her on with her own strap-on belt but she didn't let him pick a dildo; she'd already decided which one she would use and it was a longer, slimmer curving one. The two women coated their dildos with some lubricant as they walked back to where the men were kneeling.

The Baroness spread the blonde man's lower legs a bit further apart and plopped a cushion down between his feet for her to kneel on as she fucked him up the ass. She carefully knelt down, using him to support herself as she got in position; he muttered a noise in anticipation of what she was about to do to him. She was amused that he was looking forward to it so much and stroked his ass in appreciation. This caused him to give out a small moan of arousal. She positioned herself and pressed the head of the dildo against his rosebud; he gave her a heartfelt groan as he prepared to take it. She hesitated a moment, letting him feel it against him, so that he could build up his anticipation. He started to turn his head to look at her, trying to figure out why she was waiting. As he did this, she drove her hips forward as hard as she could and he took the dildo up his ass for about two thirds of its length. He whoofed in surprise.

Molly didn't give him a chance to recover; she grabbed firm hold of his hips and started pushing the dildo in and out of his asshole as fast as she could. He started moaning as he enjoyed her rough treatment of him. Molly couldn't keep up the pace for very long because she wasn't used to performing in that way; she knew the Baron could keep up that sort of pace for quite a while but he was much more experienced at fucking that way. She found that she was sweating quite profusely from her effort and slowed her thrusts down. She became more intent on seeing how deep she could force the dildo up him, making him hold it deep inside him for a while before doing it again. He grunted in pleasure as she did this to him and she wondered how it felt to him. She knew what it felt like to her and wondered if he had the same feelings of pain, humiliation and happiness that sex like that created in her. She'd wondered how other women responded to such treatment, knowing that a great deal of them refused to be fucked in that way but had never found the courage to discuss it with them. She decided that at some point she would talk to Helene about it because the brunette made her feel safe enough to discuss such matters. But for now, she thought, I should do something more for this young man that I am busy fucking in the ass. She reached around his hips and slowly stroked his cock in time to her thrusts into him. He stiffened magnificently and was soon showing signs that he was going to orgasm. She sped the pace up and soon he was crying out as he ejaculated onto the mattress. He collapsed almost immediately, groaning as he enjoyed the aftermath of his climax. The Baroness unbuckled the harness, leaving the dildo deep inside him and went over to a chair by the Baron to watch Helene finishing with the other young man. The Baron smiled widely at her and held out his hand to hold hands with her. She was quite pleased with how things had gone but knew that Helene would critique her performance later so that she could learn how to improve it.

She drew in a deep breath and took a congratulatory sip of champagne. She felt that she had done well and was quite delighted with her experience.

TOM HAS AN INTERESTING HUNTING TRIP

Tom was walking quietly through the forest in the early morning fog; he was out here hunting a deer. He heard a sound and stopped to identify it. It was a low extended moan; it sounded like someone or something in trouble. He went forward cautiously, slipping up beside a tall evergreen and moved aside one of the branches so that he could look around it. What he saw astounded him. There was a small clearing ahead with two mostly naked men in it. One man who was fairly beefy was on his hands and knees with his heavy sweater pulled up over his hairy chest, letting his pale, fat belly dip towards the ground; his pants and underwear were gathered at his ankles just above his tightly tied hiking boots. The smaller blonde haired man was in behind this chunky fellow with his pants down around his knees. He was busy thrusting his cock into the kneeling man's asshole and it was the beefy man who was making the moaning sound that Tom had heard as the man fucked him.

"Oh, God" the heavy fellow called out, fairly loudly. "It feels so good when you fuck me, Gary" he moaned softer. And then Tom recognized the pair of them. They were a couple of years older than him but had been in school a few grades above him. The blonde guy was Gary Andersen, he'd been a star wide receiver and had married a quite pretty blonde cheerleader. The fatter guy being fucked had been the fullback for the team and his name was Albert Brock. He'd also married a cheerleader if Tom remembered correctly; the least pretty of the cheerleading squad but she was still good enough looking to be a cheerleader. As Tom recalled the pair of them, he seemed to remember them giving him a hard time about looking like a queer when they were in high school. And lo and behold, here they were having gay sex together. He frowned slightly as he also remembered that they both had children with their wives.

But he dismissed that from his mind as he watched the enticing show in front of him; Gary was pumping hard into Albert's ass and Tom could easily hear the rhythmic slapping of his hips against the bigger man's fat ass. Both of them were being quite vocal about how much they were enjoying the sex; the big man being fucked was crooning almost continuously. They carried on at their furious pace for about three minutes and then Gary stopped and pushed his cock into the other man as hard as he could. From where he was standing, Tom could see the blonde's ass cheeks twitch and suspected that he was about to unload his cum into Albert. He could see that Albert was ready to receive it and kept his ass pressed firmly against the smaller man. Gary gave a muffled yell as he orgasmed and Albert moaned with pleasure as he felt the hot cum spurt up his ass.

Gary kept his spent cock up Albert's ass as he helped the larger man lay down on his side so that they could cuddle for a while now that Gary was finished fucking him. Tom could feel his own cock twitch as he watched the pair of them and gave serious consideration to going over and asking to join in. He thought about it for a while as he watched the two men lay there. Gary had reached around Albert's wide hips in order to stroke and stretch out the other man's cock. It looked as though maybe the pair of them weren't quite done with each other and Tom didn't want to interrupt them; he'd decide later if he still wanted to approach them and thought about pulling out his own hard cock so that he could masturbate. He figured that they might see the movement of him doing that and he wanted them to finish what they were doing. He reckoned that he could always call up the image of the two of them fucking later so that he could jack off to it. Then he recalled that he had his cellphone with its camera, so he took a couple of pictures of them for his pleasure later.

He could see that Gary's cock had now shrunk and had fallen out of Albert's asshole but Gary was still busy playing with the larger man's cock. Tom wondered if now Albert would be fucking Gary. But then Gary moved over the bigger man's legs and moved his head up even with his crotch. Gary took Albert's erect prick into his mouth and began to suck on it. Tom was a bit surprised about that but found it to be very arousing; he took a quick snap of that. Gary slowly worked his head so that he eventually had the other man's entire prick in his mouth.

Albert was moaning with pleasure once more, assuring the other man "Oh, Gary, you do that even better than Cheryl does." Tom was a bit perplexed, if he remembered properly, Cheryl was the prettier cheerleader that Gary was married to. The name of Albert's wife was Amy. Hmmm, he thought with wonder, maybe they are even kinkier than I thought. Still, he was interested in watching Gary's technique so he put it from his mind. Gary took his time and was obviously enjoying what he was doing. But after a couple of minutes, Albert began twitching as he fought to withhold his orgasm but then he pushed his broad hips up against Gary's face and filled his mouth with cum. Albert gave out a low groan as he pumped his jism into the smaller, blonde man's mouth and it appeared as though Gary swallowed as much as he could. Tom was again shocked when Albert moved his head down to lick off his own cum from around Gary's mouth.

Sensing that they were probably done with sex for the day and not knowing which way they may head out or how quickly, Tom decided that it would be best to backtrack and make his way away from this pair. He didn't know how they would take having him know about their activities and didn't want to find out yet. As he carefully backed up and headed off in a different direction, he mused about what he should do about the situation. Obviously, the two men were bi-sexual, the same as Tom was; Tom didn't currently have a partner of either sex, his girlfriend having left him nearly three months earlier after finding out about his one night stand with another man. She wasn't interested in a bi-sexual man and had said some hurtful nasty things to him as she left. He was definitely feeling the need to achieve some sexual relief and he liked how Gary sucked cock. He contemplated asking Gary to fuck him and then suck him off as he'd just done to Albert.

He decided that he would approach the blonde man in a couple of days to find out if there was any interest in that. He'd do it in a friendly, non-threatening manner he decided and began to whistle happily as he walked back to his car, no longer interested in hunting deer.

SORORITY INITIATION

Ashley Grillo stared at the pretty woman seated across from her at the Student's Union coffee shop, Grind or Die!, and tried to process what she had said as she took another sip of her latte. The brunette woman just gazed calmly back at her, her grey eyes meeting with Ashley's bewildered green ones. Finally, Ashley got herself under better control, found her voice and asked "Did you just say what I thought you did?"

"If you thought you heard me offer to get you accepted into one of the most exclusive sororities on campus so that I could enjoy fucking you every day, then yes, you heard correctly" the brunette said very matter-of-factly before taking a delicate sip of her black coffee. "Do you have a problem with that?"

"Uhhh, it's rather forward of you." Ashley took a closer look at the beautiful brunette and asked sharply "Do I even know you?"

"No, we've never met" the woman answered, a little prissily. "But we have some friends that are mutual acquaintances of each other and I have been made aware of your situation and demeanor. I was asked to look you over and to approach you if I liked what I saw and I do like what I see." The woman boldly eyed Ashley's long toned legs that her tight, little miniskirt showed off. She licked her lips very suggestively and repeated "I really like what I see."

Ashley eyed her with some distaste before asking "What exactly is my situation and demeanor that you are referring to, might I ask?"

The brunette looked at her with surprise and started to show some uneasiness for the first time since she sat down opposite Ashley. She said, with a little confusion "Oh, maybe I'm mistaken. You were pointed out to me by someone I thought knew you. I take it that you're not Ashley Grillo then and you're not currently couch surfing on your friend's couches so that you can attend class here at this university." The woman looked at Ashley expectantly.

Ashley felt her heart sink as she recognized that the woman indeed knew about her situation and, as for her demeanor, the fact that she felt confident enough to proposition her in public, the woman obviously knew that Ashley was very bi-sexual with a strong leaning towards lesbianism. She wondered which of her friends would go around pointing her out to women such as this brunette in front of her before deciding that there were probably too many candidates and what did it really matter. Someone probably thought that they were doing her a favour. She looked down at the table top and murmured softly "I am Ashley Grillo and you do have your facts right about me. But I am thoroughly confused as to exactly what you are offering me." She hesitated for a pause and then said "Except for the fucking me daily part. That I understand clearly but what do I get out of it."

"Besides having your brains rattled around regularly in that pretty little head of yours" the brunette said, smirking. "I guess I should explain myself better. My name is Janice Hollysmith, of the New York Hollysmiths." She paused dramatically, as if Ashley should understand what that meant; Ashley just shrugged her confusion over the matter. The brunette made a noise of exasperation before saying "We are one of the richest families in the United States of America. We get what we want, how we want it, or heads roll. I belong to Phi Phi Pho and we are arranging for new prospective members to join us. Now most of our members are among the richest in the nation and are extremely eager to join us. We require that these members show their dedication just like all members have to but then there are special cases, like what I am offering you. Those members are not among the elite but if they serve well during their sorority years, they can parlay that into a very exclusive position with one of our extremely rich, influential members." Janice eyed Ashley with some superiority. "A lot of girls would give their eyeteeth or even firstborn to be given such an opportunity." She paused for a moment to let Ashley think about what she had said as she took another delicate sip of her coffee.

Ashley thought hard about telling this presumptuous, rich, snobby bitch to stuff her proposal up her asshole sideways but then recognized that she was in no position to do so. She needed some financial help to get her through her undergraduate degree, never mind the law degree that she really aspired to. She sighed loudly as she thought about what her life would be like if she had powerful friends to help her like what this arrogant bitch in front of her was busy offering. She knew in her heart of hearts that she would have no troubles doing whatever they demanded of her; she already discerned that she really enjoyed being the object of extremely kinky sex and had no problems with either gender fucking her. She recognized that she didn't like Janice but determined that it would likely make the sex between them even hotter. She locked her green eyes on the brunette's cool grey ones and hissed "Maybe I can get by fine without you." She knew that she didn't believe what she was saying but was determined not to be too easy a conquest.

"Not a problem" the woman said coolly as she gathered her darling, little purse and the remainder of her coffee in order to get up and leave.

Ashley panicked as she realized that the woman was prepared to walk away and discard her like leftover garbage. Ashley gave a disgruntled moan as she recognized that she needed this woman and her offer more than this woman needed her. The brunette was right about there being plenty of other women who would be extremely eager to accept what was being offered. "Wait" she wailed. "I'm sorry. I shouldn't have said that. I apologize. I'd like to hear more about this fabulous opportunity. Please sit back down."

Janice gave a steely glare at Ashley as she paused to ramp up the tension in the gorgeous redhead. Once again she ran her eyes over the other woman's form, liking the hourglass figure with its slim tummy sandwiched by an impressive bust and wide hips. She knew from gossip that the redhead was a real firecracker in bed, willing to do and endure almost anything asked of her. She'd heard that Ashley had a long, limber tongue that she knew how to use and that she really liked making use of. She was far more interested in Ashley than she wanted the other woman to know. She wanted Ashley to feel exceedingly beholden to her and eager to prove it. She didn't want the redhead to think that she could refuse to do anything asked of her, no matter how small a matter it was so she decided that she had to stomp down hard on this show of backbone. So she grinned evilly at Ashley as it came to her what she wanted the redhead to do to prove that she would be a wonderful submissive slut for her. "I will sit down and tell you more about this fantastic opportunity only if you show me the respect that I deserve" she said evenly as the corners of her wide mouth twitched with amusement. "I want you to get down on all fours in front of everyone here and suck on my big toes for a minute each. If you are not down there in the next ten seconds doing that, neither I or anyone else at Phi Phi Pho will offer you anything." It only took Ashley two seconds to do exactly what the brunette had demanded of her; she knew that she really had no choice and that she also got aroused at being humiliated like that in front of others. Janice was a bit surprised by how fast that the redhead had responded but was exceedingly pleased by it. She glanced around the big room, proud that everyone was noticing what she was doing to the gorgeous redhead.

Ashley got up, brushing off her bare knees, sat back down onto the stool and focused her eyes back on the table top. She could feel a surge deep in her groin as she became tremendously aroused by her humiliation. She shot sneaky little glances around the room to see if she knew any of the people who'd witnessed her degradation. Janice gaped a bit as she saw that Ashley was exceptionally aroused by her public disgrace; boy, she thought, chortling to herself, this girl is going to be fantastic fucking fun. She took her time, settling back on her own stool and replacing her things on the table, completely ignoring the downcast woman in front of her. Finally she looked Ashley over and smiled cruelly, saying "I hope that you have learned your lesson and I won't have to repeat it again any time soon. When I say jump, you ask how high on your way up." She paused and then hissed "Is that perfectly clear?"

Ashley gulped and stammered out "Y-y-yes." When this was met with frosty silence, she looked up to see Janice glaring at her. "Mistress" she squeaked out. She was relieved to see Janice nod in approval and then ducked her eyes back down to the table in submission. She felt an increase in heat in her loins and desperately wanted to touch herself to increase her buildup to an orgasm. Janice noticed the slight twitch of Ashley's right hand and recognized that the woman in front of her was getting incredibly aroused by her humiliation and submission. It fuelled something very primal in Janice and she realized that if she didn't get this woman away from the public, they were both going to do something that was likely to get them kicked off campus.

"Do you have a class right away?" she asked the redhead, who nodded affirmatively. Oh Damn, she thought, I wonder if I should tell her to blow it off and come with me so that I can fuck her and then recognized that she shouldn't attempt that so early in their relationship. It might end in failure and she wouldn't be able to retain the upper hand. "Very well then" she snapped, frustrated. "I want you to come over to the sorority house tomorrow after your last class. Since it is Friday, you won't have to worry about getting up the next morning for any classes. I'll introduce you around and show you what some of your duties will be. Don't worry about what you're wearing tomorrow, you'll just be wearing my collar when you're at the sorority." She smiled evilly at the startled redhead and then asked imperiously "Do you know the address of the sorority house? What time do you finish tomorrow?"

Ashley meekly replied "I finish at four and can get to the sorority house by about a quarter after. I do know where it is." She thought about what Janice had said about her only wearing a collar; she was both intrigued and slightly mortified by the prospect.

"Then I'll expect you there at that time" Janice commanded as she gathered her belongings and stalked away. She didn't have a class until later and decided that she needed to relieve some of her arousal before then.

Ashley spent all of Friday in delicious agony, every time she let her thoughts stray she thought about how she would look wearing only a collar; she imagined being shown to all sorts of different women and them commenting rudely on her body's imperfections. She knew that she had a quite good body but it had its imperfections. She almost creamed her panties as she imagined how much shame and humiliation she would feel as they critiqued her flaws; she caught herself more than once coming out of a fantasy in class, panting and moaning softly from her arousal. She drew a number of weird looks from some of the guys and some knowing looks from some of the other women. She tried to hide behind textbooks to cover up her flushes. In her economics class right after lunch she slumped down in a seat that was near the edge of the lecture room, avoiding being too near any other classmates. A pretty brunette excused herself from her friends and came over to sit right beside her; Ashley gave her a frowning look as the girl settled in, she wanted to be by herself. The brunette took no heed of Ashley's unspoken warning. Once she was established, the brunette nonchalantly reached out and put her hand on Ashley's knee. Ashley startled and emitted a small noise at the unexpected intrusion; she removed the other woman's hand and glared at her. She was shocked as hell when the brunette just turned to her and gave her a broad smile before putting her hand back on Ashley's knee.

"What the hell do you think you're doing?" Ashley hissed, not wanting to draw too much of the rest of the class's attention to them. She went to remove the woman's hand once more.

"Oh, I wouldn't do that" the brunette said softly, almost lazily. "I know that Janice has claimed you for her own but I intend to challenge her for your ownership. I've seen you around campus for quite a while and liked what I saw. I'm the one who started checking you out. Janice just talked to some of the people who know you after me. I was waiting for a good time to approach you but Janice forced my hand so I'm letting you know that I am interested in you right now." She looked Ashley in the eyes and stated "I think you'll enjoy being my bitch and I can be quite generous if you please me. For now, just pay attention to the lecture and ignore my hand like a good little girl." Ashley tried to pay attention to the professor but she was too conscious of the brunette's active hand. While the other woman wasn't too forward with what she was doing, she was quite persistent and seemed to enjoy pinching the flesh on Ashley's thigh. Ashley breathed a sigh of relief when the class was over and the brunette removed her hand to prepare to leave. She delayed gathering her stuff to see if the brunette would exit without her and the woman did so. But not before informing Ashley "My name is Sonya. Remember that. I'll get to see a lot more of you later tonight. Taa. I'm looking forward to it." Ashley stared after her, unsure about how she felt about the encounter. On one hand it was fairly scary that a woman would treat her so in public but on the other it was strangely arousing that the other woman was so free about her own actions and would refuse to take no for an answer. She also wondered what was going to happen that night between Janice and Sonya and if there might be more women wanting her at the sorority. Thankfully, she only had one more class to go after this break between classes; she decided that she needed a coffee and went to get one.

At a quarter after four, Ashley trotted up the path to the sorority. She was excited by the prospects of what might happen to her that night and was breathing a bit hard from her arousal; she was also conscious that her pussy was quite wet and her panties were definitely damp. She rang the bell and waited; she wondered whether Janice or Sonya would answer the door. She was a bit shocked when a short, bespectacled blonde opened the door and stood there looking Ashley up and down. Ashley said, hesitantly "My name is Ashley Grillo. Uhh, I was asked to come here by Janice. Could you let her know that I am here." She gave the girl a tentative smile.

"Yes, I know who you are" the woman said with a small sniff of superiority. She eyed Ashley up and down very openly and said "I can see what all the fuss is about you. I might even be interested in forwarding a claim to you myself." She smiled broadly at Ashley and said "I was designated to answer the door because there are actually four members of this sorority that have already chosen to claim you. If you perform well tonight, you could very well have more members advancing their case about you. I've been told to invite you in and get you ready for the evening." She guided Ashley in through the door and then closed it before turning and saying over her shoulder "If you would follow me, please." Ashley frowned at her, totally confused about what was going on and unsure if she should proceed; then she decided that she had to go through with whatever they had planned to find out what it was. She followed the blonde who led her down to a bedroom.

As they entered the room, Ashley decided that she should try once again to get more information about what was planned for her. "I'm sorry. I've never been here before and I don't know what is expected of me. Perhaps you'd be so kind as to enlighten me." The blonde just chuckled and pointed to the items laid out on the bed. Ashley gaped openly as she recognized a lacy collar, a leather hood, a ball gag, wrist, ankle and elbow restraints and to her utmost horror, a large buttplug.

"I realize that you don't have a full picture as to what you might be in for but I've been told that you've participated in a lot of what will be required of you before. So it should be fairly easy for you. I've also been told not to discuss these matters with you. The committee wants to see how you handle it. So if you'll just strip completely and then cooperate while I put all of these things on you, we'll be ready in no time." Ashley eyed the blonde with a slight look of horror as she thought about how vulnerable she was going to be in all that bondage gear. She thought wildly, maybe she was at the wrong house and this woman was just taking advantage of her but then she calmed down a bit and realized that the woman was just being that mysterious to heighten Ashley's fear. But she could feel her heart still racing and her panties were completely soaked right through. The woman stood there, grinning slightly, as she waited for Ashley to strip off all of her clothing. Ashley took a deep breath to settle her nerves a bit and began peeling off her clothing. The blonde took the buttplug and began absent mindedly coating it with lubricant; she gave a small giggle of glee as she saw that Ashley's eyes were drawn to it.

When Ashley had all of her clothes off, including the sopping panties which the blonde had snatched from her hand and sniffed at, before Ashley could put them with the rest of her clothing, the blonde knelt and began putting on the ankle cuffs. There was exactly twelve inches of chain between these cuffs that would allow Ashley to walk, although her steps would be more of a mince than anything. Then the woman had Ashley lean onto the bed so that she could more easily fasten the wrist and elbow fastenings behind her back. And since Ashley was already in the best position for it, the blonde gave Ashley's rosebud a thorough coating of KY jelly before starting to push home the buttplug. Ashley groaned and wiggled as the woman forced it up her asshole. Ashley enjoyed the sensations that it caused but when she sat up, to her horror she noticed that she'd left a damp spot of her enthusiasm on the bed. The blonde woman just grinned about it when she noticed. The woman fastened the lacy collar around Ashley's neck and it rode tightly on her skin. Next the woman fitted the sturdy leather hood over Ashley's head, blocking her sight completely; she secured it tightly under Ashley's chin. Then she opened Ashley's mouth and pushed the large ball of the gag into her gaping mouth before tightening it firmly behind her head. Ashley sat there, shivering slightly, as she recognized that anything at all could be done to her now; she wouldn't be able to object any more than whining. The blonde reached out and tugged firmly on Ashley's right nipple causing her to try to pull back out of reach and whine her surprise. Ashley flushed with anger and shame as the blonde chuckled noisily at her reaction.

The blonde then said "Come on you big, beautiful bitch." She took a firm hold of Ashley's right tit and led her out of the room and down the hall. Ashley was led into what seemed like a large room with a number of other people in it; she could hear murmurs of approval as the occupants got a good look at her naked body. She was terrifically unsure to feel proud about that or to feel humiliated that they were able to look her exposed body over. She recognized that she felt a little of both and had to keep from thrusting her large tits out for their pleasure; she felt that she should at least keep a little decorum about the situation. Then she realized how ridiculous that was. The blonde had released her and moved away from her so that Ashley now stood alone in the room. She was unsure as what to do and was restrained from using her hands or legs to search items out.

She startled a bit when a woman laid a warm hand on top of her shoulder near her neck. "My name is Anne and I am the president of this sorority. There have been a number of claims laid on you by members of this sorority. This has happened occasionally before but not involving more than two members who were able to work out arrangements amongst themselves without having to have the initiation committee rule on matters. There are currently four claims to you. We decided that since you were so popular that we should all have a look at you for ourselves. Hence, you are here. I'm going to lead you over to an ottoman where I want you to kneel and place yourself over it, stomach down. There is a pillow there for you to kneel on and I will guide you onto it. Over the course of the evening, any member that wishes to will come over to touch and play with you as she pleases. This will give everyone a chance to determine if they want to make a claim for you. Nod your head if you understand." Ashley nodded, signifying that she understood.

Anne led her over and helped her get into position. Ashley figured that the other woman would then leave her to let the other women get a chance to inspect her but Anne settled down beside her and began caressing her. Anne slid her hands under Ashley's chest to fondle her tits. Ashley enjoyed the other woman's deft touch and soon her nipples and aureoles were swollen as big as they had ever been; Ashley was gasping hard through her nose because of the arousal that Anne was causing in her. She could hear Anne's almost tinkling laughter over the muffled moans she was making; she felt an incredible itch deep inside her pussy and wanted a dildo or cock up inside her so that she could rub her flesh against it to try to relieve her situation. She was aware that some juices were leaking out of her and most likely creating a wet spot on the ottoman but she was past the point of caring too much about it. She moaned deep in her throat, trying to convey her need for something more; Anne seemed to understand her message and slid three fingers up into Ashley's sopping cunt. Ashley willingly wiggled her hips to accommodate the intrusion and to get the fingers pressing against the right spots inside her; Anne laughed once more at her actions but Ashley was beyond caring about how ridiculous she looked, she needed some action. But Anne removed her fingers after just a minute, causing Ashley to groan in protest, and said, quite sadly "I'd love to make you climax, dear bitch. But you have a long night ahead of you and it'd be a poor example of leadership if I was to allow you to satisfy yourself with me when I've told the others not to give in to you. I'll just enjoy my taste of you and let the others have a chance to explore your body and their desire for using you." With that, Anne stood up, sucked Ashley's juices off her fingers and walked back to her seat. Ashley grunted as loudly as she could in disbelief, the damn woman was going to let her continue being in need of release.

For the next hour, Ashley moaned and thrashed as a number of women joined her for a short while and played around with her body; all of them stuck their fingers in her but none of them allowed her sufficient time to force a climax, the same as Anne had done to her. Ashley felt that she was going out of her fucking mind as they mercilessly teased her and left her in need. She attempted to clench her thighs around one or two of the hands to hold it in place long enough to climax but her restraints prevented her from being able to create any leverage; all the women did was to giggle with glee from her desperation and smack her on the ass before extracting their hands. Ashley knew from the sounds she heard that there was quite a large audience watching the proceedings and she got the impression that they were really enjoying watching her actions. She began to wonder if she would get some pity from them if she gave up fighting to achieve her climax and just meekly submitted to the attentions of the women, allowing them to simply stroke and feel her up without moving too much. Maybe one of the women would then feel enough remorse to push her into climax. She thought hard about doing this but then realized that if she meekly gave in, most of the women would probably lose some of their interest in her; she recognized that part of her attraction to these women was her desperate need for some sexual satisfaction. She also acknowledged that she was really enjoying their sadistic teasing of her; her cunt felt as hot and needy as it had ever been. So she continued to thrash and attempt to trap a woman's hand deep inside her. For their part, the other women giggled and slipped their hands out of her so that she couldn't achieve her goal. Ashley could hear the soft sounds of women playing with themselves and enjoying the results around her as they perfumed the room with their odours. It was heavenly, Ashley thought, even though she felt that she personally was in hell because of her desperate need.

This went on for quite a while, with Ashley moaning and thrashing around, before she felt the nice firm fingers of another woman probing deep into her cunt. The woman stroked in and out of Ashley's wet cunt, allowing her to climax; since Ashley had been so primed for the event, it only took her a couple of minutes of action to climax so explosively. Ashley cried and mewed as she thrashed her hips about, enjoying the mind bending feel of a truly great orgasm. Oh, I love you and want to be yours forever, she thought as a number of women pushed their heads between her thighs in order to taste her. She enjoyed the slightly rough feel of the other women's tongues against her most sensitive areas as they cleaned her up. She lay there still in a daze after they had finished with her. She wondered what her fate was going to be.

RUTH ELLEN, ARNOLD AND STEVE

Ruth Ellen was a painter; she was one of those people who worked frantically at something until they finally collapsed. She would paint for nearly twenty four hours straight before she was forced to take a break. She often found that she needed hard sex to distract her mind so that she could relax and sleep. She wasn't a pretty woman; a more apt description of her would be average. She was five foot four, dark hair that was usually scraggily, small breasted, wide hipped and had what most people would term a pleasant, not pretty, face. She knew that her nose was too big and her bottom jaw was too short but she wasn't overly worried about that. She'd always had a fairly healthy appetite for sex and even though she wasn't the best looking woman in town, a lot of men were willing to fuck her. Her main problem had been finding those men when she was in the mood to get fucked. She'd met Arnold and Steve nearly three months earlier, in the bar that a bunch of the local artists tended to favour; she'd noticed that they were spending a fair amount of time looking for women who were willing to go back to their place to get fucked. She'd found out that Arnold was a writer while Steve was a sculptor. She'd been intrigued by them and went over to introduce herself. After spending around forty-five minutes chatting with them about the work that all of them created as well as other news about the town, she'd decided that she'd fuck the pair of them to see what they were like.

"So, Steve, I notice that you and Arnold spend a fair amount of time in here looking for sex. Don't you find that it cuts into your creative time?" she asked bluntly.

Steve looked at her a little sheepishly, took a cautious sip of his beer as he formulated his answer, and replied "Yeah, I guess it does. But neither Arnold nor I have been able to attract a steady girlfriend to give us sex when we want it." He shrugged his shoulders and said "You do what you have to do to survive."

Ruth Ellen smiled quickly at him and stated "I notice that you guys often take just one woman home. Do you take turns fucking her or do the pair of you do her together?"

Arnold perked up and looked at her carefully, while Steve found the ballgame on the tv to be suddenly very interesting. Arnold asked, after a minute "Why does that matter to you? Are you interested in finding out what it's like to sleep with both or either of us?"

She smiled, a little coyly, and replied "I'd be interested in finding out how good you both are in bed. I have a similar problem to the one you guys appear to have and I think maybe we can help each other out. That is, if you guys are able to ring my bell sufficiently." She gave them a challenging smile and raised her left eyebrow.

Steve muttered "I'd be willing to give it a try" but kept watching the tv rather than meet her eyes.

Arnold took a moment longer, taking a good look at her; she was nowhere near the type that he usually liked, tall, willowy and blonde by preference, but she was better than his right fist, which is what his prospects for that night were. He knew that it was useless to try to talk Steve into letting him fuck him; Steve had fairly rigid rules for being screwed, it could only happen twice a week and by preference would be Sunday and Thursday nights. Steve liked some tv shows on those nights so was willing to stay at home from the bar and since he was home anyways, Arnold could fuck him. Arnold mused, if only Steve was willing to give me blowjobs, I could avoid the problem of looking for sex altogether but Steve didn't like having a prick down his throat. Arnold didn't mind giving blowjobs but wanted it to be reciprocal. He said, carefully, "I think that we can go see how well we all are together. And to answer your earlier question, we usually fuck the woman one after the other. Is that a problem for you?"

She smiled at the older, balding man and stated sweetly "Not a problem but I wouldn't mind if both you guys are in the room. One can watch and one can fuck me. I don't mind an audience." She grinned at him and continued "I've heard that you guys are a little more than roommates but that doesn't bother me either. In fact, if we can decide to pursue our mutual needs, I wouldn't mind watching you guys screw each other."

Arnold put on his shocked face and said "I don't know what you're talking about." He was a bad actor and Ruth Ellen didn't believe him for a minute.

"Don't bother denying it, Arnold" Steve said, in his slow, soft way. "She obviously knows about us. It's not really a great secret." He then turned and faced Ruth Ellen, looking her in the eyes. "I won't mind you watching but it's only Arnold who fucks me. I don't fuck him." Ruth Ellen nodded slowly, understanding and the three of them drank their beers and left the bar.

They drove to the small farm that the two men shared and they led her inside; she pushed aside their attempts at making small talk to get her comfortable with being there with them and suggested that they get on with business. They took her into Arnold's bedroom because it was the larger of the two bedrooms they occupied.

She looked at them boldly and then proceeded to strip off all of her clothes; she did so quickly and then stood naked before them. She knew that she didn't have a lot to show them but she wasn't shy about showing what she did have. Steve looked her over and then grunted in appreciation while Arnold spent more time examining her. Again he thought, she's better than just having to masturbate but he gave her a small smile, not wanting to hurt her feelings. After they'd had the chance to look at her for a while, she stated "I'm not going to be the only one nude here. Get your gear off so that I can see what you guys look like. Do you have a preference for which of you goes first? It really doesn't matter too much to me." Both of them just shrugged, usually the girl expressed a preference and they went with that; neither of them minded sloppy seconds. "Well, I guess the best way would be to have the man with the smallest cock screw me first so he won't stretch me out as much as the larger cock will."

The men were just pulling down their underwear when she said this and Arnold said "I guess it will be me first then. Steve definitely has a bigger cock than I do." She looked at the pair of them. Steve was taller and bigger than Arnold in every way, including cock size. He was dark-haired and almost handsome but he wasn't very comfortable in talking too much with people so he came across as being a bit abnormal. Arnold was balding and chose to wear his dirty blonde hair long as an attempt to compensate; he also appeared to think that his silly goatee covered up his receding chin and made him look better. Ruth Ellen was not impressed by either; she decided that she'd have to do something about both of those if she chose to continue their relationship past that night. She checked out Arnold to see how small his cock was, since he'd admitted that he was the smaller man, and was quite pleased to see that he was a little bigger than what she knew the average man to be. Hmmm, she thought pleasantly, these two guys had some potential for her to enjoy herself with and if she could teach them what she enjoyed, they might work out perfectly for her. She took a look between Steve's legs to see how big he actually was, she didn't want to have to contend with too large a prick because it would just hurt. Steve was on the upper limit of what she liked but she thought that she would be able to handle him fairly well, especially since he seemed so biddable. She might have trouble handling that size of cock in her pussy if the guy insisted on being too forceful with her; she'd need some time to adjust to handling it. She mused that Arnold screwing her first would probably loosen her up enough to handle that bigger prick.

Both men waited patiently for her to look them over since she'd been kind enough to do that first but Arnold decided that it was time to get the show on the road. "Do you like a lot of foreplay to get you in the mood? Or do you just like being entered and pumped hard?"

She smiled at him and said "To get me to orgasm, you guys are going to have to work me a little hard. It takes me some time to build my orgasm. And if you want to continue fucking me in the future, you're going to have to make me orgasm. Else, there's not much sense in this. Do either of you like eating pussy? I find that a good tonguing sets me in a fairly receptive mood."

Arnold stated "I've got no problem with cunnilingus and I don't think that Steve does either." Steve nodded in agreement. "Shall we start with that, then?"

"I guess you might as well" she said as she lay down on the bed and spread open her legs. Arnold decided that he would start matters and knelt by the bed so that he could place his mouth on her dark haired cunt. She was a little furrier than he liked but he could easily cope with it. He was surprised to find that she was actually fairly pleasant tasting and that her odour was arousing. He often found that most women were somewhat unpleasant smelling and tasting. She lay back and let him have his way with her, moaning her approval; she began issuing juices after just a minute or so of attention but he sensed that she would need a fair amount of work to get her to orgasm. The juices tasted fairly nice and he lapped them up. After nearly five minutes, he felt his tongue tiring and gave way to Steve. Steve wasn't near as deft with his tongue but he enthusiastically lapped at her damp pussy; Ruth Ellen wasn't sure which she liked better. But Steve tired too before she was able to cum so Arnold retook the task. He managed to get her on the throes of her orgasm after just a few more minutes. She groaned and grunted, letting him know that she was on the verge and he pressed her harder to put her over the edge. She gave a small cry, almost like the mewl of a cat, as she climaxed. She lay back and sighed as she enjoyed the feelings her climax had engendered in her. She was a bit surprised when Arnold spent a bit of time cleaning her pussy up, most men weren't interested in doing that and she appreciated it. It was also a shock to her when Steve took a moment to taste her once Arnold relinquished his spot. She sat up and offered both men a kiss of thanks, enjoying her own taste on their lips.

"Okay, fellas, that was really very nice. I guess that now it is your turn to have fun with me. How do you want me positioned, Arnold?"

Arnold didn't bother to say anything, just arranged her onto her back and stuffed a pillow under her hips before coming up between her legs to lie on top of her. He'd hooked her ankles over his shoulders so that her legs were being pressed against her torso. He pushed his stiff prick against the slit of her wet pussy and forced it inside her; he slid in fairly easily since she was aroused and ready. He grunted with satisfaction as his hips came into contact with hers. She expected him to just pound her until he came but he surprised her by alternating his rhythm of thrusts between fast and slow; he also adjusted his angle of penetration to give her a better experience. She found that he was a better fucker than she'd been led to believe. He couldn't keep the sex going much more than five minutes though and he began panting very hard from his effort. She could tell that he was on the verge of orgasming and prepared herself for his release into her pussy. In less than fifteen seconds, he pumped his cum into her and then collapsed down onto her. Though he was not an overly large man, he was still bigger than she was and he felt very heavy on top of her. She found that she had to push him over to the side so that he didn't cause her as much discomfort as she'd been feeling. She made sure that she was still quite close to him, not wanting him to think that she was rejecting him, and looked into his lightly dazed eyes. They remained there for a few minutes before she remembered about Steve. She looked over worriedly to see how he was taking matters and was relieved to see that he was sitting there comfortably and silently taking them in. She gave him a tentative smile and he grinned enthusiastically back at her. She felt more reassured.

After a few more minutes of them enjoying their post coital bliss, Ruth Ellen decided that Steve had waited patiently enough. She encouraged Arnold to get up from her by pushing at him gently and telling him to move. She patted the warm spot beside her, inviting Steve to come over. He did so in his slow, easy manner and when he sat beside her, the bed sagged. She began to worry about how heavy he would feel on top of her. He smiled at her and said "Perhaps it would be better if you knelt so that I could enter you from behind in that position. I don't think that a girl as small as you would be happy bearing my weight." She flashed him a quick grin of appreciation and rapidly got into position for him. He got in behind her and used his hands to widen out her legs a bit so that he had an easier entrance into her pussy. He was hard and he pushed the tip of his cock up against her pussy lips and just inside her. She stretched easily to accommodate him even though she did murmur with appreciation for the feel of his big cock inside her cunt. He just remained motionless to let her enjoy the feeling. Then he pulled out of her, surprising her; she looked around to see if she could tell what he was thinking. Was he having second thoughts about fucking her, she wondered. He just smiled at her and repeated his previous motion. He teased her like that about five more times and she was contemplating snapping at him to get on with matters. She was aroused and wanted to feel that big cock all the way inside her. She muttered in frustration at him and he just gave her a booming laugh. He didn't say anything to her but the next time he entered her, he grabbed her hips in his strong hands and pulled them backward towards him as he thrust his own hips forward. She felt her cunt stretching in a somewhat uncomfortable way but her overriding emotion was one of joy. He felt wonderful inside her.

She gave a little yip of satisfaction when he stopped. Once again he paused to let her enjoy her feelings and she murmured her appreciation at him. Then he pulled his cock about four inches back out of her and rammed it back into her with a fair amount of force. It was then that she realized that he hadn't been totally inside her before and she began to worry that she wouldn't be able to take his full length. But she was determined to take as much of it as she could, she decided as she rocked her hips slightly to see if there was a slightly better angle for her to take him. He just pressed down heavily on her hips with his hands, wanting her to stay in her current position. He started a slow thrusting up inside her and she panted with her effort of accommodating him. He grunted his approval as she slid up and down his big, long cock; she was nice and tight, he thought happily. She was enjoying the feeling of him sliding inside her but unfortunately he wasn't able to last much more than two minutes. She was disappointed by that because she thought a few more minutes of being fucked like that would have sent her over the edge to another orgasm. She heard him groan and felt him quiver slightly just before he filled her with a large deposit. She kind of expected him to rest upon her and braced herself for his weight but he chose to pull himself out of her while he was still erect. She grunted a bit as he disengaged his cock from her with a small popping sound. She could feel some of his cum dribble out of her.

She was going to turn around and sit down facing him when he surprised her again by dropping his head down and licking her sloppy cunt. He used his big tongue in her pussy again to slurp up all of his cum and any remaining from Arnold. She found the experience to be erotic and her nipples ached for attention so she started pulling at them. Arnold quickly came over and began stretching out her nipples as Steve continued to eat her out. She was surprised about how good it felt to have the two of them work her over.

As she lay there relishing their attention over her, she thought that this would work out well for the long term and she decided to talk to them about a more permanent relationship. She could see if she could move in here and share this house with them, trading sex with them for all of their pleasures.

EMMA WORKS LATE

Emma was at the law office, trying to make sure that she had researched all of the possible outcomes of the case that her superior had assigned to her. She knew that she had to work extremely hard and put in long hours if she hoped to compete with the richer and possibly smarter young people here in the office. She wanted desperately to become one of the associates of this prestigious firm. She heard a sound that she couldn't identify coming from down the hallway. She didn't think that anyone else was working here tonight and it was still too early for the cleaning crew; she was very aware of what time they did the office because they had surprised her more than once, even though she'd only been employed here for just over a month. She wasn't sure what she should do but needed to know what that sound was so she quietly went down the darkened hallway and peeked into the lobby.

She was surprised that the lights were still off and that the room was only lit by two fat candles that gave off a flickering glow. As her eyes wandered the room, she realized that there were two people there and that they were facing mostly away from her position. She was trying to make sense of what they were doing and who they were when she realized that they were two men and the one behind the other was bending him over and undoing his pants. She clasped her hand to her mouth to prevent from letting out a gasp as she saw that they were preparing to have sex here in the lobby. Right in front of her, she thought wildly. She gave some consideration to withdrawing back to her office to give them some privacy. It was really no business of hers what these two consenting adults did to each other. But then she reflected that she'd only been having unsatisfactory masturbation for just over two years now as she worked hard to gain her position. She felt a twinge of arousal over watching one man pound another man's ass as hard as he could. She was shocked to discover that because she'd never bothered with gay male sex previously. I must be feeling really deprived she thought with wonder. Normally I think about me and handsome men; then she admitted to herself, very reluctantly, that the occasional pretty woman crept into her dreams as well. But not two guys, she thought, feeling a bit confused and totally naughty. Perhaps it's the feeling of naughtiness that is making my cunt twinge and tingle, she thought a little worriedly. She pondered undoing her pants and sliding her right hand down into her panties to take care of the feeling. She realized that she hadn't been paying attention to the men and they might have noticed her. She looked up guiltily in case they had; but no worries, they were too intent on what they were doing to have noticed her.

She decided that she could get away with fingering herself as long as she kept fairly quiet about it because the man bent over one of the comfortable leather chairs in the lobby was making a lot of approval noises as the standing man worked some lubricant up his asshole. As she got herself ready, she studied the two men to see if she could identify them in the poor light. She realized that the standing man was one of the senior partners, the tall one with broad shoulders and distinguished gray hair, Mr. Douglas. She wasn't able to see the other man's face but judging by his youth, his blonde hair and low voice as he moaned, she would identify him as Harry Leshire, one of the other people hoping to make associate like her. So, she thought, rather smugly, this must be what they meant in this firm by taking dictation. She smiled broadly at her pun.

She'd gotten two fingers up into her pussy and was enjoying the feeling of them stroking in and out of her damp pussy. She pondered whether or not what she was seeing in front of her could be considered sexual harassment; she supposed as a lawyer, that it was. Then she worried that maybe this was the only way to get to become an associate; she'd always thought that Harry was someone who considered himself a ladies man. She'd already turned down one of his advances and she was quite new. Was he doing this because he needed to, in order to keep his position, she wondered worriedly. Would she find herself in a similar position in a month or so just so that she could keep her job. She didn't like the implications of that. She also wondered if Mr. Douglas fucked the young women trying to become associates as well or just the young men. Or, she thought, maybe he just liked Harry. If he just liked Harry and Harry was willing to get fucked, she supposed that if would be okay.

As these thoughts flitted through her head, she realized that the men in front of her had continued getting ready and Mr. Douglas was about to enter Harry's ass. She was amused to see that he had quite a large prick and she wondered if Harry had ever taken it up his ass before. If this was a newer experience, she thought, he might be in for quite a surprise; she wasn't even sure that she could accommodate that large cock in her pussy. As Mr. Douglas pressed the head of his prick up against Harry's rosebud, Harry gave a startled moan as his asshole began to stretch over the big head. "I told you I was big. Now just lay there and take me. If you fight too much, we'll end up tearing your asshole" Mr. Douglas told the other man. "Once I get my head in you, I'll let you relax a bit before we go any further. Big breath now." When Harry inhaled, he relaxed a bit and the older man forced his way up his asshole before stopping to let him get used to being filled. Emma bit her lip to keep from squealing out with delight as Harry howled in surprise and pain. He tried to move away from the older man to relieve the pressure up inside him but Mr. Douglas held him firmly in place. "Come now" he said crossly. "You agreed to being fucked and I intend to make you go through with it. If you weren't prepared to pay your debts you shouldn't have made that bet. You lost and I get my reward from you."

So, it wasn't really about getting ahead at work, Emma thought with some relief as she stroked her pussy. Her nipples wanted a little attention as well and were perking hard against her suddenly tight bra but she didn't want to bother trying to get at them. She'd just have to put up with exactly what she was doing. Mr. Douglas had forced more of his big cock up Harry's tight ass, relishing the feel of it on his sensitive organ as Harry moaned somewhat in protest of being stretched out. Emma had to smile to herself, thinking that Harry sounded almost like one of her roommates when her boyfriend was fucking her. Once she'd gotten over her jealousy, she found that she liked hearing the other woman's high pitched yips from being pounded hard and she found Harry's somewhat deeper ones to be equally stimulating. Mr. Douglas now had hold of Harry's hips and was lifting him slightly as he pushed his big cock up into him; Harry was moaning loudly and grunting hard. Emma was fairly sure that he was feeling pain from the other man's rather rough treatment of him but she sensed that he was also enjoying that treatment tremendously. She was feeling jealous that Harry was getting his ass fucked and not her; she was again shocked because not only had she never been fucked in the ass, she'd never really considered it as a possibility. She did have to admit though that Harry made it look like fun.

Mr. Douglas had finally managed to get Harry to take the full length of his cock up into his ass and was pumping hard against Harry's rather muscular, flat ass. There was a loud slapping sound as his hips struck against the younger man's ass. Mr. Douglas was pounding as hard as he was able and sweat rolled down his face from his effort; Emma was sure that she'd see sweat glistening all over his body if he'd been completely nude.

She could feel herself begin to tingle heavily in her hips as she worked her pussy over; from past experiences she knew that she still needed about five minutes or more of fast fingering to push her into orgasm. But Mr. Douglas suddenly stopped, grunted loudly and pulled Harry's ass as tight to him as he could. Oh no, thought Emma, almost giving a wail, he was finished and had already climaxed. Once again she was struck by how unfair life was; men got to orgasm easier and faster than women did. She hastened to get her hand out of her panties and fastened the top button of her pants so that she could escape without her pants falling around her ankles. She knew she had to be fairly quiet even though both men were moaning and groaning a fair bit. She didn't want them discovering that she'd been watching them.

She stopped in the bathroom down the hall to clean off her hand. She gave some thought to finishing off her orgasm but the mood had left her a bit. She decided that she'd just let her feeling die for now and go back to the office to finish her work for the night. If she should happen to be found by the men, she'd just act surprised to see them there, she thought. But she would definitely explore the possibility that Mr. Douglas might be interested in fucking her. What type of bet did she have to lose for that to happen, she wondered. And it might be interesting to cultivate a friendship with Harry. He certainly became more interesting in her eyes. So many possibilities, she mused as she went back to her now very boring research.

THE ENEMA CHALLENGE

Selena Craig was waiting beside her husband anxiously. They were waiting to be taken into the sex club that they hoped to join. They were friends with one couple who were already on their way to being initiated into the club. That couple was attempting to fulfill the requirements to become associate members of the club. As associate members, they would always have to provide sex to the full members, who paid a lot of money to retain their status, but the opportunities for them to earn money and important contacts were quite staggering by them achieving their membership. That was one of the most important reasons that the club was able to attract young, attractive couples as associate members. But in order to achieve that position, every couple had to perform seven different initiating acts and today Selena and Rob were going to do their first performance for the members. Selena had asked Dianne what these acts were but Dianne had refused to tell her about any specifics and stated that one of the restrictions placed on them was not to divulge what went on in the club in any way. Dianne was not about to risk their membership by telling Selena about what was expected of them; Selena would be as surprised by what was compulsory as Dianne was. She did hint that this first challenge was messy and somewhat humiliating but not painful. Selena was aware that Dianne and her husband would be rewarded for recruiting her and Rob; Dianne had not been shy about telling them about the rewards that being a member of the club was projected to be on that day that Selena had complained to her about mounting bills. They were having coffee at the time. Selena had just received a final notice on the electrical bill and was unhappy that paying that bill would mean another week of little food for her and Rob. She was only able to have coffee because Dianne had invited her over to her home, two doors down the street, and was supplying the coffee; Selena was almost ecstatic when Dianne also set two donuts in front of her. That was a treat that they hadn't been able to afford in a while.

Selena had questioned why Dianne was now able to afford such luxuries when she knew that Dianne and Jake had been in a similar situation to where she and Rob found themselves now. Dianne had looked at her in a very coy, calculating way and asked "How desperate are you guys? Are you willing to trade some of your principals to earn some money with a good chance of being able to earn a lot of money?" She'd given Selena a very earnest, scrutinizing look.

"We're likely going to lose our home and we really can't afford anywhere else" Selena admitted sourly. "Our bills are too high and our incomes are too low." She hung her head sorrowfully. "I just don't see any way out of our predicament. What principals are you talking about? Did you have to murder someone or something?"

Dianne laughed softly. "No, nothing like that." She grimaced slightly at Selena, recognizing that she didn't really know the other woman that well. They'd only been neighbours for just over nine months, had coffee three or four times a week and that was about the extent of their friendship. They'd had a couple of dinners at each other's homes with their husbands along and gone to a few neighbourhood parties together but not much more. They'd never had what Dianne would consider to be a truly serious and significant conversation about life, just mostly small talk. She wondered if she should bring up the sex club to Selena or not but then decided that the money and prestige of bringing the quite pretty young blonde into the club would be worth the possible loss of her friendship. "I'll tell you how we are managing to get out of our financial hole and you can decide if you want to follow us. If you do follow us, Jake and I will get a nice reward for recruiting you. I want to state that up front so that you'll know about it." Selena thought to herself wearily, great, another pyramid scheme where you had to get all of your friends and family to join. She gave the pretty, slightly plump brunette in front of her a somewhat sour look. Dianne just smiled at Selena's expression and asked "How adventurous are you and Rob? You know, sexually? Would you be willing to have sex with other people for the chance at a lot of money?" Selena looked at Dianne astounded and wondered, was the other woman suggesting prostitution? Was that how she was earning extra money and getting them out of debt? Selena paused and thought about matters for a while. She liked sex and had often paid for a nice dinner with a quick blowjob when she'd been younger and in college. Of course, that was mostly before she got serious about being with Rob although she had to admit that they'd almost been married before she'd given that up entirely. How hard would it be for her to go back to something like that, she wondered.

"Are we talking about prostitution?" she asked cautiously as she scanned the other woman's face.

"No, not exactly" the brunette admitted as she looked frankly at the blonde. "We're talking about a sex club where some rich people pay a lot of money to be full time members and people such as ourselves provide them with entertainment in return for some money, the ability to be noticed and let us into the club to use its fabulous facilities. So you know." Dianne gave a shrug to indicate that this was something that you might do for friends and family. Selena looked at her a little warily as she wondered about the sex club.

"What would I have to do to be a member?" she asked suspiciously.

"You could only be an associate member. Full time members pay exorbitant fees every year" Dianne stated as she evaded answering momentarily. She sighed and then stated "You'd have to let the members watch you being fucked by your husband in some unusual ways. It's humiliating and can be painful at times but the rewards are worth it. We're already out of debt and putting away some savings. And you're going to have to let some members of the club fuck you and your husband eventually. Once you've passed the initiation challenges and fulfill your associate member requirements, you have to make yourself available sexually about one evening or afternoon every two weeks to keep your status. Of course, if you're willing to do it more often, there are very generous rewards." Dianne paused so that the information could be absorbed by the blonde woman. Selena sipped her coffee and thought about it for over five minutes; Dianne knew what a big step this was, having gone through it herself just a couple of months earlier. They sat in silence for a while. Dianne topped up Selena's cup when she finished her coffee.

Finally, Selena gave a huge sigh and said "I'll talk it over with Rob. We'll probably have a bunch of questions for you and Jake, if we're interested. Can we come over to ask them?"

Dianne nodded, somewhat sympathetically because she remember how much shock she'd felt when Jake's aunt had told her about the sex club, and replied "As I mentioned earlier, there aren't a lot of specifics that I can tell you but I'll tell you what I can." She blushed slightly and then confided "One thing that I can tell you is that Jake and my sex lives have never been better. We'd gotten into a rut of being too tired to have sex before this, so anything would be an improvement. But, I find that it is even better with him now than any time we've been together. Even when we were first dating and trying each other out wasn't as good as it is now. And we both have some other partners fairly frequently." She paused to look at Selena before continuing "One thing that Jake and I decided upon was not to discuss any sex with other partners if the other person wasn't there to participate or watch. There's no sense rubbing one another's noses in the sexual activities. Why don't you and Rob come over for supper for the next few nights? I remember how we had to scrimp on the food budget when we were in dire straits and I'd like to treat you guys to some good meals. I promise not to pressure you into agreeing to anything but will answer your questions to the best that I can." She smiled in a very friendly fashion as Selena considered the offer. She was tempted to say no but knew that if she did, they wouldn't be eating and she hated to have to do that.

So she replied "I'll see if Rob is willing to agree about the sex club but we'll be here for supper tonight. Thank you."

"I'll break out some steaks so that we can have a fantastic meal" Dianne promised. She and Selena said goodbye and Selena headed home to contemplate matters further.

When Rob arrived home, he was tired, grumpy and expecting to go hungry; Selena told him that they were going over to Jake and Dianne's place for a steak supper and he perked up. Then she told him about the sex club and the possibility about getting out of debt. Rob wasn't in favour of the idea so Selena suggested that he talk to Jake about it to see if more information might change his mind. Rob agreed, a little reluctantly, to talk with Jake.

They got themselves ready and went over for dinner. As soon as they walked in, Jake grabbed Rob and took him down to the basement for some drinks while Dianne prepared dinner. Jake had been warned by his wife so he was prepared to convince Rob to partake in the sex club; he found it to be a wonderful idea, improving both his sexual and financial life. Selena stayed in the kitchen to help Dianne. Dianne got her to tear up the lettuce for the salads and she did so, humming a happy little tune; she'd been somewhat surprised that Jake seemed so into the sex club but was pleased to see that he was prepared to try to convince Rob. When the men joined them for supper, it was evident to Selena that Jake had poured a few whiskies for Rob. She knew that Rob hadn't been able to drink for the last couple of months because they couldn't afford it and the alcohol was hitting him kind of hard but she didn't begrudge him of it. She was actually able to settle her nerves and have a fairly nice time and a wonderful supper.

She refrained from pestering Rob about making a decision as they spent the next two nights going over to Jake and Dianne's place. Rob and Jake always spent some time together talking before supper and she didn't press Rob to tell her what they talked about. She didn't pester Dianne with any questions either because she had already decided that this was the only path for them to follow so that they could guarantee their future. She just had to make sure that Rob was in agreement with it. Truth be told, she was looking forward to getting some more sex; things had been fairly dull lately.

So when Rob told her a few days later that he thought that they should seriously investigate the sex club to see if they could qualify, she quickly agreed with him. She arranged for Dianne to set up a meeting for them and they were soon in front of a group of people who would determine if they were suitable material for associate membership.

Selena had been instructed to wear a dress and heels only, no underwear; it felt weird not wearing a bra to support her large breasts; she hadn't done that since she was fourteen and they were still maturing. She wasn't particularly happy to be without support and felt that her tits hung there like sacks of cement; she was unaware that her unfettered breasts pushed nicely against her dress, defining them in a lovely manner, and her nipples tented the material in a wonderful manner. Not wearing panties was a minor inconvenience because most of her panties were tiny scraps of material anyway but it did feel different being totally exposed to the world. Rob had been told to wear no underwear either and he felt a little too unrestrained and kept squirming around while they waited. They were led into a room where fifteen people were sitting in comfortable chairs around an area that had a small mattress on the floor. Selena gazed around at the small sea of faces and wondered if she would have the guts to go through with this interview or not. They would be required to show off their bodies and answer all the questions of the group before demonstrating their knowledge by performing sex in every position that they knew. They had gone over those positions last night to ensure that they both understood them. Selena was a bit amazed that she knew a few more positions than her husband and realized that the two of them rarely used more than two positions anymore; so blah had they become in their sex life. As she stood in front of the group, awaiting instructions, she felt her pussy and nipples tingle in anticipation of being fucked in front of this crowd; she realized that she relished the notion.

"Hello, Selena and Rob. We'll be the people evaluating you today" a pretty blonde woman in her early thirties and wearing a predominantly dominatrix outfit said pleasantly. "Don't worry about our names because you're probably too nervous to even remember them. You'll get to know us better once you become associate members and we're being more intimate with you." She flashed them an encouraging smile as she said that. "The important thing to do today is get over your nervousness as quick as you can and show yourselves off to us. We have a lot of very pretty people in our sex club and both of you are attractive but we'd like to get to know a bit of your personalities and more importantly, if you have any reservations about sex. The more flexible you're willing to be in regard to sexual activities, the more likely we are to welcome you to the club. Now we should start by seeing both of you naked. Please take off your clothing and display yourself to us. You first, Selena."

Selena reached around behind her back to pull down the zipper of her short dress. She used her left arm to hold it up against her as she did this; she'd decided that it would be best to perform a small striptease and since she was wearing very little, she'd have to work the tease fairly hard. Once the zipper was fully down, she slowly exposed her large left breast, gave them a quick flash of her exposed nipple and pulled the dress up again. She repeated the process with her right tit; several of the watchers chuckled at her coyness. Then she flashed both tits at once and two of the men gave her a couple of claps of applause in appreciation. She grinned at the watching people and got smiles back from them; she wanted to show them that she had an adventurous, playful personality and she felt that they were seeing that in her. She also realized that the butterflies that had been in her stomach were gone and she was feeling confident about what she was doing. She worked at exposing herself briefly to them for about five minutes before she simply stripped off the dress and stood in front of them with her legs spread slightly so that they could all see her fully. The watching people gave her some applause as she stood there and then a couple of them motioned that they wanted to see her rotate around so that they could see all of her naked body. She did this for about two minutes before the blonde dominatrix said "Thank you, Selena. That was a good job and I think that we all appreciated it and your nice body, as well. You can go sit on the mattress for now while we have a look at Rob." Selena moved over to the mattress and sat cross-legged, exposing her pussy.

Rob stepped forward, he'd been nervous about showing his cock to all of these strangers, but Selena's little performance had distracted him enough that he now felt at ease. He could feel his cock pressing against the front of his pants from his arousal of watching his wife tease these strangers. He knew that he couldn't possibly perform as well as Selena had so he didn't bother to try. He stripped off his shirt and did a few quick flexes to show off his muscles. He wasn't overly built but he wasn't skinny either. He didn't take too much time to do this, just enough to let them see him. He dropped his pants and stepped out of them, his eight inch cock bobbing nicely in front of him. He gave it a couple of strokes with his right hand so that they could see it fairly well. After a minute, he made some turns around so that all of them could see his body quite well. He also received some applause. "Excellent, Rob" the dominatrix said. "You may go over and sit by Selena. We will now ask you a number of questions so that we can get to know you better. Please answer them honestly." Rob went and sat by his wife, reaching out to clasp her hand briefly.

A woman in the watching group asked "Hi, how often do you two have sex?"

Selena responded "We try to have sex daily, most of the time more than once. The best that we've ever achieved is five times in one day. Uh, things have been a little more sparse lately because of our troubles financially. Also, I usually masturbate at least once a day."

The woman nodded and asked "Rob, do you masturbate also?"

Rob coloured just slightly and admitted "No, I find that Selena takes care of my needs quite well so I don't have the desire to masturbate. I am aware that she has the stronger sex drive of the two of us so if I feel the need for sex, I just ask her and she usually complies." He looked around a bit anxiously that these people might see him as less of a man for admitting such a thing but he saw nothing but pleasant understanding on their faces. He felt a bit of warmth in his heart.

"Are both of you bi-sexual?"

Selena replied "I'm fully bi-sexual, I guess. Back in university, when I had a lot more chances of being with different people and before I'd committed to Rob, a lot of my friends thought I was more lesbian than straight. I guess I just found my female friends more interesting to be with than my male ones back then. I find I like men more than women, these days, but I have no problem eating pussy or getting eaten by a woman. I don't think that Rob has had very much experience with men."

He said "Before I met Selena, I did some experimenting with other men. I sucked a bit of cock and got fucked a few times. I enjoyed having a man's cock in my ass a couple of times but more often didn't really like it." He shrugged his shoulders and continued "I guess it really depended on how well the guy fucking me, treated me. I never got offered the chance to fuck another man in the ass, so I don't know if I'd like that. I probably would. Selena gets me to fuck her in the ass when she's in the mood for it and I kinda like that. I haven't been with a man since I've been married."

The blonde dominatrix asked "So, are you both willing to be bi-sexual in the club?" Both of them nodded, Rob more slowly than Selena.

They spent about forty minutes or so, answering questions from the group. They were asked a lot of questions about how they felt about a lot of things, what their expectations and goals were by joining the sex club and what sort of sexual encounters they would be willing to participate in. Selena was asked if she'd be willing to be a submissive for a bondage and discipline session and answered that she would be very happy to try that out. She had to hide a smile as the pretty blonde dominatrix perked up about that. She found that she wanted to impress the other woman with her eagerness to be with her and could feel a twitch deep in her hips whenever she caught the blonde looking her over. Rob agreed to try B&D a little more reluctantly; Selena noticed that the blonde dominatrix never even bothered to glance over at him regarding this. Selena concluded that the other woman was likely a lesbian and found that this fact intrigued her a lot more than it turned her off. She imagined being in a B&D session with Rob and a couple of others, where she and Rob could watch each other being beaten and she almost came right then. She recognized that she'd missed hearing the next question and had to ask for it to be repeated to her; she also pushed that image from her mind so that she could concentrate and answer all of their questions because she didn't want to appear too distracted.

When the questioning was over, the blonde dominatrix spoke again. "Okay, that was good. Now we'd like to see both of you in a little action. So, I'm going to ask you to demonstrate the sexual positions that you know. Rob, we'd like to see you stroke your cock in and out of Selena's pussy about a half dozen times or so in each of the positions. We're not expecting you to make her orgasm at this point. And you're not expected to cum either but if you do, we'd like to see both of you clean that up. After you show us your knowledge, we'll want to see both of you climax by masturbating in front of us. Do you understand or would you like me to go over it again?" Both of them nodded their understanding and proceeded to show the group the sex positions that they knew how to get into. Selena was intrigued to notice that more than half of the women perked up their interest when Rob's thrusting into her made her large tits bounce. She made sure to grin invitingly at them when that happened.

Finally, they had shown all that they knew and the blonde dominatrix signalled that they should now masturbate for the enjoyment of the group. Selena decided that she should go first so she arranged herself on her back so that most of the group could easily see up her cunt. Then she used the fingers of her left hand to stroke her wet cunt while her right hand played with her nipples. She closed her eyes and pictured the blonde dominatrix riding her hard with a big dildo as she worked her body over. She moaned and twisted in her enjoyment of what she was doing to herself. She found the soft mutterings of the watchers to be stimulating when she'd thought that she'd find them a distraction. It took her just over ten minutes to make herself climax but when she did cum, she squealed out her pleasure. She was a little embarrassed when the watchers gave her a round of applause. She looked over at Rob to signal that he should start and was amused to see that his cock was already standing hard at attention from her arousing performance.

Rob wondered if he should try to extend his performance or if he should just go ahead and cum; he knew that he was quite excited because of what Selena had just done and probably wouldn't last too long. He decided that he'd just go ahead and make himself cum as he would normally without a crowd watching him. He was slightly shocked to realize that he wasn't intimidated by their presence. He lasted just over three minutes.

Once they were finished, the blonde dominatrix thanked them, told them to dress and that they would be contacted regarding the group's decision about them. A couple of days later, Selena received a phone call that set up the situation they were now involved in.

Their guide led them into the club; they were both naked but they tried to be unconcerned about the fact as they realized there were probably nearly two hundred people examining them. They were led up to a small inflatable pool and the guide told Selena to kneel within it. She complied and another woman came over quickly to help her position herself better. The woman rubbed some KY jelly onto Selena's asshole and Selena wondered if their first sex act would be her getting fucked up the ass. But then the woman reached over and retrieved some equipment and Selena slowly recognized it as an enema set up. Selena didn't say or do anything as the woman inserted the nozzle up her ass and pumped about three litres of warm, soapy water up her ass. The woman then instructed Rob that he was to enter Selena's pussy and fuck her while she was loaded with the liquid. She told Rob that they would receive a payout of $10,000 if he could do a hundred full thrusts into his wife without her losing control and bathing him with her enema. Rob looked at Selena dubiously, unsure as to whether or not he wanted to participate. Selena urged him to try quickly as she felt the pressure of wanting to rid herself of the liquid. She'd finally realized what was meant by people telling her this would be messy and humiliating. And why she was in this pool. She didn't know that very few of the previous couples had come anywhere close to winning the grand prize. The game was severely stacked against them.

Selena withstood the first few strokes of Rob's cock inside her fairly well and began to wonder if she'd be able to complete the required task but then after about a dozen thrusts, she could feel the pressure of the liquid wanting out of her. She gritted her teeth and tried desperately to keep it under control. But shortly after Rob's twenty-third thrust into her, she lost her ability to hold onto it and she spurted the liquid out her asshole and all over a startled Rob. Selena hung her head in shame as the watching people laughed uproariously at the sight of the two of them. The woman who'd put the enema into Selena came over with a hose and bathed them both quickly with warm water, washing away the mess. She gave them towels and then led them out of the main area down to a smaller room.

The beautiful blonde dominatrix that had led their interview was seated there waiting for them. She bade Rob to sit in a chair nearby and patted the loveseat beside her for Selena to sit there. Selena gave Rob a slightly inquiring glance and he just shrugged his shoulders back at her and took the offered chair. Selena sat near the gorgeous blonde as requested; she was unsurprised when the dominatrix immediately reached out and opened up her towel to expose her nude body. She was a little shocked when the other woman began fondling her tits right after that. She noticed that the blonde was looking at Rob challengingly, daring him to object or intercede. Rob just sat there and looked her in the eye; he knew that if Selena objected to the dominatrix's handling of her, she would not be shy about saying so. And if his wife was willing to let the woman fondle her, he had no objections to the matter. He was aware that Selena had organized a few affairs during their marriage because she told him of them as they were happening; he'd gotten over the fact that they were all with women because Selena felt it wasn't really cheating if she had lesbian affairs. Rob knew that she had the affairs because he wasn't able to fully satisfy her sexual needs and that she needed to go elsewhere to achieve some release.

Selena was enjoying the other woman's fondling of her tits for the few silent minutes that the standoff lasted; she thrust her upper torso forward so the woman had easier access to her. When the dominatrix decided that Rob wasn't going to object in any way to how she was treating Selena, she focused more on Selena. She gave a quick grin of possession as she saw how Selena was leaning into her caresses and then decided that she needed to teach her to be less forward. She removed her hands from Selena's plump tits and without saying a word, used both of those hands to smack the heavy tits hard. Selena gave a gasp of astonishment when she was struck but didn't say anything else or move away from the woman. The blonde dominatrix nodded at her approvingly and then began to talk to them.

"Congratulations to the pair of you. You've successfully passed the first test that we give all of our candidates." She noticed both of them frown at her as they thought that they had failed miserably and laughed lightly. "Almost nobody succeeds in winning the grand prize. It's pretty much impossible to do. I've heard that it was won once but I've never seen anyone even come close. Most of them fail about where the pair of you did. Your test was not to succeed at that task because that was designed just to provide entertainment to the members. Your test was how you handled doing it and being the object of everyone's laughter at your failure. The fact that you are still here and didn't storm out of here means that you are of suitable material for us to look closer at you." She gave them a smile of encouragement and continued "I'm very interested in you, Selena, as you are undoubtedly aware. My name is Mistress Helga. I am strictly a lesbian in all matters. If we are to develop a relationship, it will be just you and I. Rob, you would not be included, not even to watch. If this bothers either of you, let me know and I will seek my pleasures elsewhere. As it is, what I can offer is to sponsor the pair of you as associate members. You don't necessarily need that at this stage of the process but it will come in very handy for the future. If you are not interested in accepting my sponsorship, I am confident that you'll receive other offers. I won't go too deep into that for now but if you are interested, Selena, we can meet at a later date and I will explain matters further." She leaned back against the loveseat and gave them a toothy smile. "As for now, there are a pair of showers in that room beyond so that you may clean up better. There are fresh towels there for you to use. I suggest that you make use of one of them." She broadened her smile and continued "Nobody's going to begrudge you if you spend a few minutes screwing each other to reaffirm your commitment to the other. I will talk with you at a later time, Selena." With that, she got up and left the room.

Selena and Rob looked in amazement at one another and then without saying a word, went down to do as Mistress Helga had suggested.

DARBY'S BAD DAY

Darby Cooper was having a bad day; their two young girls, aged three years and eighteen months, had been a handful all day and she was presently fighting with them to get them to eat their suppers. The youngest was busy spitting out her strained beets while her older sister was balking from eating her chicken nuggets. Darby knew that her eldest loved chicken nuggets and fries and would eat it by preference most days but today she was just being obstinate. Darby sighed as she got a face full of strained beets. Then her husband Don walked in the doorway; he looked at the fussing children and then at his tired, stained wife. He knew by the slump of her shoulders that she was nearing the end of her rope. It was Friday and he was hoping to start off a fun weekend with his family, starting with some great sex with his wife; it looked as though he may have to change his hopes, he thought sorrowfully as he surveyed the mess. His perturbed wife glared at him and he gave her a broad smile as he suddenly figured out a way to save at least some of the weekend. He shrugged off his shirt so that it wouldn't get messed up and went up to the table; he took the strained beets out of his wife's hands and said softly "Why don't you go treat yourself to a bubble bath, honey? I'll take care of cleaning up and getting the kids to bed. Have yourself a glass of wine and use some of your aroma candles. You look as though you've had a hard day. I'll rub your back for you when you're done and I've got the girls bedded down safely." Darby looked at him with suspicion, she recognized that he was just treating her nicely because he hoped to fuck her later in the evening. Still, she thought, she was tired, pissed off and in need of some pampering; she could always refuse his advances after the back rub, she thought. She knew that she was unlikely to say no to him because she enjoyed sex; it put her in a wonderful frame of mind and relaxed her totally so that she could sleep well. She was aware that her husband knew this about her too but it was a nice gesture on his part to acknowledge that she needed some time away from their two, usually adorable, kids.

She left him to it, refusing to say anything, even when he blew her a kiss; she trudged up to the bedroom so that she could run the hot bath to soak in and stripped out of her dirty clothes. She looked at herself critically in the mirror once she was nude; dismayed to see that she retained some of the fat that she'd put on for the baby. She squeezed her plump breasts in her hands, thinking that they were the only good thing she retained from her pregnancy. Her belly still had a layer of fat and her ass was huge in her estimation. Her thighs now had a wobble whereas before the children, they had been very well toned. She sighed and wondered who would love such a wreck, well aware that her husband loved her very much and frequently showed her that affection. She relieved herself in the toilet before slipping into the hot water. Oh, that felt fantastic, she thought as she felt her cramped muscles begin to unwind. She spent a leisurely forty minutes in the bath, sipping a glass of wine and only left it because it was starting to cool and she didn't want to run more water into it.

She climbed out, toweled herself off and wrapped her raggedy plush pink housecoat around her before heading into the bedroom. She settled herself on the bed to await her husband, pouring another glass of wine to enjoy. Less than five minutes later, Don wandered in, whistling a jaunty tune. She looked at him, feeling a bit of envy that he felt so happy; she wasn't as unhappy as she'd been earlier but she wasn't back to feeling her usual self either. He smiled brightly as he entered, even though he noticed that she was still scowling somewhat, and stated "Kids are down for the night. Time for me to show you my appreciation of all the work you do for this family. Take off your robe and lie on your front so that I can give you a fantastic back rub." She gave him a tentative smile and then did as he asked; she really enjoyed his back rubs, even though she knew that 99% of the time it was just a prelude to him fucking her.

He stripped off the rest of his clothes except for his boxers and then got out the scented oils so that he could rub her down. He climbed on top of her, straddling her well-padded ass and began rubbing her tight neck muscles without any oil. He dug his fingers in and worked her muscles hard, knowing that she liked that; she moaned and muttered approval as he worked the kinks out of her neck. Oh, she thought, that almost felt better than sex. He could see that her neck and back were both loosening up so he got the vanilla scented oil, a scent that both of them liked and felt aroused them, pouring a large dollop of the thick liquid between her shoulder blades; she gave out a small moan as the oil hit her back. He dipped two fingers into it and started rubbing it across the back of her neck and over her shoulders. She muttered happily at him as he lightly worked the oil over her soft pale skin; he could feel his dick stiffening, both from the warmth of her soft ass and the intimacy of what he was doing for her. He knew that he would be able to talk her into fucking and was pondering what to ask her to do for him; he wondered if he could talk her into anal sex after her bad day. Better be a hell of a back rub, he thought with a small snort.

Darby was getting lost in the intimacy of the moment, the pleasant feel of his hands on her and the wonderful scent wafting up her nose. She could feel the tension of her anger leaving her to be replaced by the tension of her building arousal.

Her nipples were rubbing lightly and pleasantly against the sheets as he pressed her against them with his rubbing; she was pleased that they were erect and could feel their fantastic tingling. She knew that he was just getting her in the mood for fucking but she still appreciated his effort and also acknowledged to herself that she enjoyed the sex between them as much as he did. Even after two kids, she liked being fucked and preferred that it alternate between hard and soft; she liked sex in all sorts of different positions and methods depending on her mood.

He'd worked the sweet smelling oil all over her back now, leaving her feeling very loose and invigorated, and was now at her waist. He poured another tiny dollop at the small of her back and started rubbing it roughly into her ass muscles; she wiggled and moaned as she relished his treatment of her tight muscles. She could also feel her pussy tingling and knew that she'd be begging to feel his cock up inside her in a few more minutes. She wanted the back rub to last as long as she could stand it but both of them knew that once she started getting aroused, she wanted him to forget the back rub in favour of him fucking her. He ran oiled fingers gently but quickly down the crack of her ass and she realized what his goal for that evening was. The dirty bastard wanted to fuck her up the ass, she thought, a little crossly, and after her hard day. Then she thought about it for a minute as he continued to rub and manipulate her ass cheeks. She reflected on how she was feeling and decided that she could handle taking him in her ass. Her asshole puckered magnificently at the thought of it and her tight pussy began to leak a bit of her liquid. She sighed as she recognized that he'd manipulated her once again into giving in to what he wanted; she wasn't upset about it or that he did it to her, she was just a little peeved that he knew how to do it to her so easily. She reflected that it really helped them get along in their marriage, knowing that each of them could be so giving to the other even when their day had been bad.

She turned her upper body so that she could see his face as he continued to stroke her ass and stated "You want to fuck my ass, don't you?" He gave her a big grin and nodded, knowing that since she brought it up, she was going to accede. "Okay, I'm game for it. But I want you to make me cum with my vibrator before you get off inside my ass. Okay? None of this fucking my tight asshole and forgetting about my pleasure, making me do the work of creating my orgasm."

"Sheesh" he muttered in mock exasperation. "Leave you in need one time and I have to hear about it forever." She gave him a steely glance and he said "I promise that you get to cum first." Then she grinned at him. He decided that she was randy enough to want to get started so he abandoned the back rub and went to get the items needed for the anal sex. It took him less than a minute before he was back with everything. He helped her roll over onto her back so that he could start preparing her. He lifted her ass up and stuffed three cushions under her before folding her legs up against her chest. He poured some lubricant onto her damp pussy hair and began rubbing it along her drooling slit. She murmured her enjoyment of his activity and he could feel his dick twitching from her sounds and facial expressions. He felt as though he could do this to her forever but knew that she would very soon want more as her orgasm built up. So he started pushing the lubricant up into her cunt with his fingers, enjoying the feeling of her vaginal muscles closing on his fingers as she rocked her hips in pleasure. While he was doing this to her, she'd taken her favourite vibrator and was running her tongue along its smooth surface; she knew that he'd coat it in lubricant before sticking it up her but she liked to do this.

Finally, he decided that they were ready to proceed so he pushed her legs up toward her chest so that her pussy would gape, giving him much better access into her. Then he took the vibrator from her, lubricated it and started to push the head of it against her entrance; he teased her with it, popping it quickly in and out of her. She could feel her mind start to cloud with arousal and she moaned encouragingly at him as she enjoyed the sensations he was creating in her. He knew that she required a fair bit of fondling to totally build up for her climax and he really enjoyed her reactions to the foreplay, so he took his time. He used his free hand to isolate and stroke her clitoris as she whined in pleasure. He occasionally reached up and pulled on her nipples as he worked her pussy over. He smiled at her as she groaned each time he did that to her.

After more than five minutes of that, he decided that she was aroused enough that she was aroused enough to push her vibrator fully into her so that she could enjoy the feel of it while he prepared her ass for his penetration. She grinned at him as he pressed the toy up into her and when he'd finished, she rolled over to give him access to her ass. He spent a few minutes stroking her soft skin and teasingly running a finger along her crack. She shivered with delight and he enjoyed watching her plump ass shake for him. He got out the lubricant again and started working some up her asshole. He hummed a happy little tune as he took his time greasing her up; he knew that she really enjoyed all of the attention he paid to her rear end so he was happy to take his time on the job. Within a few more minutes, he began working his fingers in and out of her asshole. He knew that she was ready for him when he could easily slide three fingers into her gaping asshole. His attention to her ass and the toy vibrating in her pussy pushed her to a level of arousal that made her start to ignore what was happening around her. She was becoming lost in her own world of pleasure.

He was already very hard so he just coated his prick with a layer of lubricant as he climbed onto the bed behind her. He adjusted her positioning so that he could more easily push his cock into her asshole; she was very compliant about being positioned. As soon as she was ready, he placed the head of his dick up against her rosebud and gently pushed it forward into her; he slipped in without any problems and she groaned at the full feeling she had in her hips with his prick in her ass and the vibrator in her pussy. He could see that she was leaking a lot of juices out of her cunt and knew that she would be fairly close to her orgasm. He wanted to be fully inside her ass when she climaxed because the pressures of her anal muscles on his cock would feel wonderful. But he knew that he probably still had some time so he guided her hips back and forth so that her tight asshole created some friction on the head of his prick. He relished the sensation of her warm, greasy skin rubbing up and down on his very sensitive head. She was now grunting and panting fairly rapidly, giving him notice that she was very near her orgasm so he thrust deeply into her, pushing her hips roughly onto the bed. She gave him a whine of ecstasy as he did that to her.

He quickly pulled his prick back out of her and drove forward again, putting all of his weight behind his thrust; she screeched loudly in both pain and pleasure as he spread her open. After three more tremendous thrusts, she started to buck her hips around and he pushed her hard back onto the bed, using his weight to hold her in place. He knew that she was just reacting unconsciously to his fucking of her; she was panting very heavily now and growling her pleasure at him. He slipped his hands up under her heavy breasts, grabbed her nipples and pulled as hard as he could on them; she screamed again and began to orgasm. He had to fight hard to keep her squirming body below him as her ass closed down hard onto his cock. He whined as she forced his climax out of him. Oh God, he thought wonderingly, it felt simply incredible to be so deep inside her as she orgasmed.

He continued to hold her in place on his dick until she was completely finished with her orgasm. It took her more than two minutes to finish. Then she needed some respite to recover so she attempted to push him away from her but she was too weak from her exertions to do the job; nonetheless, he knew what she wanted so he separated his cock from her ass and reached between her legs to turn the vibrator off. He took firm hold of the toy and worked it out of her. She murmured her thanks and lay there in a daze. Don lazed beside her, sucking in tremendous gasps of breath, feeling almost totally exhausted but incredibly satisfied. She'd provided him with a fantastic fuck. He knew that she'd be feeling happier about herself and their situation in life and he was feeling extremely good about things as well. It was an exceptionally pleasant way to end the week, he thought smugly.

CARLENE AND DARLENE

Carlene and Darlene Schultz were identical twins; they were tall, just about five eight, blonde, stacked and beautiful. Men were instantly attracted to their intelligent, pretty faces with their bright blue dazzling eyes, straight pointed noses and large mouths framed by pouting lips. Of course, most men checked out their toned legs, flattish stomachs and prominent busts before reaching their faces. And a lot of men were attracted to the fact that they were so similar to each other that most people, including their parents, couldn't tell them apart; they both knew that Carlene was slightly heavier in the tit department while Darlene was a trifle wider in the hips. And they knew where they differed in freckles and moles because they examined their differences with extreme interest. The girls were both very adventurous sexually and found each other attractive as well as other men and women; they enjoyed their personal rendezvous with each other quite a bit but liked other partners almost as much. They'd often thought about how wonderful it would be to have sex with another set of identical twins but they had yet to find such a pair.

They had moved out of their parent's home the week previous so that they could attend university. Their many friends in the large town had been heartbroken when they'd expressed their desire to move to the large city to study to attempt to become lawyers. They'd cut a wide swath through the sex life of many in the large town so that a number of the older adults that they had not been involved with were ecstatic to see them leave. A number of their friends had wanted to join them but they had made it clear that they wanted to have new sexual adventures and that they would not share themselves with anyone from their own town until they were satisfied by their escapades. That had put a huge damper on the enthusiasm but still a few friends had followed them in hopes that they might change their minds. They were aware that their parents had allowed them quite a bit of freedom while they were growing up, not saying anything when they led a pair of boys or girls up to the bedroom they shared but they wanted to experience sex that they knew their parents wouldn't tolerate in their house. So they had taken an apartment with a large single bedroom just off campus and bought a large, springy king sized bed for it. Their parents hadn't said anything when they helped them move into the apartment and saw the bed because, although their room at home had twin beds, their mother was fully aware that the two girls shared only one of them. It didn't bother her as long as the two of them were happy; she knew that they occasionally fought and could carry on a fight over a number of days but that didn't seem to affect the fact that they slept together. She often thought that they reminded her of her and her husband in how they handled their fights; sex was never used as a tool against the other and even if they were thoroughly pissed at each other, they would still fuck one another.

But the gorgeous twins were now preparing for their first sex party; they had spent the previous day inviting the best looking men to join them tonight and only one of the six they approached had refused them. They had informed the men that there would be a number of them at the party while they would be the only females there. The men would get to fuck them until either they or the men could no longer perform; the girls thought that they would easily outlast the men. It was a bit surprising that, even though at least two of the men had their girlfriends with them when the twins made the offer to them, the men had accepted so readily; it just went to show how easy it was for a pretty girl to get a man to do her bidding, they thought. Neither of them cared if they made enemies of other women and even at home, they were proud of their lurid reputation. They enjoyed the jealous and envious stares of other beautiful women, knowing that they had an advantage in the fact that they were identical twins; what man or woman could resist two such perfect beauties, they thought smugly.

Carlene was the slightly older, slightly more dominant of the two of them, although many people would classify both of them as dominant and quite pushy about matters. She was the one to take the lead when it was just the two of them and Darlene was happy to comply. When they were with more submissive women, they were both very happy to control them. She was busy looking at her makeup in the mirror, giving it a final check; she wanted to look perfect and alluring, even though she knew that the makeup wouldn't survive the first few energetic encounters she was planning to have. She saw Darlene approaching in the mirror and reached back behind her to fondle her twin between her legs. Darlene gave her a delighted smile as always and pushed her hips up against her sister's hand. Carlene reached around and gave her twin a smack on the ass; she smiled with pleasure when Darlene wiggled her bum under her hand. "We don't have the time to get into anything right now" she stated with regret. "Besides we wouldn't want to wreck our makeup before the guys get here. Did you prepare the wine for tonight?"

"Yes, my darling older sister" Darlene cooed at her as she leaned in and planted a light kiss on the cheek of her twin. "There are also some snacks out for the guys to nibble on while they wait their turn with us. I figure that we'll be too busy getting fucked to participate in eating them. Especially early on while the guys are still feeling their oats." She smirked knowingly at her older twin, who nodded her agreement and acceptance.

Both of the twins liked to dress identically and they owned two of every outfit that they had but for tonight those chose similar outfits that only differed in colour. Carlene wore a baby blue bustier with thong panties, garter belt and stockings; her five inch heels were white laced sandals. Darlene wore the same outfit but hers was a very soft pretty pink. Both girls were prepared to ditch the bustier and panties once all of the invited men had arrived; they wanted to show off their lithe bodies as much as they could. They hadn't yet decided on how they were going to choose the order in which they would allow the boys to mount and fuck them but they had discussed the matter quite extensively over the past day. Carlene was in favour of letting the boys decide amongst themselves, knowing that it might just provoke some fighting amongst them because she liked to see some blood and Darlene wanted it to be more by chance. They decided that they would wait until the boys had all arrived to make the final decision. They had informed the boys to arrive by seven pm and the first arrival was at five to and the last one was just seconds after the hour. Carlene was happy that they had all arrived so promptly and all of them had done a double take when the twins greeted them at the door in their outfits. Both girls had hugged and kissed the arrivals, pleased that all of them were sporting nice hard erections as they pressed their hips against the men.

They led the final arrival to the living room and then looked at each other so that they could coordinate their actions; they both discarded their bustiers and then stepped out of their panties, dropping both items to the floor near the walls. They stood there proudly in front of the five young men, who greeted their beauty with gasps and the inhalation of breath; one man stood up from his seat and began giving them a standing ovation that all of the others quickly joined in. Both twins blushed slightly, excited that they could arouse these men as much as they did. Carlene could feel her buds hardening into little points as her blood pressure increased from her arousal and a glance at Darlene told her that the same was happening to her twin. "Now, boys" she purred. "We're happy that you all appreciate how good we look but we are anxious to get started because we're both in danger of dripping on the floor from our desire to get fucked hard. We just have to decide who is going to be first. Do you have any ideas about how we should make the decision?" She flashed them all a brilliant smile as she glanced around at them.

"How about dick size?" one of them asked, half in jest.

"What? Do you mean that the smallest should go first so that the girls aren't too stretched out by those of us with more monstrous dicks?" another asked, laughing.

Carlene looked over at Darlene, who nodded happily back at her, figuring that this method was probably the best one and one that they hadn't thought of doing. "Okay" she said sexily. "Drop your pants and line up. Darlene and I will put you in the correct order and don't worry about us being too stretched out." She grinned naughtily at them and continued "We recover our shape very quickly. You'll all feel how tight we are." The men quickly did as asked and the twins rearranged them into the correct order, only having trouble deciding which man was third versus fourth because their cocks were so close in size. They eventually decided that it didn't really matter that much and just arranged the pair to their satisfaction. They spent a moment admiring the five hard dicks before taking the two with the biggest dicks into the bedroom with them. Carlene called over her shoulder as they went "Help yourselves to wine and snacks while you wait your turn, boys. We'll be back for you in a fairly short while unless you guys can last longer than the normal man, that is."

Carlene held the hand of the man with the longest cock; his prick was almost two inches longer than that of the second place man and was almost as thick as the thickest of the five men. She salivated at the thought of all that meat up inside her. She'd been quite pleased that all five men were larger than the average; the smallest of the five cocks was about seven inches in length and that man had the thickest cock of the five. She knew that she and Darlene were going to be well pleased that night. She led the man with the over eleven inch cock over to the right side of the bed while Darlene led hers to the other side. Darlene lay on her back on an angle on the large bed so the man with her could fuck her in the missionary position while Carlene knelt from the other side of the bed over her twin so that her man could enter her from behind. The way that they were positioned would allow the twins to look into each other's eyes while the men pounded them. They would be able to kiss each other while they were being fucked as well. The men understood what their roles were to be and quickly got started entering both girls. Carlene wasn't too surprised that Darlene was able to engulf her man's cock before she was able to accept all of hers because this man was easily the longest that she'd ever taken. She moaned with happiness as he struggled to get her to take his full length and hoped that he would be able to fuck Darlene later in the evening so that she could also experience his size. As he started to thrust into her with a more regular rhythm she pushed her hips back at him to increase both of their pleasure. She could tell that the man riding her twin was already well on his way towards orgasming while her own man was just starting to build towards his own climax. She was a bit disappointed that they wouldn't be cumming together inside her and her sister but she wouldn't have traded the experience of feeling his large cock in her for that pleasure. She huffed her breath and gave a small squeal of joy as he drove his cock deep into her. She noticed that Darlene was grinning a little superiorly at her and decided to wipe away that smile by kissing her lips. The twins were engaged in the kiss when Darlene gave a small moan of surprise as her man erupted inside her cunt. The man fucking Darlene grunted his satisfaction at his climax and climbed off of her. Darlene continued to lay there kissing her twin as her man kept thrusting inside her. The man who'd finished seemed unsure as to whether to leave or not and then he decided that he might as well watch them continue to fuck. He was quite impressed as to how big the other man was and that Carlene was able to handle taking it quite easily. He hoped that he'd get the promised chance to fuck Carlene later in the evening so that he could see if the twins screwed differently or not; he was quite curious to find out because he'd never had the opportunity to fuck twins previously. It was a full minute and a half later that the man with the biggest cock began showing signs that he was about to cum. The watching man was surprised when it took him over twenty seconds to stop spurting and when he pulled his cock out of Carlene, she dripped a few rather large gobs out of her pussy.

He was shocked when Darlene rolled over and scooped up the gobs with her fingers, sucking them into her mouth before sharing them with her twin in a wet kiss. He found that to be quite a turn on. He was even more shocked when the man with the biggest cock decided to separate the twins and share in their wet, sloppy kiss; the girls eagerly complied, impressed with his willingness to taste his own cum. The twins turned to include the other man but he declined, not wanting to be associated with the cum of another man.

So the twins then led the two men back out into the living room where they gave the man with the biggest cock a sloppy, wet kiss from each of them, leaning their lush bodies against him as they did so. The man, John, just smiled knowingly at the other men in the room as they looked enviously at him; he enjoyed the notoriety he was receiving. The other man was hoping for similar treatment but both girls just strode by him as they grabbed the hands of the next two men and led them to the bedroom.

Carlene and Darlene reassumed their positions on the bed and the men quickly entered them; both of these men were just a bit smaller than the second man had been and were almost equal in size. Carlene could easily feel her man inside her and enjoyed his nice size. She was happily surprised when it appeared that both men seemed to understand although the twins wanted to be fucked, it didn't mean they wanted to be mindlessly pounded. It became evident that the men were holding their orgasms back and varying their rhythms to help the girls enjoy the sex. Carlene started kissing Darlene as the man stroked in and out of her wet pussy; she liked what he was doing to her and moaned her approval to the man. Darlene similarly rewarded her man. The men were able to keep going for nearly ten minutes and the twins were in a state of bliss; they knew it would take more for the men to orgasm them but recognized that the men could be taught what would push them over the edge if they spent a little more time with them. But Darlene could tell from the face of the man riding her that he was tiring of his pace and wouldn't be able to hold himself back much longer. She grunted to attract her sister's attention before she pushed her hips up against his thrust. The man recognized her movements as a signal that she was satisfied and that he could let himself release.

Carlene realized what Darlene was doing and pushed her hips backwards into her man and was pleased when he groaned and began to spurt into her. The two men orgasmed within seconds of each other and the twins were very pleased by the result. The girls were happy to let the men stay up inside them until their pricks shrank enough to fall out on their own. They'd enjoyed the sex and therefore rewarded the two men with a little cuddling and kissing before returning them to the living room. Carlene decided that she'd see if Darlene agreed with her that the two men should be considered for future encounters given how well they had performed but she was quite sure that her sister would agree.

When they were back in the living room, both girls gave both men a quick kiss of reward. Darlene looked hopefully at John to see if he'd recovered enough from his encounter with Carlene; she was looking forward to taking his big cock up inside her. She could only imagine what that was going to feel like and she could feel her arousal level increasing. She noticed that Carlene was just smirking at her, aware of what she'd been thinking. It turned out that John was fully recovered and ready for a second go at the twins so Carlene got the man with the smallest cock while Darlene got John. The twins were quite amused that they were going to be experiencing such a difference and couldn't help but giggle as they took the men to the bedroom. Carlene recognized that part of their amusement stemmed from their state of exhaustion and decided that they should take a break once these men had finished their task. She knew that they would be able to handle the men once more once they'd rested a bit and hoped that at least two of them would be able to rouse themselves for a third time.

Once back inside the bedroom, the twins started to lead the two men to their favoured positions but John balked a little; he didn't feel comfortable trying to fuck Darlene in the missionary position and would prefer to take her like he'd earlier taken Carlene. He told them of his preference and the two girls looked at each other for a few seconds before deciding that it probably made sense. So Carlene ended up on her back while Darlene knelt over her; the twins smiled happily at each other over the change in their positions. Carlene watched Darlene's face intently as John worked his massive cock into her. Darlene cooed with pleasure as John filled her sloppy pussy; she really relished his size and how it stretched her out. She was somewhat surprised about how deep inside her he was but groaned loudly with pleasure. Carlene was so intent on her sister that she barely registered what the man fucking her was doing; he was an okay fuck but nothing fantastic. He came before five minutes had passed and Darlene was still fighting to establish a good rhythm with John and his massive cock. Carlene remained on her back, watching and stroking her sister as John worked his prick in and out of her. She could tell that Darlene was likely primed enough to orgasm with the big prick inside her and she wanted to watch it happen. John took his time with Darlene, being a little more tired than he had been previously. Darlene was arousing him quite a bit with her constant moaning of pleasure and the rocking of her hips as she accepted his thrusts but his earlier bout had robbed him of some of his stamina and affected his ability to cum. Therefore he was taking longer inside Darlene. He could sense that she was on the verge of an orgasm and he desperately wanted to take her there. He was hoping that the twins would make him a regular part of their sex lives and he was looking forward to repeat performances but knew that he had to impress them with his style for that to happen. He changed his rhythm and realized that he'd made a mistake when Darlene hissed "No" at him so he re-established his pace. Darlene moaned her approval and he worked in and out of her for about a minute more.

Suddenly, Darlene squealed as she felt herself let go and she clamped down her vaginal muscles around his big cock. John felt the powerful squeeze as she orgasmed and he couldn't prevent himself from letting go inside her. It felt as though a massive, warm vice had fastened itself around his prick. He enjoyed the wonderful sensation as he emptied his balls into the willing woman. He felt tremendously tired once he was finished but it was a wonderful feeling of exhaustion. Darlene was flopping, moaning and writhing beneath him as she enjoyed the aftermath of her orgasm; she pulled herself off of John's deflating prick. Carlene quickly rolled up to her knees and pushed Darlene over on her side before working her fingers between her twin's legs. She exposed and rubbed her sister's clitoris, attempting to push Darlene into a second orgasm. It took her less than a minute to accomplish that task and Darlene was soon spurting John's cum out of her pussy with the force of that second orgasm. Carlene happily licked it up off the bed and her sister as Darlene lay there panting with exhaustion. Carlene could tell that Darlene was fairly dazed by the force of her orgasms and would need some time to recover. She gave John a big grin and looked around for the man who'd fucked her before realizing that he had left the bedroom sometime during the proceedings without her even realizing it. She shrugged her shoulders before pulling John to her to give him a long congratulatory kiss.

They went out in the living room to find that the second man had left and the fifth man was just leaving; both of them realized that the twins weren't really going to be interested in them so they moved on. Carlene wasn't disappointed that they had recognized their future and she was sure that Darlene would feel the same way. John went over and sank into one of the armchairs, he knew that he needed time to recover and probably was done performing for the evening. He was extremely pleased by his encounters with both twins, if it was never repeated, he was sure that he'd remember it until his dying day but he was hoping for repeats of it. Carlene went and squeezed in between the two remaining men who were seated near each other on the couch. She kissed and fondled them both in turn while allowing them to return the favour; she needed some time to recover a bit and then would check to see if Darlene would be interested in continuing. She thought there was a real possibility that Darlene would want to rest for the remainder of the night. She decided that if that were the case, she'd fuck these two men herself and then see if she could get John aroused for a third time. As she looked at him, she was doubtful that she would be able to do that. But, she thought, never mind, it had still been a great evening and they would be able to recapture some of it in the future.

ABBY FUCKS HER NEIGHBOUR STEVIE

Abby was in a truly miserable mood. She'd broken up with her boyfriend John because he wanted to become too serious about their relationship and she was nowhere near ready to settle down to become a good little wife. She loved getting screwed and usually craved more than one man at a time; she knew that John wouldn't put up with that if he married her. And the bastard had made it clear that he wasn't about to continue fucking her unless she made a commitment to that marriage. He'd even mentioned that what they were doing was sinful, she thought disbelievingly. As if Abby gave a damn about what the church and its members thought about her. She recognized that John would demand that she take more heed about their wants if they were married. I'm not about to agree to that straitjacket, she thought determinedly. But it did leave her without a guy to give her a regular plowing she thought sadly. She pondered just going to the bar and letting whatever man pick her up and fuck her but she knew that most of the men in the bars in this town were married or dating women that she probably knew. She would be returning to college in the fall and didn't want to cause any other woman distress just because of her needs; she believed in sisterhood. So she faced the prospect of going the whole summer with just her fingers and dildo to satisfy her needs; that was more than three months, she thought miserably. She would probably explode from her need by that time.

Then her neighbour Stevie lumbered into the kitchen; he'd been cutting the grass out in the hot sun, was sweaty and bare-chested. He went over to the refrigerator to get himself a cool drink; she knew that he often cut their lawn for them and that her father had told him to help himself to the drinks. Abby eyed him with interest, watching the sweat roll down over his nicely defined chest muscles to his flat stomach. He was wearing a pair of shorts that were fairly tight and if he wasn't enhancing himself, he had a nice bulge in them. She was aware that he had turned eighteen just six months earlier, which did make him legal. She was only fifteen months older than him and would be turning just twenty in the fall. She was also aware that by the time she'd been his age, she'd had quite a few sexual encounters with a number of men. She'd often teased him with her body in the ten years that they had lived next door to each other and she wondered if he came over so often just to get a look at her. She'd always been with men older than herself and began to contemplate the possibilities of teaching a younger man; Stevie looked as though he still didn't have too much in the way of sexual experience. Hmmm, she thought wickedly, the possibilities abound; she knew that she got extremely aroused when she played the bad girl. Something about breaking societal conventions just pumped her brain with hormones making her body respond in kind. She'd enjoyed breaking her parent's rules when she was younger to get lectured by her angry mother; the mental picture of her mother screaming at her could still make her pussy twitch. And then, they'd moved on to her father spanking her when that wasn't working. That had quickly stopped when her mother caught her fingering herself to orgasm in her room after one really hard spanking. Her parents then realized that she was getting herself caught just to be disciplined. She was aware that her mother wanted to talk to her about her abnormal sexual needs but was afraid to; both her parents had tried to talk her into seeing a psychiatrist but she steadfastly refused. She knew that she was unlike all her friends but she relished her differences.

She noticed that Stevie had observed her careful scrutiny and was busy taking in an eyeful of her in return. She grinned broadly and pushed her firm, round tits forward against the scraps of material that barely covered her erect nipples. She giggled as she saw his eyes widen and was ecstatic to see his shorts bulge. He seemed unable to decide whether to look at her tits, where her nipples were hardening enough to tent their coverings or down between her legs, where she was aware that some of her pussy hair was sneaking out of the legs of her short cutoffs. Abby knew that she was considered beautiful; she was five foot five with a trim body that displayed its share of curves and had a lively, pretty face. It was oval, with a cute nose, wide, plump mouth and a set of dazzling grey-blue eyes. Most men would do anything if she just smiled at them in hopes of getting inside her pants; the fact that she had a reputation of allowing that often just enhanced her effect on them. She was currently taking the pill and had an IUD jammed up her cunt to prevent her from becoming pregnant; besides, even if those two precautions failed, she was prepared to have any baby aborted. One of the reasons that she had to break from John had been the realization that the bastard was hoping to impregnate her in order to insist that they get married. He hadn't been made aware of her precautions, she thought smugly.

So, she thought, rather coyly, there really wasn't a good reason not to fuck her younger neighbour and plenty of delicious ones why she should. She arched her back to give him a good look at her tits and purred "Do you have a girlfriend, Stevie."

She could see him gulp and look miserable as he watched her tits strain her bikini top even more. "No, I don't, Abby" he said shyly as he ducked his eyes briefly before returning them to her erect nipples. Abby wondered briefly why that would be, he seemed nice, well-built if too shy for his own good; he should be good boyfriend material. She wasn't aware that all of the girls who knew him were also aware of her and his desperate attraction to her. He wasn't boyfriend material as far as they were concerned.

"Maybe I can give you some help in that department" she said, flashing a brilliant smile at him.

Stevie just moaned as he pictured what she would look like, nude and writhing underneath him. He was tired of taking care of his own needs and the fact that his neighbour was so beautiful and frequently barely dressed really pushed his buttons hard. He felt that he was spending most of his life up in his bedroom, stroking his cock. He was aware that he shouldn't be looking at his neighbour in that way but she seemed to enjoy teasing him with her body any chance she got and it was hard not to respond. He was only flesh and blood, he thought miserably. He was fully aware of her reputation and had seen the results of her dalliances by the number of men that left her home early in the morning. He knew that her parents had long ago decided that they couldn't possibly control her and left her to her own devices. He'd begun to suspect that living next to her was a version of Hell.

She smirked at him and purred "I'm gonna fuck you until your balls are dry and you're gonna beg me for more. You're gonna learn a lot this summer, neighbour." Then she smiled in a menacing way and hissed "And if you know what's good for you, you're gonna learn it the first time. I'm gonna train you well enough that I'll be proud to acknowledge the fact to any future wife that you might have." Then she smiled sweetly as Stevie cringed, both at the implication of punishment to come and that she might enjoy telling his future wife that she'd been the one who taught him to fuck. But he pushed both thoughts aside as he contemplated what fucking her was going to be like; he could feel his cock straining and began to worry about premature ejaculation. He remembered cumming in his pants a few times when she'd hugged him hard and rubbed her wonderful tits against his chest. Then he wondered if she'd recognized what she had done to him and realized that she did it a number of times during a six month period of his life and must have known her effect on him. As he looked at her right then, he could see that she was eying how large the bulge in his shorts was. She knew what she'd been doing to him, God damn it, and he'd tried very hard to convince himself that she'd been doing it without realizing his reaction. He knew that she was an evil bitch but he hadn't quite realized how evil; God, he wanted to fuck her so badly, it tortured him as he pictured her writhing and moaning under him. Oh fuck, he thought as he pushed that image down, I'm gonna cum before she even touches me.

Abby watched as Stevie processed what she'd said; she could see his cock grow and assumed that he was picturing her. Men were so predictable, she thought, hiding a grin, flash them a bit of tit and rub their little cocks and they'd do anything for you. She admitted that she got aroused at the prospect of making Stevie her little bitch; the poor bastard had no idea about what she was going to put him through that summer before she was satisfied that he'd learned how to properly fuck a woman. She knew that she liked to see men in pain and if they bled as well, she creamed her panties. She licked her plump lips in anticipation. Of course, she thought, she'd have to start him fairly slow and suck him in so that he'd agree to whatever she wanted. She'd hold back her urges and let him have some rewards from her so that she could have her way with him at a later date. Of course, she'd always hurt him a little bit so that he would have a reminder of their time together. He might not appreciate her little presents but she would and that was really all that mattered to her. She'd be able to smile sweetly at him when he winced because of something she'd done to him. Besides, she thought, he deserved some pain for wanting to fuck her so much; that was an immoral thing to do, sex outside of marriage, and God said to punish people if they acted immorally, didn't he. She let out a little giggle.

Stevie was a bit worried about the expression on her face and the intenseness of her eyes as he stood in front of her wondering what he should do next. She solved the problem by reaching out her hand and when he took it, she led him up to her bedroom. As they entered, he breathed in deeply; the room smelled of her perfume and underneath that was the wonderful musky smell that must be her own scent. He'd often tried to get whiffs of it from her room whenever he passed her doorway. To him it was ambrosia; he remembered jacking off a number of times when he'd been lucky enough to inhale a dose of it. She was fairly messy and he could see some of her clothes lying around. He almost groaned aloud when he saw a pile of her tiny panties lying near the corner. He'd always fantasized about having a used pair of her panties to use as a prop to masturbate but she was fairly careful about ensuring that he was never able to get them. He wondered why that was. She led him over to the bed and pushed him down onto it before she whisked off her tiny top. He gaped as he got a good look at her round, plump tits, having only gotten quick glimpses of them previously; her nipples were a reddish-brown and stood prominently from the small encircling aureoles. He noted how white her skin was, she didn't like tanning because she felt that it would wrinkle her skin, and her nipples stood out from her paleness.

She saw him looking intently at her breasts and reached down to caress herself; she grabbed hold of her right breast with her left hand and gave it a good squeeze so that the nipple popped up. She rolled the nipple in between her thumb and forefinger, enjoying the sensations that she felt; she heard Stevie moan and stare harder. As she continued to fondle herself, she regarded him as she thought about how she was going to handle him; it was obvious to her that he was going to cum as soon as she touched him in any way. That would be disappointing she thought but he was so revved up there didn't seem to be any way around it. "Do you masturbate, Stevie?" she asked as she let her breast drop.

Stevie coloured a bit and muttered, feeling shame, "Yes I do."

"Well, I do too. Almost everyone does it. Most people just don't have the confidence to admit it. It's not a big thing. How long does it take for you to recover? I assume you've done it more than once in a day" she asked, in a slightly soothing tone because she didn't want him being too ashamed to tell her the truth.

"Uh, about fifteen minutes or so and then I can get hard again."

"Wonderful. Do you find that it takes longer to achieve your second orgasm? Most men I know do."

"Yeah" he replied, a sheepish look on his face. "I find that it takes me a few minutes longer to ejaculate the second time and longer for the third."

Abby was quite happy to hear him talk about a third ejaculation; perhaps she would be able to enjoy herself for longer than she'd thought. Of course, one of the first things she'd have to train him to do would be to hold back on his initial ejaculation but that would take some time and punishment to do. She knew that he wouldn't be able to do that today, given his obvious condition. "Okay" she said sweetly. "That's fine. You seem pretty excited right now and I'm guessing that you're gonna cum if I stroke your dick, aren't you." She waited while he nodded shamefacedly and then continued "That's okay for now. We will work on that. The first thing for you to know is this. Any sperm that goes into or onto me is going to go in your mouth and you are going to swallow it like a good little boy. Do you understand?"

Stevie looked at her with a very confused look on his face. He'd heard the words and understood what she was telling him but he couldn't believe that she meant what she was saying. "What?" he asked slowly.

She looked crossly at him. "It's really simple. If you want to continue to fuck me, you lick your sperm off of me. If you blow cum all over my tits, you clean them off with your tongue. If you cum in my pussy, your tongue hunts down all of the sperm in it until I am clean. If you're not prepared to do that, then we won't fuck." She turned around and walked to the door. "You can leave anytime that you want" she said angrily, holding her door open.

Stevie sat there with his mind whirling; he desperately wanted to fuck her but was hesitant to agree to what she was demanding. What should he do, he wondered as he gave a small moan of desperation. Abby heard him moan and waited. She knew that if he agreed to this, he'd be easy enough for her to manipulate into more intense measures in the future. She figured that he was horny enough to agree to it and it gave her a good handle over him; besides, she liked it when men licked their cum off of her body. She could see him trying to tense up to leave but he couldn't;

she knew that she had him then. She smiled at him and fondled her tit again. He moaned once more and stated "Fine. I agree to lick any of my cum off of you."

"No" she corrected. "Any cum that you put onto me or into me goes down your throat."

"Fine, that's what I agree to" he said quietly, feeling his dick straining hard against his shorts. God, he wanted her so badly, he thought desperately.

"Good" she said as she shut the door and came back over to him. "Since you're gonna cum quickly, I'm going to give you a quick blowjob. Once you've orgasmed in my mouth, I'm gonna kiss you and transfer your cum into your mouth. Then you're gonna hold it in there until I give you permission to swallow it. I want you to roll it around your mouth so that you get a good taste of it." She gave him another intense look and hissed "Do you agree?"

He gave her a miserable look, thinking she can't really mean that; she's just bluffing to get me to do whatever she wants. Then he realized that she really did mean what she said and that if he wanted to fuck her, he was going to have to enjoy the taste of his own cum. He wondered what it tasted like. He knew that girls had to learn to tolerate the taste of their boyfriend's cum so he was sure that he could too. He wondered briefly if swallowing your own cum would be considered a gay thing to do. He thought that the fact that he would be taking it from his hot female neighbour would kind of negate the gayness of the act. Besides, what did it really matter. He knew that he was going to agree to do it so that he could fuck her repeatedly. "I agree" he replied, his voice cracking.

Abby stood there a moment longer, looking him over, examining him for any signs that he might try to renege. She knew that she held all of the cards, if he balked, she wouldn't continue fucking him but she wanted him compliant and willing to do as she demanded. If he balked and she didn't continue with him, she'd have to find another amusement and it might take a while. She had needs that she wanted taken care of immediately. She decided that he meant what he said and proceeded. "Take off your shorts, underwear and socks" she commanded. "Then stand there so that I can look you over. You will focus your eyes on a spot in front of your feet and keep focused on it no matter what I do to you. If you move or look away, your balls will get smacked. Do you understand?" He nodded his head. She struck him across the face as hard as she could, bloodying his lip. He sat there in shock. "When I tell you to do something, you say 'Yes, Mistress' in a clear voice as you are complying. If I feel that you are slow at doing what I want, you get punished. Now, do you understand?"

"Yes, Mistress" he replied as he stood up and took off his clothes before standing there looking at the floor.

"Excellent" she purred, thinking that he deserved a reward. She could be a kind mistress when her pet obeyed her so quickly, she thought. She decided to reward him and stepped up to him and kissed his bloody mouth lightly. He tried to put his arms around her and bring her closer to him so she punched him in the stomach. She didn't hit him as hard as she could but it was still a fairly solid shot. He bent over, surprised and she stepped back from him. "Your hands always remain behind your back unless I direct you otherwise" she told him firmly. "Now stand up, spread your legs and let me see you."

He stood up and moved his feet about twenty inches apart; she stood back and took a good look at his bobbing prick. It appeared to be about seven or seven and a half inches long, was a nice girth and had a nice pink, velvety head. It was nowhere near the biggest that she'd seen but it wasn't the smallest either; it would do quite well and she knew that she'd enjoy riding it. But for now, it was twitching fairly rapidly, showing his intense arousal level. She'd have liked to have examined him further and rubbed her hands against him but she knew that he'd explode as soon as she touched him. Well, she thought, I better take care of matters before he cums on the floor. She pictured making him lick his cum up off the floor and was amused by the image but decided that it would be easier for him to take his first load from her mouth. No sense pushing him so hard that he refuses, she thought pragmatically. She knelt in front of him and placed her hands on his thighs as her mouth engulfed his erect member. He gave an excited guttural groan and reached forward to put his hands on her head. She tensed as she sensed him doing that but he remembered himself and quickly thrust his hands back behind him. She thought about punishing him but decided to let this small indiscretion go for now. She swallowed about five inches of his prick and used the base of her tongue to rub against his sensitive head. She quite liked the taste of a man's cock and his cum so having him in her mouth was no chore for her. She immediately tasted his pre-cum and readied herself for his load. It followed about five seconds later. She'd known that he would be on a hair trigger this first time but he'd have to work hard so that he wasn't so anxious in the future, she thought as she milked his cock. When she thought that she had most of his load in her mouth, not that she could really fit any more into it because he'd pumped out a healthy amount, she stood up and pulled his head down to hers. She pushed the salty liquid up into his mouth and then stood back to watch to see his reaction. He obediently rolled his cum around his mouth and she could see his surprise as he got its taste. She was pleased that he neither spat it out or swallowed it without permission. He began choking a bit and she said softly "Breath through your nose. You should be able to do that." He complied and shot her a grateful look.

She found it quite funny that he could stand there with a mouthful of his own cum and look gratefully at her but she didn't want him to see her laughing at him because it would ruin the mood she was trying to develop. So she stepped around him so that she could look over his backside. She wanted him to hold that warm cum in his mouth for quite a while anyways so that he would understand its taste and his own obedience. She was pleased with the muscular definition of his ass but slightly disappointed that his ass cheeks were fairly flat. Oh well, she thought, you can't have everything. She contemplated stroking his ass and running her finger up his crack but she figured that he'd most likely swallow his cum in surprise and she didn't want that yet so she refrained.

After a couple of minutes of standing behind him, admonishing him when he tried to turn towards her, she said softly "You may swallow." Then as he was doing that, she knelt in front of him to suck up any remaining cum so he could have that in his mouth. He was deflated but still not a bad size as she sucked his dick fairly quickly. When she was satisfied, she transferred that cum into his mouth again; this time she commanded him to swallow it right away. He did so with a bit of a sheepish look on his face. She ran her long fingernails through his chest hair, he wasn't too hairy yet and she liked what he had. He seemed to enjoy that action as well. She tweaked his nipples lightly while thinking about what she would be doing to them in the future; she pondered whether or not she could get him to have them pierced, well, she would see. Then she decided to get on with things. "Lie down on the bed" she commanded, giving him a firm pat on the ass.

When he complied, she straddled his face, looking down his body; she pushed her damp pussy down onto his mouth and commanded "Lick my cunt. I want you to make sure that all of it is sufficiently wet." She rocked her hips as his tongue was pressed against her crotch. She sat on his face for over five minutes, instructing him on how hard or soft to lick her various parts. His tongue felt pretty good but she thought that he would need a lot more practice before he could be considered to perform well. Oh well, she thought mockingly, I guess I'll have to sacrifice myself and get him to eat my pussy a couple of times a day. She could feel her arousal level rise at that prospect and felt the tingle that usually preceded her orgasm. She looked down at his crotch and saw that his prick was stirring nicely.

She pressed her wet cunt down over his face so that she covered both his mouth and nose; he made a muffled sound of protest but didn't try to dislodge her. She was pleased about that and removed herself after about twenty seconds. She slipped off of him and looked down at his face. He had a ring of her juices around his mouth area; she thought he looked quite cute that way. "You're going to lay there while I fuck you" she told him firmly. "I want you to hold onto the bars at the top of the bed while I ride you. If you remove your hands from the bars, I'll smack you. If you do it too often, I'll climb off of you and we won't continue unless you agree to be bound. I would prefer for you to do this voluntarily. If you can't obey me, then there is no reason for me to fuck you. Do you understand?" He nodded eagerly and started to say "Yes" but she held her finger to his mouth to shush him.

He looked at her with eyes sparkling with excitement as she slid her leg over his belly before scooting down lower on him to straddle his crotch. She saw that she'd left a wet trail across his skin and was amused by the fact. She was fairly excited and could feel her heart pounding in her chest. She reached down between her legs and found that he was stiffening nicely once more. She pressed the head of his prick against her wet, lubricated slit and pressed down on him, putting three inches of his cock into her pussy. She stopped and looked at him expectantly. He looked back at her, puzzled, until she indicated with her eyes that he should be holding the bars above his head. He shamefacedly grabbed them and she pushed herself further onto him. She rocked her hips against him, enjoying the feeling of his cock up inside of her. She began a slow thrusting against him, putting her hands on his chest to steady herself. She kept up the slow motion, moaning low in pleasure, as he filled her and then didn't as she rode him. She kept that up for three minutes or so and he joined her in moaning his approval. She wondered how long he could last at the slow pace, knowing that most men needed more friction to maintain their erection. She decided that since it was their first time and she didn't want a failure that she would make him cum fairly quickly. It wouldn't be as satisfying for her but she knew that she had to make the sacrifice so that he would remain in her control. If he got too frustrated with her, he would balk at being commanded about what to do; besides, he'd been fairly good and she was willing to reward him for that. She leaned hard onto her arms, sucked in a deep breath and started lowering and raising her body against him rapidly. She could feel the friction between them increase and he moaned with pleasure.

She kept her pace up for about a minute and a half, feeling sweat break out over her body from her effort. He was grunting now as she smacked her hips against his and she could sense that he was about to climax. Suddenly she felt his spurt into her and she enjoyed the warm sensation deep in her cunt. She stopped her motion on him to let him finish without letting any of his cum escape her tight cunt. She wanted to make sure that she kept most of it in her so that he could lick it out of her wet pussy. She watched as he strained to shoot a second load into her and smiled happily. They were going to have such fun together, she thought.

MERRY OLD MRS. CLAUS

The elves were all a twitter, Christmas Eve was here and Santa would soon be away with a packed sled to deliver all of the presents to the good little boys and girls of the world. Once Santa was safely on his way, Mrs. Claus would be in charge and for twenty-four hours the elves would have to do everything that she instructed them to do. Every elf knew that the crafty old lady had big plans for what was to happen this year and she had been working on something in secret for over six months. No one was quite sure about what was planned by her but for about a month now, her favourite elf Susannah had been seen staggering around some mornings looking exceedingly tired. There was only two more hours until Santa left and Mrs. Claus had a bunch of the elves baking cookies; which was good, because all of the elves loved cookies, especially Christmas ones.

Santa was off and as soon as he disappeared past the horizon, Mary Claus called all the elves together in the workroom. The workroom had been emptied of all the tools and parts; it now was filled with tables that were covered with cookies and there were a number of different areas that had a video game console, tv and a number of comfortable chairs. The elves entered, chattering noisily amongst themselves and Mary Claus sat on a chair and waited patiently for them to settle themselves and quiet down. She knew that she had lots of time to put her plan into action and was actually enjoying the anticipation of what was about to happen. She hummed one of her favourite Christmas carols as she waited. Susannah was nowhere near as patient; she'd been the one that Mrs. Claus had practiced on and she was anxious to get her turn at being the one giving than the one receiving. Mrs. Claus hid a smile as she watched Susannah fidgeting, knowing exactly what was going through her mind; Susannah finally stepped forward and called for silence so that Mrs. Claus could tell them what she wanted them to do.

When they had all quieted down, Mary Claus stood up and in clear tones said "I want to thank all of you for your hard work this year. As you know, we could never achieve what we do without your exhausting labour. For you male elves, these tables of cookies and video games are for you to enjoy for the time that Santa is gone. We all know that we will have to start on the new year as soon as he gets back so enjoy your break. You've earned it." She smiled warmly at them as they cheered her welcome present. "Now, you female elves, please follow Susannah and I. We have something special planned just for us ladies." The nineteen other female elves all began to gather near the doorway as they wondered what it was that Mrs. Claus had planned for them, most of them would have been happy to share in the cookies and video games with the guys. Nevertheless, Mrs. Claus led them out of the workshop and down to one of the now empty storage buildings that she and Susannah had been setting up and decorating for this occasion. The elves murmured happily amongst themselves as they made their short way over to the hut.

Mrs. Claus led them into a sexy wonderland; there was soft furnishings gathered in a number of areas, with tables loaded with every sex toy imaginable and a number of small sets of sexy clothing draped nearby. There were erotic paintings and photographs adorning the wall in amongst the Christmas decorations, streamers and wreaths. Best of all, thought the female elves, there were plates of cookies that looked even more fabulous than the ones the boys had. When they turned to look at Mrs. Claus, she had removed her heavy red cloak and was now clad in only a tight red leather body suit attached to black silk stockings. What had seemed to be fashionable, high leather boots suitable for trudging in the snow now took on a slightly more sexy, menacing meaning. Mrs. Claus grinned sexily at them as she reached back and unfastened her bound hair, shaking it out and making them realize that it really wasn't grey as they had always assumed but was more of an ash blonde. She was also displaying a very nice young figure with a plump bust, narrow waist and wide hips; in her leather outfit she looked like a wet dream. Most of the female elves stared hungrily at her as they began to realize exactly what she had in mind; there was a small rush as they ran over to claim their favourite costumes. They were all cute little women with slightly pointed ears, narrow foxy faces and lush figures themselves; they certainly didn't have a problem with sexuality and all considered bi-sexuality to be the norm.

Susannah brought out the costume that she had put away for herself; it was a short slinky black dress that fit her like a second skin with garter belt and stockings. She lifted her hat and shook out her long black hair before proceeding to change into the outfit. She admired herself in the full length mirror before going over to where Mary Claus now sat in the middle of the room on a straightback wooden chair. Part of their practicing had been for what was going to happen now and Susannah was extremely excited about her part in it. She could feel her tight pussy getting exceedingly wet. She noticed that most of the elves were busy getting into the spirit of things and there were only two who appeared to be still looking around uncertainly. She saw that Mary called them over to her and talked to them in a low voice so she delayed making her way over to them. After the conversation, both of the elves nodded and one left, while the other went over to join in with the other elves. When she walked up to Mary, she asked "What did you tell them?"

"I just told them that if they weren't comfortable with what we had planned for here tonight, they could go over and join the guys. That there would be no hard feelings from anyone here. I only want elves here who wish to be here. This is a present, not a punishment." Susannah nodded her agreement and went up to lean against Mary, seeking a kiss; of course, Mary responded and they kissed deeply with Mary probing Susannah's mouth with her long, pointed tongue. Susannah could feel her arousal rise even more as Mary wiggled her tongue around. By now, most of the other elves had changed and were gathering around them, regarding them with keen interest. A number of them had realized what the large, soft pillows scattered around were intended for and brought them over to sit on.

Mary finally broke their kiss and looked around, noticing that some of the elves were still scattered around the room and she decided that it was time to gather them all in. She was very pleased that there had only been one dissenter in the group because she had expected more. She called out, loudly and firmly, "If all of you ladies would finish your preparations and join us over here then we can get started. There is a lot that we would like to do and although it may seem that we have lots of time to do it in I think we will find that time goes by very quickly when you're having fun. I want everyone here to remember that what we want to do here is have fun. If you find that something isn't fun for you, feel free to not participate." There were a few minutes that passed until everyone was ready.

Then Mary Claus assisted Susannah off with her dress, leaving her clad only in garter belt, stockings and heels; the watching group of women ohhed and ahhed their appreciation for her boldness and beauty. Mrs. Claus arranged her outfit slightly and patted her knee. Susannah quickly leapt into her lap so that her bare rear end was just on her right knee and sticking up towards the roof. Mary gave the plump little bottom a soft caress and then raised up her hand and brought it down sharply; Susannah squalled slightly in surprise and appreciation. There was a murmur of shock and anticipation as the elves could see the red imprint of Mary's hand on the pale white ass of the pretty elf. Some of them moved forward or sat up slightly to get better points of view to watch the proceedings; Mary was happy to see that some of them were starting to fondle themselves somewhat as they got further into the spirit of things. She had figured that this would be a good ice breaker for the party and they had discovered that Susannah really liked being spanked. She delivered another nine blows to the proffered ass in rapid fashion with Susannah making noisy protests each time she was struck. As Mary looked around the room, a lot of the elves were openly stroking their own pussies because of their arousal and she could smell the pleasant odour of stimulated female; she thought that it made a enjoyable change from the usual scent of pine and cookies.

She reached down and tilted the elf's head toward her to determine if she should continue or move onto something else; Susannah was crying, with big fat tears running down her cheeks, but she gave Mary a saucy grin, confirming that she wanted more spanking. So Mary straightened the elf's head once more and slapped her a further five times before stopping and giving the flushed, red ass a few comforting strokes. Susannah was very noisily sobbing now and the remaining elves watch anxiously, wondering if she was really hurt or not. Both Mary and Susannah were aware that Susannah could take a lot more punishment but she liked being the center of attention, so she cried as hard as she could; Mary could feel the dampness on her thigh and knew that the elf had orgasmed during the punishment. She was happy and somewhat aroused by the other woman's enjoyment of the spanking, knowing that she would never be interested in being the one spanked. A number of the elves crowded around them, interested in receiving the same treatment but they had decided that Susannah would be the only one spanked that night. Susannah liked that decision because it would leave her with a mark of distinction and Mary didn't want to hurt her arm spanking a lot of eager elves, there were more fascinating things to do. So Mary eased the sore elf off of her lap and was amused that three other elves immediately came up to comfort and caress her.

"Now, we're going to move onto something different. Do I have a volunteer?" Immediately about eight hands shot into the air. Mary surveyed them and made her selection. She chose a blonde who had chosen a naughty school girl outfit. The elf skipped her way to the front as Mary reached behind her and brought out what looked like a small leather saddle from the items piled behind her. The blonde elf looked at it, confused, until Mary demonstrated that there was a dildo attached to the seat; then the elf knew exactly what it was for. She grinned appreciatively as she walked her way up to beside Mary. Mary helped her to remove her skirt so that it wouldn't interfere and the blonde sat down on the saddle slightly behind the dildo so that she could find the best position in which to ride it. She raised herself up somewhat and shuffled forward over the dildo; she used her right hand to ensure that the dildo would go where it should and pushed her hips down on it until it entered her a few inches. She muttered some noises of appreciation about how it felt in her before raising up and then pushing down a little harder. The blonde could feel the dildo spreading her pussy lips and groaned a little more in enjoyment. She continued her movements until she was engulfing the dildo completely and then she worked on how fast she wanted it penetrating her. The other elves watched her raptly. She could feel that there were a lot of liquids starting to drip from her excited pussy onto the soft leather saddle and that she was building to a climax. A few more thrusts onto the plastic dong and she came, pushing her hips down hard so that her cunt spasmed with the dildo deep inside her. She let out a tremendous screech of happiness. The hubbub of the watching women increased and there was more than one moan of climax from them; Mary smiled slyly as she could see that the party was heading towards a great success. She let the blonde elf remain where she was impaled on the saddle and called for another volunteer; almost all of the group of watching elves put up her hand and waved it vigorously.

Mary looked them over carefully and then chose a really short redhead who had chosen a sexy reindeer outfit. She beckoned the elf forward and the girl pranced prettily up to her; clearly she was enjoying her playacting and was milking it for all that it was worth. "Take off the clothing but leave your antlers on" Mary commanded imperiously. The girl began to do as ordered and Mary continued "You know what the reindeers like being done to them, don't you?" She waited as all the elves smiled and shook their heads negatively. "They love to take it up the ass" Mary crowed loudly.

"No" shouted the shocked elves.

"Oh, yes. Why do you think that Prancer prances so much." The elves looked at each other, confused; none of them thought that Prancer acted any different than the other reindeer. Then Mary Claus cackled with laughter and the elves realized that she was kidding with them and began to laugh as well. "Nonetheless, Vicky here has just volunteered to take a vibrator up her ass" Mrs. Claus said with a grin. Vicky looked at her with wide eyes and then started to smile; she was into anal play in a big way and looked forward to what was going to be done to her. The rest of the group cheered loudly as they looked forward to the show. Mary brought out a long slim anal vibrator and motioned for Vicky to bring over an ottoman she could perch on while Mary sodomized her with the pink toy. Vicky enthusiastically brought over the ottoman and perched herself on it with her rear end up and facing Mrs. Claus. Mary spread the small elf's ass cheeks and put a large dollop of KY jelly on her rosebud; she spent a few minutes working it up into the elf, noting with some amusement that the girl really liked having that done to her and was vociferously voicing her approval. Mary then spent a moment coating the long, pink toy so that it would slide in easier. When she was satisfied that all was ready, she pushed the slightly bulbous end up against the redhead's asshole and began teasing her with it to get her used to what was going to happen to her. Vicky moaned loudly as she felt herself getting very wet from arousal and began to wish that Mrs. Claus would work a little faster; she felt a need to be penetrated.

Mary determined that the short elf was as ready as she'd ever be so she pushed nearly three inches of the toy into her; Vicky gave a loud moan of ecstasy as the toy entered her. She was in heaven and wanted even more. Mary just let her feel the toy's penetration for a moment before she started working it even deeper; once she had nearly five inches up the elf's asshole, she started up the vibrator. Vicky felt the toy's movement deep inside her and gave a small yelp of surprise before settling into a steady moaning of appreciation. She began bobbing her small ass, pushing back against the thrusts of Mrs. Claus. Mary could see that Vicky was really getting aroused by what was being done to her; Vicky's thighs were coated with liquid and a small damp spot was forming on the ottoman. She decided to tease the small redhead and began pulling the toy out of her; Vicky let out a squawk of outrage and tried to follow the retreating toy. Mary laughed, a touch cruelly, and then pushed it back deeper inside the elf. Vicky let out a gasp of pleasure. Mary spent a few minutes twisting the toy around and thrusting it in and out of Vicky pushing her close to an orgasm. She could see from the quivering of the redhead's small pussy lips that the elf was about to blow so she reached down between Vicky's legs and tugged on her erect clitoris. Vicky shouted as she came and the small damp spot became a large wet spot. Mrs. Claus decided to leave Vicky alone so that she could recover and went looking for her next partner.

"Okay, who's volunteering to be next?" she asked with a smirk and all of the remaining elves lifted their hands and shouted for her attention. They were all very happy about what was going on and wanted to be involved. "We're going to take a break after this one for some cocoa and cookies. Then I want to see all of you girls in action with one another, entertaining me for a change. But first, I select you" she said as she pointed to one of the tallest of them, a brunette with a nice body and pretty face. The elf quickly came up and joined Mrs. Claus; she was wearing a naughty nurse outfit that barely covered her chest and showed off a lot of her legs. Mary got out a mat and a strap-on belt with dildo and began arranging the mat in front of the group. The brunette fastened her eyes to the dildo, certain that Mary was going to use it on her; she was joyful that she was going to be able to participate in that way. Mary knelt on the mat and pulled the elf towards her, unfastening her outfit as she did. Mary wanted the elf to kneel down in front of her so that she could penetrate her pussy from behind and she guided the other woman into position.

Once Mary was satisfied that the elf was in a good position to receive the dildo and she could see the small cunt gaping in readiness and anticipation, she entered the brunette with the long, baby blue toy. The elf bucked her hips slightly while making a noise of happiness as the tip penetrated her; she was quite happy about the size, it seemed to fill her up completely. Mary kept the thrusts shallow and slow initially, to get the elf to lubricate the dildo and allow her to widen her cunt to accommodate it entirely; they spent about five minutes in this type of foreplay before Mary started pushing it deeper into the other woman. As soon as she had the elf fully breached, she began using her right hand to guide the elf's hips at the rate of speed that she wanted the elf to move them at while her left hand caressed the bobbing left breast of the other woman. The elf began to make a lot of sound regarding how much she was enjoying the fucking and Mary smirked with pleasure, feeling her own pussy twitch in response. Mary decided that after the cookie break, she was going to seek out Susannah and have the elf give her some oral relief from her sexual tensions. But she remembered, now was the time that she was busy screwing another of the elves and she concentrated on assisting that elf to set a pace that allowed her to stimulate her orgasm. Mary grinned as the smaller woman started panting and groaning loudly as she felt the pressures build within her; Mary began hesitating a bit as she thrust in to allow the woman to enjoy and respond better to the toy spearing her wet cunt. A few more minutes and the elf climaxed with a din that made Mary want to cover her ears for a moment; she was overjoyed that the elf had enjoyed it so much but her reaction was rather high pitched for the normal human ear. She carefully unsnapped the belt and worked her way out of it, leaving the long blue toy inserted in the elf's pulsating cunt. She'd let the elf deal with it once she'd recovered her senses enough to do so.

"Okay" she called to the other elves, most of whom had fingered themselves into orgasm. "We'll take some time to enjoy cookies and cocoa. I can see that most of you will need a little time to yourselves before you join us. So go ahead and take that time. Afterwards, we are going to continue the fun and frolics." She smiled at all of them and looked forward to continuing; knowing that so much more entertainment was going to happen in the near future.

CHARLEY-GIRL'S FIRST JOB

Charmaine Armstrong, better known to her friends and family as Charley-Girl, was a healthy young eighteen year old woman with a strong sex drive that she'd inherited from her mother. She'd approached her mother about sex back when she'd been barely past her eleventh birthday and her mother had explained a great number of matters to her, including why she often heard her mother's squeals of joy from her parent's bedroom. Her mother taught her the mechanics of sex and the restrictions she should be using until she wanted to become pregnant. Her mother suggested to her that she should pursue a solo act of satisfaction for a while and had taken her to a sex shop so she could pick out her first vibrator. Of course, Charley-Girl's eyes had lit up at the size of some of the toys in the shop and she'd begged her mother for the largest one. Her mother had laughed uproariously at her, before suggesting a much smaller one, barely four inches in length; Charley-Girl had been tremendously disappointed and showed it until her mother promised that they could come back to get a bigger one if she wasn't satisfied after trying it for a while. The woman running the sex shop knew her mother and was prepared to look the other way regarding the age restriction about the shop for Charley-Girl and her mother. She'd smiled brightly at them both as they went to pay for the purchase.

Then, the two of them had spent some very interesting afternoons together as her mother taught her how best to pleasure herself with her new toy. Charley-Girl had been very interested to see how easily her mother handled her bigger thicker dildos. She'd been incredibly turned on watching her mother push herself to orgasm and had wanted to become involved with her mother but the older woman had dissuaded her. Her mother explained that lesbianism could be immensely fun and that she herself enjoyed it but that Charley-Girl should learn about her own needs and desires first. Her mother told her that once she'd learned those, they could revisit whether or not they became more intimate with each other. Charley-Girl had eagerly shared her sexual knowledge with the girls she knew and was astounded to find out that none of their mothers had bothered to explain anything to them. She'd talked to her mother about that fact and her mother confided in her that she, rather than the other uptight mothers, was the one that most people in their small town considered to be abnormal. Charley-Girl could not understand that thinking at all and wondered why society seemed so fucked up. She knew of at least two of the older sisters of her young friends that had been impregnated by their boyfriends before they were done high school; she thought that a mother being frank with her daughter about sex and preparing her for her sexual life was a tremendously good thing.

Of course, openness about sexuality meant that one occasionally had to put up with some ribbing about sex; there had been the one morning, just before her sixteenth birthday when Charley-Girl had come down for Sunday breakfast to find a bag from the local sex shop sitting at her place at the table. Her younger brother and sister were already eating their pancakes and were watching her with interest as she sat at the table. She wondered what was in the bag; she had a fairly new vibrator that her mother had purchased for her and was still quite happy with it so she didn't think that it would be that and she hadn't expressed an interest in anything else lately. She opened the bag to find a leather ball gag with a bright red ball fastened to it. She had an idea of what the item was used for and wondered why her mother would think that she needed one; she wasn't prepared to start with any B&D practices just yet. She looked at her mother curiously and asked "Mom, why did you buy me a ball gag? Did you have something in mind?"

"Yes, I did, honey" her mother replied in a weary voice. "I know that you are a healthy young girl who has strong needs and that you enjoy taking care of those needs. I don't begrudge you that. But, honey, you like very early morning sex and you're goddamn noisy about it. You've woken the rest of the family from their sleep every morning this past week and we're getting a little tired of it. So, do us all a favour, and wear the ball-gag when you're masturbating in the early morning." She then favoured her somewhat embarrassed daughter with a smile and asked "Okay?"

She'd then looked at the grinning faces of her younger siblings and turned red a bit. She felt that it was unfair of her family to talk about her sex life in that way and then she realized that her mother had always been quite frank with her about anything sexual in nature. And, she thought, a little miserably, she could recall her mother suggesting that she learn to bite the pillow in the mornings which she hadn't bothered to do. So, she thought evenly, maybe she did deserve this somewhat. "Okay, I'll do that" she promised solemnly.

Then her father had spoiled her seriousness by coming into the kitchen and asking "Has the early morning rooster agreed to curb her activities a little so that the rest of the family can get their beauty sleep?" That caused her brother and sister to break up into convulsions of laughter.

But now Charley-Girl was starting a new job as a clerk in a large warehouse; she would be responsible for all of the paperwork required by the head office and she would report to the woman who ran the administration. She would be the only female on sight and her new boss had warned her that the men at the warehouse, mostly fairly young in age, could be very rough on women in general. They'd had a number of instances where the previous clerks had been harassed and had quit the company. The administration head had been quite worried about putting this young, dynamic, fairly pretty young girl in the job but her boss, the CEO, had directed her to do it. The CEO knew Charley-Girl's father and he'd been assured that she would be able to handle the harassment of the men.

Charley-Girl was about five foot five, had a fairly average body shape and long dark hair. She had a pleasant, plump, inviting face with a large mouth, straight nose and big blue eyes. She was intelligent, confident and had a very bawdy sense of humour. She'd been a girl that a number of boys had dated in high school and it was generally known that she'd awarded most of them with sex. But she currently didn't have a steady boyfriend. That meant that most of the girls were somewhat apprehensive with their boyfriends around her but she was still fairly friendly with most of them. The girls recognized that it was their boyfriend's fault if they strayed with Charley-Girl and that the boy wasn't worth their while if he succumbed to her charms. So she actually had a number of female friends.

On her first day, she wore a tight navy blue dress that exposed a great deal of her legs; she knew that it looked great on her. She arrived at the office of the yard, got out of her low-slung little car and strode confidently to the door. Some of the men were already working in the yard and three or four of them chose to catcall to her as she entered. She shot them a disdainful glance and then just ignored their juvenile attempts to attract her attention. The overall boss of the warehouse had been waiting for her in the lobby and was upset that she had received that reception; he had spoken to the men about how they treated women on the sight but felt powerless to do anything more. He didn't want to fire anyone because otherwise, he considered them to be good workers. He apologized to Charley-Girl and led her over to her desk in the reception. She told him that she would take care of matters before the week was out and he looked at her astounded. He wondered what she thought she could do with the men to change their attitudes.

At coffee the men were in their lunch room and Charley-Girl walked by, giving them a good look at her legs again. Once more, catcalls rang out and she just ignored them. She simply wanted to make sure that they all were aware of how good she looked.

When she left at the end of the day, a dozen or so of the men were waiting for her to come out and go to her car. They shouted their silly suggestions at her as she strode by not bothering to acknowledge them. These types of actions went on all week until Friday. The boss was quite worried that she was going to quit because of the men's harassment.

At lunch on Friday, about fifteen minutes before they were due back at the job, Charley-Girl entered the lunch room. She was wearing a black dress that exposed all of her assets to their full advantage. There were a number of catcalls and rude suggestions thrown about but she just stood there in front of them waiting for them to settle down. It took about five minutes for them to do so.

"You men seem to get some sort of perverse satisfaction about putting women down" she said firmly. "It really is too bad. If you children were real men and willing to act maturely around a person of the opposite sex, I'd be willing to reward you. But you appear to be uninterested." She paused, knowing that the men were keenly interested in what sort of reward she was talking about. "Think about this on the weekend. On Monday at coffee, if I am not molested on my arrival, I'll give you all a taste of what I mean." She gave them a winsome smile and then left.

That afternoon Harold, whom everyone called Hoss because of his size, issued a challenge; namely that anyone who catcalled or harassed Charley-Girl would answer to him. He'd never really participated in their harassment of the other women but he'd never bothered to say anything against it either. The two main culprits who'd encouraged the others to follow suit, looked at the size of Hoss, thought about his reputation for almost literally destroying other men in fights and decided that they would curtail their activities. All of the other men decided that discretion was the better part of valour as well.

Charley-Girl was expecting that the men would be waiting for her to leave and that she would have to endure some rude remarks from them since she had stated that the ban would start Monday morning. She figured that they would want to get in their last licks at her. She was surprised to see that although the men were working not too far from her car that they were very polite and just wished her a goodnight or nice weekend. She thought that she had done very well at handling the situation. It just took someone to be firm with them and promise them a treat, she thought smugly to herself. The men were very conscious of the big silent man amongst them, watching their actions.

Charley-Girl arrived on Monday morning wearing a small pink dress that displayed her charms quite well. She also wore her highest heeled pumps that made her ass wiggle tremendously when she walked in them. Once again there were a number of men who were working in the yard near where she parked. She displayed a fair bit of her legs as she worked her way out of her small car and wiggled her way over to the entrance. The men greeted her politely and she smiled back invitingly to them. The boss was surprised by her revealing outfit as she arrived and looked at her confused; he hadn't heard the usual catcalls and remarks, he thought. She smiled at him and he just nodded back to her. He decided that he would have to investigate what exactly was going on.

He called in his foreman and asked what was going on. "Well" said the foreman, reluctantly. "Apparently Charley-Girl visited them at lunch on Friday and promised them a reward if they stopped harassing her."

"And that did the job?"

"Well, no, not really. The fact that Hoss told them he'd pound the shit out of anyone who continued to harass her did the job. I guess that she influenced him enough to do that, though." The boss nodded and wondered if she knew about Hoss; somehow he really didn't think that she did. So he decided that he needed to let her know about it before she did something stupid.

He called Charley-Girl into his office and told her about the situation. She was upset that it hadn't been her actions that led to the cessation of the harassment but the actions of another man. She decided that she would give them the treat that she had promised them and then see what this man looked like. If she liked him she would reward him further, she thought.

At the morning coffee, she went into the lunchroom to fulfill her promise. She'd dressed very specifically for doing that. She was wearing a tight lace body suit that supported and displayed her breasts and had straps that held her stockings up under her pink dress. When she got their attention, which was almost immediately, she stated "I offered you guys a treat to stop harassing me. I understand that someone threatened bodily harm if you didn't stop harassing me." She paused and looked at Hoss, she didn't have any problems picking him out because no one else was really near his size. She gave him a smile. "Hopefully some of you changed your minds because of my offer but I've been told that it is more likely that most of you did it because of the threat. No matter. I am a woman of my word so I'll provide the promised treat. And Hoss, if you wouldn't mind waiting around after work, I'd like to go out to dinner with you to thank you for your participation in this matter." And with that, she pulled off her pink dress and stood in front of them for a minute in only her white lace body suit, her white stockings and high heels. Then she pulled her dress back on and left. One of the main culprits opened his mouth to say something to her as she was leaving, caught sight of Hoss glowering at him and swallowed his remark.

Hoss arranged so that he would finish work at the same time as she did; the foreman was happy to let him take the half hour off considering what was waiting for him. Hoss was a good, dependable worker who caused very few problems. He was actually waiting at Charley-Girl's car for her when she left for the day. When she arrived at her car, she smiled up at him and he said "You really don't have to do anything to thank me. I really should have spoken up sooner and put a stop to matters." He shrugged his massive shoulders and confessed "Sometimes it is easier just to go with the flow."

"No" she said smiling brightly at him. "I am happy to go to dinner with you. And it is not just because of what you did. The boss told me a bit about you and I'd like to get to know you a little better. You sound like someone that I would enjoy spending some time with."

Hoss looked at her for a moment, pondering what she might have heard about him. He knew what he'd heard about her. He looked her over carefully, liking what he saw. She was pretty, lively and smart; qualities that he liked in a woman. He knew that a lot of people considered him to be big and dumb but he was actually very intelligent; he just chose not to show it all of the time. "Okay, where would you like to go?"

"How about Burger Heaven?"

Hoss pondered going to the fast food joint that tended to cater to younger people like them but decided that she deserved to go to a better spot than that. "I'd prefer La Chez Noir. They do a really fine steak there."

"I'm not sure that I can afford that" she confessed.

He looked at her in total surprise. "Why would you pay? I'll buy you your supper for going out with me."

She frowned back at him. "But I invited you."

He chuckled and said "Yes, but I've been working longer than you. You just started here. Tell you what. You let me buy you dinner tonight at La Chez Noir and I'll let you buy me a burger at Burger Heaven when you get paid. Deal?"

She smiled at him, liking the way that he handled the situation. She'd been told that he was very bright, dependable and kind and she did want to get to know him better. He was bigger than any man she'd gone out with before and she wondered what he'd be like on top of her. She decided that if he continued to be as charming as he currently was, she'd see if she could find out at the end of the night. She didn't mind that she had the reputation of being an easy lay because she often slept with men on the first date; if she liked the guy enough to go out with him she might as well see how good he was in bed, she thought.

So the two of them went off to dinner and had a wonderful time. He kept her entertained with lots of talk about the many subjects that he knew about and she was happy that he was willing to listen to any thoughts that she had on matters, as well. He didn't treat her as just a brainless woman but actually talked about matters with her. Towards the end of the dinner, just as he was finishing up his steak, she asked casually "So, what have you heard about me?"

He smiled at her and stated "From what you did at coffee today, I could have surmised that you are adventurous and sexually provocative. That would have made me have some interest in you because I like that in a woman. But I also do have a younger sister still in high school with your sister, so I've also heard quite a bit about your reputation."

"And what is my reputation" she challenged.

He shrugged and looked her straight in the eyes. "That you like sex. That you often fuck on the first date. That you're not shy about being yourself."

"And does that bother you?"

"Not at all. In fact, it intrigues me. I'm not really a lady killer. I find that most women are interested in me because of my size and muscles but that they hold limited interest for me because they can't hold a decent conversation."

"And me?"

He grinned and stated "One of the best conversations that I've ever had has been tonight."

She looked him back in the eyes and said evenly "You know that I'd fuck you without you having to compliment me."

He stated as evenly "I'd like to go out with you again even if we don't fuck. I truly find you intriguing and hope that you feel the same about me."

"Well" she said as she fiddled with her wine glass. "I do find you intriguing and will go out with you again." She paused and then looked more intently at him. "But you definitely are going to fuck me tonight. Dessert?"

He choked slightly but said "Maybe we should skip it and just get the check."

"That would be wise."

They drove back to the warehouse so he could pick up his car and lead her back to his place. After they entered, he offered to show her around the place even though it wasn't very clean; he hadn't been expecting anyone over. She just smiled at him and said "I'm just interested in the bedroom right now." He led her down there and she shrugged out of her pink dress before letting him look at her in her lingerie. He reached out to touch her and hesitated, unsure if she just wanted to be looked at for a while. She grabbed his hand and placed it on her tit, covering it with her hand. He smiled joyously and squeezed her plump breast, enjoying the feel of it. She let him hold his hand there for a moment and then guided it over to the zipper up the side of her body suit. He got the hint and undid it for her. She felt the release of the restrictive suit, knew that her skin was a bit marked from its tightness and waited to see if he'd remark on it. Instead he just took a quick look at her now nude body before meeting her eyes again and smiling at her. She liked how he was treating her; letting her know that she interested him in both body and mind. But she wanted to get fucked so she dropped to her knees in front of him and started undoing his belt to get his pants off.

He quickly grabbed her hands and pulled her back to her feet; she looked at him, confused. He just pushed her gently onto the bed and put his head down between her legs, tonguing her pussy lightly. She'd received oral sex a couple of times before but she'd given it much more. She indicated that she'd be willing to sixty-nine him but he just shook his head and continued to lick her cunt. She decided that she might as well relax and enjoy it. He kept it up for about five minutes before she stopped him. He looked at her, questioningly. "That feels fairly nice but I'd really rather feel your cock inside me" she told him boldly. He nodded and undressed quickly, letting her lay there watching him. She liked how big his chest was and how strong looking his legs were. When she looked at his cock she found it to be a very nice size, about eight inches long and probably three inches in circumference. She knew that she could handle that size and enjoy it very much. She went to lick the head of it but he just shook his head at her and helped her onto her back again. She was compliant.

He lifted her legs up so that he could get up against her hips and pushed the head of his cock into her wet pussy. He didn't penetrate her too deeply at first but began to work his hips against hers, making her take more of his prick into her cunt. She moaned with delight to encourage him to work her harder and he gradually picked up speed and depth. Soon they were both panting from the effort of their fucking and he was being very careful not to put too much of his weight on her. She found it to be extremely pleasant to be ridden by him and she cooed with delight. He grinned at the pleased noises that she was making, finding that they really turned him on. He began to feel the start of his orgasm and he moaned a bit in frustration, knowing that it was likely too soon for her. He would've liked for them to cum together their first time but knew that wasn't about to happen. So be it, he thought as he pumped against her harder wanting to fill her with sperm. She recognized that he was on the verge and bucked him hard with her hips, encouraging him. He spurted into her and held himself on top of her, still trying to keep most of his weight off of her. She ran her hands over his back and down to cup his ass. He eased himself off of her and sat by her, running his fingers into her sloppy cunt. She lay there and let him do that for a moment while she caught her breath. Then she pushed his hand away gently and sat up.

"I enjoyed that and I hope that you did too." He nodded eagerly and she asked "Are you good for a second go around or is that too much to ask?"

"I'll need about twenty minutes or so to recover" he admitted. "Did you have anywhere that you needed to be?"

She grinned at him and replied "No. What do you think we should do for those twenty minutes?"

"Oh, I'm sure that we can think of lots of things to amuse ourselves with."

SISSY BOY TAKES IT UP THE ASS

Billie groaned mightily and shot his eyes wildly around the room, trying to find something to focus on to distract him from what Kimmy was doing to his ass. He was truly regretting agreeing to this endeavour and gave some thought to calling the whole thing off; unfortunately, he knew that if he were to do so, Kimmy would move on to other men and he desperately didn't want that to happen. Kimmy was a tall, stacked, gorgeous blonde with a usually pleasant personality, although she did have a fantastic cruel streak in her, and had men at her beck and call. Billy knew that he would be unable to land anyone else nearly as beautiful and interesting as Kimmy in his whole life. He wasn't entirely sure how he'd managed to do it in the first place. So, when Kimmy wanted him to do something, no matter how painful or kinky it might be, his only response could be an enthusiastic question about how soon did she want to do it to him.

So that is how, on this morning, he found himself kneeling on her bed with her spreading a generous dollop of lubricant all over his rosebud. He found the lubricant to be quite cold against his sensitive skin and shivers ran up his back. Kimmy laughed a loud, almost tinkling laugh at the sight; she was enjoying herself immensely and part of her pleasure was from the fact that she knew that she had Billie in a very tight spot. She knew he would do anything for her in order to keep her and intended to make sure to take full advantage of that fact. Since she'd been a very little girl, she'd always enjoyed charming others into doing things for her and had learned to be very successful at it; of course, she found things much easier with men once she'd grown into her figure. It was amazing what men would agree to do if you had a great set of tits, she thought exuberantly; she literally had men falling at her feet, trying to gain favour from her. So far, Billie had been the most pliable and therefore he was her main boyfriend. She made no secret of the fact to him that she enjoyed a varied sex life with other men and some women. He was just the one that she let stay over on a regular basis and took to parties where he got introduced as her boyfriend; it wasn't like she was tremendously serious about him. However she was ready to play it like it was, just to get him to agree to do some of the kinkier things for her. She'd done that to many men and some other girls over her relatively short life so far and had gained incredible satisfaction from it. She smirked cruelly at the back of his head as she greased him up; he wasn't aware how much pain she was going to inflict on him, she thought as she felt her brain begin to bubble in arousal.

Billie became aware of the odours percolating in the small bedroom; there was the smell of both of their sweat, an old one of sex, his fear and if he wasn't mistaken, her arousal. He could feel himself calming just slightly, if she was being turned on by what she was doing to him, then he was accomplishing his goal; that was exactly what this was all about, he thought happily to himself. He wanted her to have a reason to keep him around and he was prepared to go to any lengths to achieve that. He didn't care at this point if he wasn't able to sit for a week or more; as long as she was happy, he'd take pain from her. He recognized that he was in a fairly vulnerable position and trusted her not to take too much of an advantage of it; he didn't realize how wrong he was about that. He wriggled his ass a bit as he settled in to enjoy the feeling of her nimble fingers dancing along his asshole; in truth, it felt fairly good, he thought. He could feel the sharp little bite of her long painted nails as she worked the lubricant into his tight brown rosebud. He could feel his cock stiffening, even though she'd put his prick and his balls into a leather sling and had tightened it up; she hadn't tightened it too tightly, just enough for him to really feel that it was there. It served to remind him what could actually be done to him. He felt his balls swell a bit as he got aroused and began to feel uncomfortable. "Hey, babe" he said, softly but plaintively. "That fastener on my balls is starting to cut off my circulation somewhat. Could I get you to loosen it a bit for me?" He turned his head to her and gave her a winsome smile as he raised up his arms that she'd bound with velcroed restraints behind his back. He frowned and felt a sharp bite of fear lance through him when she just looked coolly back at him while ignoring his request. She just calmly kept on lubricating his asshole; in fact, she slid an index finger with its long sharp nail deep into him and gave him a superior smile. He sucked in some air to protest mightily and she noticed, so she quickly grabbed a nearby ball-gag and slapped it hard into his gaping mouth. She wrapped it around the back of his head and fastened it securely at the back. He moaned into it, surprised at how much it muffled his cries; he hadn't agreed to that, he thought in panic. He was supposed to be able to end things by using the safe words "red light"; how was he going to be able to do that now, he wondered.

Kimmy smiled viciously as she looked down at his restrained and gagged form and she began to hum a happy little tune. She had to work fairly quickly to make sure that he was completely helpless before she really began on him. She'd convinced him into most of the gear she'd be putting on him by only fastening it quite loosely to him, telling him that she just wanted him to feel what it felt like and that she wouldn't be tightening it up without his approval. She grinned and chortled loudly as she pulled hard on all of the different items forcing him into a more helpless position; she'd lied, she thought deliciously as the feeling of power ricocheted throughout her mind. She felt the competing senses of supremacy, disgust and fear dash through the stew of endorphins bubbling in her mind. She rapidly analysed each of them, she knew where the superiority came from and led so she just savoured that for a while as she tightened the bonds across the twitching Billie's elbows. She gave a small gasp of excitement as she pulled on the belt hard enough to make his elbows touch together behind his back; she knew that a lot of women were flexible enough to be placed in this position but that it was harder for a man due to his usually larger muscles. She watched intently as beads of sweat popped out on Billie's forehead as he endured the pain she was causing him. She hummed happily as she checked the security of the fastenings of the leg spreader she'd put on him just before she forced it open even further. She contemplated the feeling of disgust and carefully weighed whether it was aimed more at him or at herself. She recognized that she felt contempt for him for allowing her to do what she was about to do to him and that he was so easily betrayed. She had the sense that even though she was about to hurt him considerably, he would eventually crawl back for even more. She also recognized that she was somewhat disgusted with herself for taking advantage of another person in such a vulnerable state; she grinned as she realized that it just excited her that much more. And of course the fear came about because he could have enough strength left in him when she released him and could inflict damage on her or he could choose to inform on her to some of the authorities, although there was little likelihood of that, since he'd have to admit what he'd allow her to do. She savoured all of those things like she'd savour the complexities of a fine wine. She bit at her upper lip to keep from giggling out loud with glee.

Kimmy gave a quick double check on all of his bonds, tossing back her fine, long blonde hair as she did; she had to make sure that he couldn't break free because he was really going to strain against them shortly. She was satisfied that he was completely secure so she reached down between his legs and pulled on the strap to tighten the fastener around his cock and balls; she noted with derision that he'd deflated quite noticeably and she ran a hard fingernail along his sensitive ball sack as she pulled on the strap. He bucked his hips up as she performed these actions but she'd ensured that he wasn't able to throw his body off where she'd set him up. Once again she chortled with pleasure and anticipation. He now stank sharply of fear and she could sense her arousal growing within her body as her pussy began to drool onto her constricting panties. Time for her to lose some of her confining clothes and put on the studded leather outfit that she'd be wearing to fuck him, she thought with pleasure. She smacked his ass hard with her left hand as she leapt off the bed to go get her outfit and the equipment she'd hidden from him. She drew pleasure from the grunt it caused and by watching his ass cheeks jiggle just a bit.

She raced over to her closet, stripping the more sedate but still nice underwear she'd been wearing so that she could put on her kinky outfit with its leather, buckles and studs. She suppressed a shout of glee as she wriggled her way into her tight, studded leather bustier; she felt fantastic as it squeezed her considerable breasts tightly together. She gave the tops of them a playful rub and felt her nipples pop to attention; she grinned inanely at her image in the full length mirror she kept by her closet. She slipped on the crotch less leather panties with the studs up across her groin area and pulled on her fancy fishnet stockings. She slipped on and fastened her pointed high heel shoes; she liked how the points gouged the skin when she kicked someone with them. She took out her heaviest strap-on harness and fastened it on with some difficulty; it was so much easier to do with someone helping you, she thought as she imagined how much Billie would be interested in assisting her right now. She giggled and then snorted as she tried to regain her breath. She gave a small whistle as she plucked her largest dildo from her large collection and imagined forcing that up Billie's virgin ass; she gave her head a shake to clear the image and selected a smaller dildo. It was still going to do quite a bit of damage to him, she thought maliciously and gave herself an evil grin. She hunted in her items for her leather lace-up gloves, found them and put them on. She grabbed a few more items including a rowel, a butt plug, a whip and her nipple clamps and rushed back to where she'd left Billie.

She was ecstatic to see that he hadn't moved, although by the amount of sweat and colour on him, he'd certainly tried. To be fair, she thought evenly, I can't blame him for trying but I'm certainly going to beat his ass for it. She placed the stuff on the bed and then went over to put on her favourite music for fucking someone up the ass with. She snickered over the fact that she actually had a soundtrack to do that. She danced around a bit to the fast paced music she'd put at the start; it helped her to get further into the mood and psyched her up. She considered attaching the dildo to the strap-on belt because she loved the way it felt as it bobbed between her legs but decided to forgo that pleasure. She dance-stepped her way back to Billie and leapt onto the bed beside and on top of him; she made sure her knee caught him in the upper stomach area. She could hear the breath whistle out of his nose as she ground it into him. "Relax, baby" she cooed soothingly as she stroked his hair. "We got a long way to go and an awful lot of pain to be dealt before I'm through with you. You're going to be screaming for mercy and I don't plan on giving you any. Just think of how much you hurt the first girl you ever fucked. That's going to be you but much, much worse today." She smiled broadly as she gazed into his panic stricken eyes and stated boldly "I'm gonna enjoy this. You, not so much." She giggled and moved around behind him, leaning her studded leather against him so he could feel the metal studs.

She moved the loose hair off the back of his neck and began kissing it; he started tossing his head to dissuade her so she slammed her left knee up between his legs and dealt his testicles a severe blow. His strangled moans of pain just heightened her arousal; it was so thrilling to be so totally in control, she thought. "Behave yourself or you'll get hurt much worse. If you're a good boy, I'll use you as I want and then release you. If you're a bad boy, then..." she let the sentence drift off. His imagination was likely to be worse than anything she could actually do to him. She reached over to the side of the bed and retrieved an old fashioned glass milk bottle with a leather tie around the neck. She reached between his legs and took a firm grip on his prick, she was thrilled to hear him whimper with fear; she stuffed his cock into the bottle and tied the string to his restraint so the bottle was held in place. "Now" she said as she stroked his back gently. "I don't want you pissing all over the place so you have a bottle to catch any accidents. However, you're gonna drink any contents I find in there before I release you. So you better think before you piss. And if you try to shit on me, I'm gonna take that shit and stuff it up your nose." She goosed his asshole hard with her finger to emphasize her point and snarled "You got me, you sissy little bitch!"

She waited a moment to see if he'd have any reaction but he chose not to respond in any visible way so she went back to kissing the back of his neck. After five or six kisses, she bit him hard just above his right shoulder, giving him an extremely visible hickey. As she continued to hang onto him with her teeth, even though she could hear him whistling breath through his nose in pain, she reflected to the many times that men had chosen to give her hickeys. Billie, himself, had given her a few in their previous times together; she was aware that she was essentially paying him back much worse than he'd ever done to her but was content with that. She finally released him and inspected her handiwork; there was a trickle of blood and she could easily see the gouges of her teeth in his flesh. She felt a warm feeling in the pit of her stomach and even lower; she was positively dripping. She rubbed her fingers around the mark as she continued to admire what she had done; it was a truly satisfying feeling to be able to get away with something like that, she thought. She bumped her hips against his ass, ensuring that the studs caught him well and then backed away to look at the dimples she caused in the skin. She ran her hand soothingly over his backside. She gave careful consideration to giving him a hickey on his ass or inner thighs but decided that she'd refrain from doing that as long as he was a good boy and controlled himself. There's always time to inflict further pain, she ruminated happily.

She did however feel a need to mark his ass up and therefore raked her long fingernails down his left ass cheek leaving shallow gouges; he winced but didn't move any more than that. Once again she petted him and complimented him. "Good boy. Keep behaving like that and your pain will be over in no time and I'll be letting you go" she cooed again. She stroked him softly between the legs, enjoying the fact that he flinched but then held still. She picked up the beat from the music and began humming with it; it was a little bit early in the playlist for her too move on because she'd anticipated having to discipline him more to get him to comply. She was fairly happy that he'd succumbed so easily and she could feel her anticipation growing. She rubbed her damp pussy against his ass, carefully avoiding both her scratch marks and the studs on her leather bottom; she wanted to reward him, not punish him, at the moment. She could tell that the music that she wanted would be starting shortly so she began to get prepared. She picked up the dildos she'd brought over and decided that he'd been a good enough boy that she would use a slimmer, shorter one so she affixed that one to her harness. She gave the slightly bulbous tip a quick little coating of lubricant and raised herself into position.

She rested her hands on his hips and waited for the music to hit its crescendo and then she pushed forward against his tight rosebud while pulling his hips back with her hands. He was so startled that the pointed tip and about two inches of the shaft entered him before he clamped his asshole down against it. She was content for a while to wait him out to see what he would do so she stopped pushing into him and let him feel the object inside him. She could sense that he wasn't too sure about how to feel; much like she'd been the first time a man had forced anal sex on her. She knew from experience that it felt very different but didn't have to be terribly unpleasant. She recognized that she still intended for him to end the day in pain but she was considering tempering it somewhat if he continued to react well. She hummed along with the music, knowing that the hard driving beat she liked to fuck asses with was still to come. She smirked as she reflected as to how much pain she was going to inflict on him once that started. She quickly slid two fingers under her harness and gave her cunt a quick stroking.

Billy could hear her give off a few moans of pleasure, much like she did when he ran his tongue along her turgid clitoris and tried to puzzle out what was going on. She was enjoying herself but wasn't doing anything to him so he finally figured out that she was busy playing with herself. He took advantage of the respite to assess his position and condition; neither one looked very rosy at the moment he thought. His balls still ached from her kneeing them. Suddenly he became aware that she had stopped fiddling her cunt because she pushed the dildo deeper into his ass; he'd been too distracted to try to keep it out of him as best he could. He moaned into his gag as she ruthlessly spread him open further.

Now that she had more than half of the dildo up in his tight ass, she started thrusting with her hips up against him in a more determined manner; the dildo attached to her harness was pushed and pulled through his asshole. He gave a long, low, muffled moan of fear and pain as she did this but she studiously ignored his protests. As he lost the battle of trying to keep from being totally penetrated, he actually found that the plastic gliding into him actually caused him to become more aroused. He found that his cock was hardening and the feel of the tight restraint around them was causing him to grow as large as he'd ever been. He felt her hand reach down between his legs to give his cock a quick pull. He moaned once more in protest and she laughed her tinkling laugh once more before smacking his ass with her hand.

"Suck it up, sissy boy" she chortled happily. "Just think about how I feel when some man takes me hard and tells me just to endure it. You've tried to do that to me. Now the shoe is on the other foot." She increased her rhythm and he was amazed that he was enjoying what she was doing to him. He could feel his balls swelling as he tried to push his cum out of his cock but the restraint prevented him from doing that. He could feel a horrible ache beginning in his swollen balls. He attempted to dislodge her from riding him by bucking his hips but she'd secured him too well for him to do much about that. She grinned and said sadistically "If you're going to act like a bucking horse, I'm going to have to use spurs on you." He wondered what she meant until she picked up the rowel and ran the sharp spikes of it along the soft skin of his ass. He gave a muffled squeal about the feeling of that; it was more surprising than painful. She then slipped the tool down between his legs and ran it along his swollen balls. Oh God, he thought despondently, was she trying to cut his balls off with that tool. She smiled happily as she sensed his increased fear of her. It felt wonderful to feel so in charge of things, she thought as her pussy began to drip even more.

She ceased using the rowel on him to let him recover his composure somewhat but increased the frequency and depth of her thrusts into him, smacking his ass with her hips. She kept that up for nearly five minutes until she was tired and covered with sweat from the effort. She was pleased that he moaned and bucked the whole time she rode him. She used her weight to push the dildo as deep into him as she possibly could before releasing the harness and moving away from him. She didn't back off too far, just enough so that she could observe the wonderful sight of him crouching there with the dildo crammed up his ass. She grabbed his swollen balls with both of her hands and gave them a firm pull. His squeal hit new heights as she did this. She decided that he'd been a good enough boy that she wouldn't use the butt plug or nipple clamps on him that day; he did deserve some punishment, though, so she picked up the whip and spent nearly ten minutes applying it to his ass and occasionally his balls. She was in a joyful mood when she stopped and admired her handiwork; his ass was crisscrossed with welts. He was sobbing with pain.

She looked at him with her lip curling with a touch of disgust. She felt that he should be a man and take what she dished out to him. She gave him a final hard smack in his engorged balls with the whip before deciding to leave him for a half hour or so to recover himself. She'd come back then and see if he was prepared to being released or not. She knew that she had to let him out eventually but he'd survive being bound for more than twenty-four hours if she determined that she didn't want to let him go before then. She decided that she was hungry and wandered into the kitchen, humming happily, as she went to prepare a bowl of soup.

Thank you for reading these short stories.

Please rate this story. I would like to remind you that all independent authors rely on you as the reader to help them to spread the word about their works and you can help them continue to publish by letting your friends know about them or rating them on the different websites. If you would like to send a comment or two to the author, please email lizrshaw@nili.ca. You can also check me out on Goodreads and any feedback is gratefully accepted.

If you enjoyed these short stories and would like to see more of them, I'll be happy to write them. If you would like to see your name, a friend's name or maybe even family member immortalized in a story, send me the name and a brief outline of plot or situation and I will see what I can do with it. If I write something, I will be happy to send you your own copy and include it in one of my future volumes.

You may also be interested in the following works by me:
Danni Archer: The Making of a Mistress The Beginning
Danni Archer: The Making of a Mistress Continuation of Learning
Danni Archer: The Making of a Mistress The Audition Tape
Baroness Molly: Bi-sexual Dominatrix And Other Erotic Stories Volume 1